Praise for Cheryl St.John

"St.John's books are emotionally charged and her characters are well rounded."
—*RT Book Reviews* on *The Preacher's Wife*

"A satisfying, rough-and-tender novel brimming with true-to-life characters and an understanding of the era that fulfills western readers' hankerings."
—*RT Book Reviews* on *Her Montana Man*

"A beautifully crafted and involving story about the transforming power of love."
—*RT Book Reviews* on *His Secondhand Wife*

Praise for Ruth Axtell Morren

"A light, airy romance with a strong-minded character who has the faith to see herself through some hard choices."
—*RT Book Reviews* on *Hearts in the Highlands*

"Ruth Axtell Morren's *A Man Most Worthy* is a sweet, entertaining book with characters hoping for a second chance at love."
—*RT Book Reviews*

"Morren does an extraordinary job of putting two unlikely people together and showing us how love and romance can flourish despite difficulties."
—*RT Book Reviews* on *A Bride of Honor*

CHERYL ST. JOHN

A peacemaker, a romantic, an idealist and a discouraged perfectionist—these are the words that Cheryl uses to describe herself. The award-winning author of both historical and contemporary novels says she's been told that she is painfully honest.

Cheryl admits to being an avid collector, displaying everything from dolls to depression glass as well as white ironstone, teapots, cups and saucers, old photographs and—most especially—books. When not doing a home improvement project, she and her husband love to browse antiques shops. In her spare time, she's an amateur photographer and a pretty good baker.

She says that knowing her stories bring hope and pleasure to readers is one of the best parts of being a writer. The other wonderful part is being able to set her own schedule and have time to work around her growing family. Cheryl loves to hear from readers! E-mail her at SaintJohn@aol.com.

RUTH AXTELL MORREN

wrote her first story when she was twelve—a spy thriller—and knew she wanted to be a writer. There were many detours along the way. She studied comparative literature at Smith College, taught English in the Canary Islands and worked in international development in Miami, Florida, where she met her future husband.

She gained her first recognition as a writer when her second manuscript was a finalist in the Romance Writers of America Golden Heart Contest in 1994. Ruth has been writing for Steeple Hill since 2002, and her second novel, *Wild Rose* (2004) was selected as a Booklist Top 10 Christian Novel in 2005.

Ruth and her family divide their time between the down east coast of Maine and the Netherlands. Ruth loves hearing from readers. You can contact her through her Web site, www.ruthaxtellmorren.com, or her blog, http://ruthaxtellmorren.blogspot.com.

CHERYL ST.JOHN
RUTH AXTELL MORREN
To Be a Mother

Steeple
Hill®

Published by Steeple Hill Books™

STEEPLE HILL BOOKS

Steeple Hill®

PLEASE RECYCLE — THIS PRODUCT IS RECYCLABLE

Recycling programs for this product may not exist in your area.

ISBN-13: 978-0-373-82833-3

TO BE A MOTHER

Copyright © 2010 by Harlequin Books S.A.

The publisher acknowledges the copyright holders of the individual works as follows:

MOUNTAIN ROSE
Copyright © 2010 by Cheryl Ludwigs

A FAMILY OF HER OWN
Copyright © 2010 by Ruth Axtell

www.SteepleHill.com

Printed in U.S.A.

CONTENTS

MOUNTAIN ROSE
Cheryl St.John

Mountain Rose is lovingly dedicated to the Love Inspired Historical authors, an amazingly talented group of clever, resourceful and supportive women. I am honored to be in their company.

Are not five sparrows sold for two farthings,
and not one of them is forgotten before God?
But even the very hairs of your
head are all numbered.
Fear not therefore: ye are of more value
than many sparrows.
—*Luke* 12:6–7

Chapter One

Mercerville, Pennsylvania
1866

Olivia Rose stood at the window in the upstairs hall of the Hedward Girls Academy as the last young woman was being escorted into a carriage by her father. Well, not the last.

She glanced over her shoulder at the eight-year-old who sat alone in the once-bustling alcove used for reading and studying. Emily Sadler had stacked books on the worn divan beside her, and now focused intently on the one she held. The shelves behind her were empty. Everything had been sold to pay debts.

Every time Olivia thought of the war and resulting financial crisis that had forced the school to close, her stomach clenched in fear at the unknown. This was home. She had nowhere else to go.

Mrs. Hugh, the school's headmistress, stood on the curb, watching the last carriage pull away. She held herself stiffly, her posture as perfect as that of the students she'd taught for the past thirty years. Once the carriage turned the corner, the woman gathered the hem of her brown serge skirts and hurried toward the door below, disappearing from view.

"I'm going to see about our supper."

Emily acknowledged Olivia with a polite nod.

Downstairs, she met Mrs. Hugh in the hallway and followed her to the office. "I see Jeanette has taken her leave," Olivia said.

"Yes." The lines radiating from the corner of the woman's eyes had deepened over the past months. "Only Emily remains, and we still haven't heard from her mother."

"If I may have her address, I will continue to try to reach her," Olivia offered.

Mrs. Hugh picked up the only thing on the desk and handed her the folder.

Olivia glanced at the headmistress hesitantly before opening it. Emily had come here on April fifth of the year eighteen hundred and fifty-eight. Her approximate length and weight were recorded, as were eye and hair color. She'd been an infant.

Her mother, Meriel Sadler, was listed. A Mr. Roman Terlesky paid the tuition regularly.

Puzzled, Olivia looked up. "Is Mr. Terlesky her father?"

"I don't believe so. He may be her stepfather or merely her mother's…close friend."

"Has anyone ever visited her?"

"Her mother came once or twice in the first few years," the woman answered. "I doubt the child remembers."

Emily's situation was painfully similar to her own, except Olivia's anonymous tuition had stopped coming when she'd turned twelve. She'd been forced to work in the kitchen and laundry to pay her keep. All these years and she'd never known where she'd come from or who had abandoned her. Her heart fluttered, but she managed to ask, "May I see my own file?"

Without hesitation, Mrs. Hugh turned to a crate and flipped through the meager stack of remaining papers. "You may have it—and the girl's. I have no further need for them."

Olivia's stomach dipped as though she was perched on a precarious limb. She'd never had the courage to ask... though she'd wondered aplenty.

After skipping a few beats, Olivia's heart raced. Fortifying herself for whatever she found written within, she opened the folder. In black ink, the same penmanship recorded the date that she'd arrived at the school. She hadn't been a year old. Aside from the date and her physical description, the page was glaringly bare. She stared, her eyes dry and burning. "There's nothing here."

"We weren't given contacts." Mrs. Hugh moved a page to find her handwritten record on heavy stationery. "You were brought to the front door by a lad along with an envelope that contained money to pay your keep for a year. After that, bank drafts came from an anonymous source." She looked up at Olivia with regret. "Until December 1856, at which time there was no check, no notice, no anything. We never heard from your benefactor again."

Olivia had always known she'd been abandoned. That wasn't news. But she'd imagined—or dreamed perhaps— that one day she'd learn who her parents had been. Even if they hadn't wanted her, she would know their names. She would have an identity.

But this... A soul-deep ache defied her to ignore the humiliation. She wasn't even a person if she lacked parents and a date of birth. She frowned. "Where did I get my name?"

"From one of the teachers," Mrs. Hugh explained. "Miss Porter. Do you remember her?"

Olivia nodded.

"Her mother's name had been Olivia, and she always said your mouth looked like a pretty little rose." Mrs. Hugh actually smiled, something Olivia had seldom seen. "You were a beautiful baby. One of the prettiest we ever had."

Her parents hadn't cared enough to name her, and if they had, they hadn't cared enough to see she kept it. The overwhelming lack of identity made her feel like a nonentity.

"And my birthday?"

"Miss Porter guessed your age and selected a date."

With a stoic lack of emotion, Olivia thumbed through the pathetically few pages and notations. Her grades and academic achievements had been listed. She noted her first date of employment at age twelve and her gradual promotions from the kitchen and laundry to teaching. Her entire life consisted of a list of financial records and class grades.

Refusing to sink beneath the rising tide of hopelessness, Olivia closed the folder and picked up Emily's. "Thank you."

"The academy did its best by you, Olivia," Mrs. Hugh said.

She'd always had a bed to sleep in and meals three times a day. This place had been her entire life.

"There is other family listed in Emily's file. An uncle, I believe."

Olivia quickly reopened the folder. Flipping over a page, Olivia found the notation. "Jules Parrish. Oregon City, Montana."

"I only wrote him last week," Mrs. Hugh said. "I kept thinking I'd hear from her mother."

"Did you telegraph?"

"Selling off the furnishings and supplies barely fed us these last weeks. I was hard pressed just to afford postage to notify all the parents."

During the past few years, wages had ceased, and all the teachers had dipped into their own money for food and supplies.

"I'll take care of Emily," Olivia reassured her.

"The new owners will be here Thursday," Mrs. Hugh reminded her. "You only have until then."

"We'll be gone," Olivia replied.

"You haven't had good fortune with finding a teaching position?"

All she knew how to do was teach young ladies, cook and clean. She had no prospects to continue here in Mercerville. She'd queried as far as Ohio. Even the paper mills were no longer operating. The war had taken a toll on the entire country. "I'm sure I'll find something soon."

She wasn't as confident as she let on, but she'd never given in to fear in her life, and she wasn't going to start now.

Their beds had been sold, so Olivia and Emily prepared pallets in the room Olivia once shared with another teacher. Emily hadn't asked what was going to happen to her.

"Your mother still hasn't replied to our letters," Olivia told her as she spread the last blanket.

"She probably didn't get them wherever she is," Emily replied, her voice and expression void of feeling. She'd always been a quiet and undemonstrative child, and Olivia understood the need to keep thoughts and feelings private.

Olivia knew well the importance of holding oneself together. "The gospels tell us that our heavenly Father knows how many hairs we have on our heads, remember?"

Emily nodded. "Yes."

It had always meant everything to Olivia to know how much God loved her. "Even as He cares for and feeds the sparrows, He cares for us even more. We are valuable and special to the Lord."

"And He said not to fear because He is with us," Emily added.

As good as it was to know God loved them and was with them, it wouldn't hurt to know there were one or two people concerned for them, as well.

"I'm going to take care of you," she assured Emily. That was the only promise she could make and keep to the best of her ability. Olivia knew exactly what being unwanted felt like, and she wasn't going to let this girl think nobody in the entire world cared about her. Emily had become the closest thing Olivia had to family.

For the past several years, Emily and Olivia had remained at the academy over the holidays, just the two of them, celebrating with minimal fuss. As the only two without any family whatsoever, they were bound by yearnings and inadequacies only they shared. Olivia understood every unspoken dream and glimmer of trembling hope that shone in Emily's eyes. Her dearest wish was to care for her as her own, but she had no means to provide for her.

Since her conversation with Mrs. Hugh, she'd been thinking. Emily had at least one relative besides her mother. She deserved to know her uncle. Perhaps the man and his family would be ecstatic to learn about their niece. And once Emily had been united with her family, Olivia could find a teaching job, maybe even nearby.

Olivia sat cross-legged on her pallet. "You have an uncle in Montana."

Emily studied Olivia with solemn brown eyes. Was that

a flicker of hope Olivia detected? "I do?" Emily appeared to digest the information, though her expression remained guarded. "How far is Montana?"

Olivia stood and picked up the oil lamp from the floor. "I'll be right back."

Her bare feet padded on the wood in the empty silence of the hallway and alcove. She found several rolled maps, located the one she wanted and returned. Unrolling the map, she used the lamp to hold one side and Emily's book the other.

Emily folded back her blanket and leaned over the map opposite Olivia. Her dark braids fell forward with the tips grazing the paper.

Olivia pointed, locating a far western spot in Pennsylvania with her fingertip. "Here we are."

Emily ran a finger across states and cities. "Here's Montana, Miss Rose."

The distance was a good ten inches. They studied the vast gap for several minutes.

Their eyes met, Emily's dark and filled with questions. The child was so dear, her fears and concerns had become Olivia's own. Olivia had no idea what being a mother—or having a mother—felt like, but she expected a mother felt toward her child the way Olivia felt toward Emily: Protective. Concerned.

"How far is that?" Emily asked.

"Let's figure it out using the scale," Olivia answered in her teacher's voice. "Do you have a bookmark?"

Emily reached for a slip of paper she'd had positioned between pages.

Olivia painstakingly marked the paper with her thumbnail, and together they laboriously followed the marks that represented railroad lines.

After several minutes of tallying, Olivia sat back on her heels. "Seventeen hundred miles. Plus about another inch or so, because I'm not certain where Oregon City is."

The distance was inconceivable to someone who'd rarely left the safety of this house. At that moment Olivia knew desperation at its peak, but she kept her expression and her voice calm for Emily's sake. "I have a little savings left for train fare and food. We could go to Jamestown tomorrow and learn about the train schedule."

Emily turned beseeching eyes on her. "Do you really think we should go to Montana?"

Olivia yearned to comfort the child, but she was at a loss as to how. No one had ever been affectionate with her, so physical demonstrations didn't come naturally. She reached out and gave the girl's shoulder an awkward pat. "We will find your family, and then I'll acquire a job."

Emily's gaze turned to the hand on her shoulder, an unaccustomed touch that clearly puzzled her, before picking up her book. The map rolled back into a cylinder against the oil lamp. The girl set the book aside and crept back to her pallet. "Maybe my mother will come tomorrow."

Olivia didn't have the heart to support the girl's hope with an encouraging reply. She moved the map and lamp aside and turned down the wick.

She lay down, darkness closing around her. This wasn't the same secure cover of night she'd known until now. She focused on remembering one of her favorite verses from the Book of Isaiah. *Fear not, for I am with you. Be not dismayed, for I am your God. I will strengthen you. Yes, I will help you. I will uphold you with My righteous right hand.*

She had no choice but to put her trust in God's Word.

Nothing remained for her in Pennsylvania. She had no connections to anyone in the entire country. No one else needed her—no one except Emily.

Emily had people somewhere, and that meant she had a chance for a good future. She was going to do whatever it took to unite Emily with her family. Every child deserved a chance, and Olivia was her only hope. She would trust God to help her do whatever it took.

Corbin's Bend, Montana, 1866

The afternoon sun was still blistering when Jules Parrish slowly rode toward his stable, leading a horse with mud fever. He needed to treat the animal's legs and get back to the herd.

Half a dozen mares, bellies heavy with foals, stood in the shade of the slope-roofed shelter built for their protection inside a fenced pasture. One of them whinnied, and the bay he led replied with a snort.

Jules took a moment to admire the structure. The stable was a thing of beauty, built in the style of a traditional barn, though a hundred and fifty feet long to comfortably accommodate twenty-four horses. It had only been constructed last fall, but he'd given it a fresh coat of white paint this spring. Besides the bunkhouse, this was the only structure he'd had time to build. His one-room cabin and the supply sheds had been here when he'd bought the land before the war.

All he'd thought about during his four-year stint in the army had been getting back. Sleeping on the ground during freezing winter nights, tromping through sweltering heat and eating meager rations, the dream of what he could make this land into had kept him going.

Jules appreciated the shingled roof and twelve symmetrical windows with a nod of satisfaction. Could be it was the most impressive stable in all of Montana. And his herd was taking shape.

A flicker of motion caught his eye, and he squinted from beneath his hat brim, certain the waves of heat were playing with his eyes. A lone hemlock and a hedge of chokecherries stood twenty feet from the squat cabin, transplanted by someone who'd long ago given up his dream and moved on. A stack of trunks had been abandoned in the shade of the tall tree, and two females—one wearing a blue dress, the other green—stood as he approached the stable. Even from here, it was clear one was a woman, the other a child.

The woman separated from the girl and walked toward him, her skirt hem stirring clouds of dust that rose with each step.

Jules dismounted and, holding the reins to his mount and the lead rope for the bay in one hand, approached her. "What are you doing here?"

The woman stopped several feet away. "Mr. Parrish?"

"Yeah. Who are you?"

"I'm Olivia Rose. I'm an instructor—or I *was* an instructor—at the Hedward Girls Academy in Mercerville, Pennsylvania."

The name of the school meant nothing to him, but at the mention of her home state, unwelcome images of Gettysburg clouded his vision. He closed his eyes, willing the gruesome memories to fade, then snapped them open to study her.

Her bonnet hid most of her hair, but the drooping ringlets visible underneath were a shiny reddish-blond. She wore long sleeves and white gloves to protect her arms and hands from the sun, but the pale skin of her cheeks and nose had burned. "You're a long way from home."

"Yes, well…" She glanced back over her shoulder at the girl who watched them, and he studied her delicate profile for that moment. "My young charge is Emily Sadler."

She seemed overly interested in his reaction, evident in the way she turned and studied him intently.

"What are the two of you doin' way out here?" he asked again, impatient to move on with his work.

"Emily is the daughter of Meriel Sadler."

She had his attention now. Sadler meant nothing to him, but he hadn't heard his sister's name in years. *Meriel.*

Chapter Two

"You're listed in Emily's file as her uncle. The academy was forced to close, and her mother didn't respond to our letters. We're here because I thought Emily should be with family."

His sister's child? Jules turned and quickly led the two horses toward the stable, where he rolled back the door, urged them inside with slaps on their rumps and closed off the entrance. They'd be fine until he came back to tend them.

He covered the ground to the hemlock with long strides, the woman close behind.

The child widened her eyes in surprise and took a step back. Her teacher slid up protectively close to the girl, but without touching her. The girl wore a bonnet, too, one with a broad brim that partially hid her face. He glanced at the ribbons that held it on. "Take off the hat."

Obediently, Emily untied the satin bow and pulled the bonnet away from her face.

Her dark hair was thick and lustrous, her eyes the color

of a strong cup of chicory. She had a smattering of freckles across her nose and full, unsmiling lips.

Jules felt as though he'd been transported back twenty years. This child could have been his sister standing there staring back at him. For a moment he smelled the lemon wax that had always permeated his childhood home, and he wouldn't have been surprised to hear his father's voice raised in a tirade.

Her expression of stoic determination was like Meriel's, as well, and he detected the familiar look of well-disguised fear. There was no denying their relationship.

He turned to study the teacher more closely. "What are you doing with her?"

Her face flushed bright pink, probably due to the heat and anxiety, but the color made her eyes vividly blue, even in the filtering shade of the tree. "Emily has been my student since I first acquired a teaching position more than three years ago. When the headmistress could no longer afford to keep the academy running, we contacted all the parents to come for their children."

"No one came for me." Emily's pronouncement came out of the blue, apparently surprising her teacher, as well as Jules.

"When was the last time you saw her—or heard from her?"

Emily gave him a blank look.

"Your mother?" he clarified.

She said nothing this time.

"I don't believe Emily remembers her mother," Miss Rose told him.

He raised his eyebrows in surprise. "How was her schooling paid?"

"By cashier's note regularly, even during the war," she replied.

"You still haven't explained what you're doin' here."

The teacher glanced at Emily and back. "May we speak in private?"

"There's a whole lot of private," he pointed out. "But it's all blazing sun, and you look ready to wilt." Her face had become as red as a ripe tomato.

"I assure you I'm fine."

He turned to Emily and jabbed a thumb over his shoulder. "Head for the cabin. It's cooler in there."

Emily looked to the woman for affirmation before gathering her skirts and walking away.

"You're her family," Miss Rose told him matter-of-factly once Emily was inside. "I was hoping you and your wife would want to—"

"Hold it, missy. I don't know where you got the idea, but I don't have a wife."

"Oh." She frowned. "I just assumed that you— I'm not sure why I— My mistake." She recovered and continued. "Regardless, you're the only family she has, so I brought her to you."

"How did you find me?"

"You're listed as her next of kin."

"But how'd you find me here? I only got out of the army eight months ago."

"Her file listed your location as Oregon City, Montana, so that's where we went. I checked at the post office first, then finally found a record at the deeds office that placed you in Corbin's Bend. I cleaned and cooked for the telegraph man for two weeks to pay for a room and earn more train fare. We hired a ride to the ranch."

"The two of you have been alone out West for *weeks?*"

"Decidedly so."

Jules got a little sick to his stomach at the thought of two helpless females traipsing around this wild land. There'd been recent attacks by Cheyenne; women and girls were vulnerable to being taken captive. "That's probably the dumbest thing I've heard in a long time."

She flattened dry but prettily shaped lips into a straight line and avoided his eyes. "You'd rather we were tossed out on our ears in the streets to survive any way we could?"

"There's nothing out here for the two of you. And it's dangerous. Not just the trip, but being out here at all. What would you have done if I'd stayed out with the herd and not come home tonight? No, this is no place for Emily. We'll find her a new school."

The teacher's blue eyes blazed at his words. "I suppose she's too much of an inconvenience. You would prefer to palm her off as someone else's worry, just as her mother did. Even the fact she's flesh and blood makes no difference."

He scowled and drew a breath to deny her words.

Her eyes took on a glazed, unfocused look.

"Look, lady," he said. "I—"

Before he could finish the sentence, her eyelids fluttered and she slumped sideways.

Jules grabbed her before she hit the ground. She didn't weigh much more than his saddle. He adjusted her in his arms and carried her toward the cabin.

The door wasn't barred, so he kicked it open, and it flew back against the wall.

The little girl jumped up from where she'd been sitting on a wooden chair and gasped. "What did you do to Miss Rose?"

"She fainted." He placed her on the rope bed, which was covered with a Hudson Bay blanket.

Emily moved to her teacher's side and leaned to peer into her face. "Miss Rose?"

"I'll get some water." He strode out, filled a pail from the trough and returned. "It's warm, but it's wet."

After wringing out a cloth, he bathed her face, then removed her gloves, so he could moisten her wrists and hands.

Emily took off the woman's bonnet, and her curls spread across the blanket in a strawberry-gold wave. "Miss Rose?" she said softly, then looked him dead in the eye. "This happened yesterday, too. She gave me her food."

The woman's sacrifice made Jules's stomach dip. She'd forfeited a lot to get his niece to him, in hopes he'd be able to help. "Let's sit her up. We'll get her to drink, and then I'll find something for you both to eat."

"May I have a drink, too, please?"

"Of course." Her simple request stabbed him with remorse. She shouldn't have had to ask—he should have offered. He grabbed a dented tin cup from an open shelf and dipped it in the bucket. After the harsh journey they'd endured, he never should have left them standing in the sun so he could ask questions. "Have as much as you like."

Together, they sat Miss Rose up and got her to drink two cups of water. She roused, flushed in embarrassment, and tried to stand.

"Stay put until you've eaten," he ordered.

Miss Rose glanced at Emily and then nodded.

He sliced ham and bread, and the two of them shared a sandwich. He found an apple and cut it in half.

After they'd eaten, he asked Miss Rose if she felt up to taking a walk out to the stable.

"Yes, of course," she replied. "I assure you I'm not usually prone to spells of vapors. I apologize for my light-headedness."

"May I look at your books, Mr. Parrish?" Emily asked.

Meriel had always liked books, too, getting caught up in fairy tales and stories of faraway lands. He didn't have books like that, but she was welcome to what he did own. "Help yourself."

Olivia felt much better after the food and water. How embarrassing to have fainted in the presence of this imposing man who, for now, held Emily's future in his hands.

He opened a door in the side of the enormous barn and ushered her inside. The interior smelled strongly of hay and horses, odors completely foreign, but not unpleasant.

Still saddled, the horse Mr. Parrish had ridden up on clomped over to greet him. The man stroked the animal's neck, and then turned it away. The beast walked over to a stall gate and stood nose to nose with another horse.

"I'm afraid the situation is such that Emily has nowhere to go and no one to look out for her," Olivia explained. "When her mother didn't reply, the headmistress sent a wire to Oregon City in hopes of reaching you."

He took off his hat and raked his fingers through hair as dark and wavy as Emily's. No wonder he hadn't questioned his relationship to the girl.

"You don't doubt that Emily is your niece."

He shook his head. "Plain as day that she's my sister's. That look in her eyes—like she's scared to death, but not about to let it show—just like Meriel's. She has a little of my mother around her nose and mouth, too."

His perceptiveness touched Olivia. "Then you'll make a home for her?"

"Lady, I spend every waking hour working horses and cows. I eat under the sky, and when I come back here, I sleep in a one-room cabin. You saw it. That's all there is. Sometimes I sleep out there with the herd. I don't know anything about kids—and especially not girls."

Olivia's disappointment was nearly crushing. She'd come an awfully long way to get nowhere. "What do you suggest?"

He hung his hat on a protruding nail and sat on a hay bale, resting his forearms on his knees. "I don't know. I haven't had time to think. You just sprung this on me." He ran his palm down his jaw. "All I know is, she can't stay here. The best thing will be to find a new school. I have no idea how to go about that. You can help."

He glanced at her again. "What are your plans? Did you think to dump her here and take off?"

"Of course not. I intend to stay until she's settled."

He shook his head to indicate the thought of two females was worse than one. "How long?"

"I—I don't know. As long as it takes."

"No one's expecting you? You don't have family to get back to or a job lined up?"

She answered matter-of-factly and without revealing the pain his words caused. "No. No one. I grew up at the academy like Emily did."

He appeared to think that over.

"Then you can help."

Olivia knew exactly what it felt like to be unwanted and rejected, and her heart ached for Emily. She raised her chin to say, "I won't take part in abandoning a child."

"Wouldn't be abandonment," he argued. "I'll take responsibility, make sure she's taken care of. I just can't take care of her here by myself. It's impossible. She needs to be somewhere civilized, where she can learn and be safe."

Olivia stubbornly shook her head. "I won't be an accomplice."

She was going to change his mind, no matter what it took. As long as Olivia was drawing breath, Emily would not be swept under the rug.

Chapter Three

"You make finding a school sound like a crime."

Olivia said nothing. In her opinion, deserting a child *was* a crime. She didn't want Emily to feel as unwanted as she always had. Not having parents made a person feel insignificant. At least Emily had some family, and she knew her name and her mother's name. Olivia swallowed hard. She had none of those things. If she fell into a pool of water, she wouldn't even make a ripple. But that was all the more reason for her to convince Mr. Parrish to let Emily stay. The last thing she wanted was for Emily to feel the same rejection.

At her silence, Emily's uncle shook his head. "I'll wire my mother for help. It's possible she knows where Meriel is."

Olivia stared at him in surprise. "Your mother?"

He nodded. "Last I knew she was in Ohio with her husband. She may have heard from my sister."

"How long ago was that?"

"Ten years, maybe. I wrote her a couple times during the war to let her know I was alive, but I'm not sure the letters reached her. Afterward, I didn't let her know where I was settling."

Ten years? "Why not?"

"Long story." He stood. "I have to tend this animal, and then I'll ride into town to send a wire." As though remembering Emily back in the cabin, he thrust his fingers into his hair. "I can't leave her alone."

"I'm not going to abandon her," Olivia assured him. "I'll stay with Emily while you figure out what to do."

"It could be a week or more before I even hear back from her."

"What are you saying?"

"I don't know." He glanced toward the horse. "I have work I can't let go. Men and animals to oversee. I can't take her with me."

"I'll stay with her," Olivia assured him. She had nowhere else to go.

He looked at her. "I'm going to build a house eventually, but all I have is that cabin. One of my hands has a family, and they live in the wagon you saw out a ways, but they and the hands are the only people within miles. Soon as I tend this horse, I'll take your trunks into the cabin. I'll stay in the bunkhouse."

"We don't need much," she assured him. "We've slept aboard the train and even at station houses for the past few weeks. Shelter and privacy will be adequate."

He nodded, dismissing her, and turned to the horse.

Olivia walked back to the cabin.

Emily sat reading at the table. She laid down the book and looked up, her question plain in her dark eyes.

"We're going to stay here, in this cabin, for now. Mr. Parrish is going to send a wire to his mother—your grandmother—in hopes that she will know how to reach your mother."

"I have a grandmother?"

"Apparently so."

Emily seemed to digest that information slowly.

Olivia could almost imagine the questions spinning in her head. Did the grandmother know about her? If she did, why hadn't she ever visited or sent for her during holidays? Those were the things Olivia was wondering, as well.

"So." Olivia placed her hands on her hips and glanced around the dusty interior. "I guess the first thing we need to do is clean. Mr. Parrish is going to bring in our trunks. We can change into clean work dresses. I'll ask him where the washtub is, and we can do our laundry and then bathe."

It felt good to have a plan and work to do. Olivia was taking care of Emily, yes, but she would also be staying under Mr. Parrish's roof and eating his food, and she would earn her keep. It was a good feeling to be needed.

Jules hitched a wagon. All the way to Corbin's Bend, turbulent thoughts kicked up a tornado in his head. Already his supplies and accommodations were inadequate. The Rose woman had started asking him about laundry tubs and soap and clotheslines before he left. He'd scrounged up a galvanized tub, but he would have to buy more supplies while he was in town.

After sending a telegram to Ohio, he paid extra to have the message delivered to the ranch if he should get a reply. Then he made a trip to the mercantile and the hardware store, paying for an assortment of items and storing them in the bed of the wagon.

Upon returning, he showed Olivia how to let water through the troughs fed from the windmill to the pump in the cabin, and then dug a hole for a post. For a clothesline, he strung heavy cord from the tree to the post. He'd always taken his laundry to town. He didn't have time to do all this, but here he was making concessions for his unexpected guests.

But she and Emily looked busy and content when he left them scrubbing and rinsing clothing and headed back to the herd.

He didn't return until the sun had set. There were a few items waving on the line, but most must've dried and been put away.

Jules stood outside awkwardly, finally knocking on his own cabin door.

The door opened and Miss Rose stepped back. "Mr. Parrish."

Behind her the room had been transformed. The floor was clean, the bed and narrow cot made up with fresh bedding and all the items on the open shelves were neatly arranged.

"I came for my clothes."

She gestured for him to enter.

He stacked two crates with his belongings. "I'll just move these to the bunkhouse." As he moved past, he happened to think about a meal. "The cook fixes supper for the hands. I'll bring you each a plate."

He washed at the tank on the opposite side of the stable, where the hands bathed and shaved. By the time he'd donned a clean shirt, Wayland, a tall, bearded fellow, had a kettle of stew and stacks of bowls on the end of the bunkhouse table. The tired men stood in line for their grub.

"There are ladies stayin' in the cabin," Jules told them. "My niece and her teacher. Until I figure out what to do with them, is all. I expect you to stay clear and mind your own business. If you do run across one of them, behave like gentlemen."

The hands gave each other looks, and a few replied with compliance. No doubt they'd already seen the clothing on the line and had been curious.

"Didn't know you had a niece, boss," Coonie Boles said.

"Neither did I." Jules filled three bowls and placed them, along with biscuits and a small pitcher of milk, on a wooden tray, then headed out.

Miss Rose must have been watching, because she opened the door as soon as he reached it and stood back. The table had been scrubbed cleaner than he'd ever seen it. She positioned the three bowls and took the utensils from him, arranging them neatly.

"It's stew," he said, as if she couldn't see that for herself. The woman had to wonder if all his lights were working.

Miss Rose gestured for Emily to take a seat. The girl obediently took her place and sat with her hands folded in her lap.

Miss Rose folded her hands above her bowl and lowered her head with her eyes closed. Emily's eyes were closed, as well.

Jules picked up his spoon and dipped into the stew.

"Thank You, Lord, for delivering us safely to Mr. Parrish," the woman began.

He halted with the spoon halfway to his mouth and lowered it to the bowl. It had been a long time since he'd heard anyone pray aloud. Jules rested his spoon in the dish and bowed his head.

"We are grateful for Your infinite mercy and grace and for Your watchful eye as we traveled to this distant land. Lord, bless the hands that prepared this meal set before us, and thank You for providing nourishment for our bodies. Watch over us this night and comfort us with Your Spirit. In Jesus's name. Amen."

"Amen," Emily echoed, and picked up her spoon.

Jules hesitantly lifted his gaze. Emily took a bite and chewed. Miss Rose did the same. Both reached for a biscuit at the same time. Obviously hungry and giving manners priority, Miss Rose gestured for Emily to go first, and then took her own biscuit, neatly breaking off a piece and taking a delicate bite.

Jules took his first bite. Wayland had a way with game, so he often made deer and elk tender and tasty. This, however, was one of the nights the cook stubbornly insisted that squirrel made a good meal. The hands had learned not to grumble. Wayland said he needed variety to keep the job and the food interesting, and their complaints insulted him. As usual, the squirrel stew was greasy, the meat stringy.

Apparently, the meal was no hardship compared to the travel conditions his two guests had endured. Neither female showed any indication that the food was less than adequate.

The teacher's prayer had humbled him. She was thankful for greasy squirrel stew and this drafty cabin. It was disturbing to imagine the risks she'd taken to get here. A hundred bad things could've happened, and no one would've been the wiser, because he sure hadn't been expecting them.

No doubt she did owe their safe arrival to God.

Eating in silence, he thought back over their brief conversations and her obstinate refusal to help him relocate his niece.

He slanted a glance at Emily. The child ate slowly, taking her cues for composure and conduct from her teacher.

He'd been only a little older than her—ten, maybe—

when his older sister had run off. Their home life had been chaotic. Their father had never behaved rationally, often lying in bed for days at a time, waking only to demand food and drink. Other times he took a job that lasted weeks, and those were rare days of peace. However, when he was in one of his better and more energetic moods, he often took a notion to move them to a new town.

Jules remembered more than one time when his father had simply disappeared for months, leaving his mother to take in laundry and scrape by the best she could.

Jules secretly liked his father's absence better than the rest of the time, because his mother had been less on edge, and life had flattened into an even routine. But the man inevitably returned and soon had them packing yet again.

Meriel hated moving, had cried and begged to stay at school, but their father scoffed at her. Their mother always appeased him and packed their belongings.

His sister had been thirteen or fourteen when she'd had enough. She'd told Jules she was leaving, had given him several silver coins and disappeared. That was the last time he'd seen his sister.

Their mother had been heartbroken, but nothing had stopped her from joining her husband in yet another move that same fall.

That winter, during one of his spells of silent despair and sleep, the man had taken ill. He'd coughed and caught a fever that raged for days. He'd shouted in his delirium, thrown things at his wife and had eventually run out of the house and dropped dead in a snowdrift.

Jules had stayed with his mother another year until she'd married again. And then he'd packed a bag, bought a rifle and a revolver and joined a cattle drive.

In all these years he'd never heard from Meriel or known where to find her.

He'd kept in touch with his mother off and on. She had loved him. He didn't blame her for anything. What was done was done, and he'd grown up fine, discovering he liked pushing cows and taming horses. He'd learned as much around campfires as he ever had in school, and then his stint in the army had proven he wanted land and a herd of his own.

At least he'd known his parents. He had some good memories of his mother. Emily had nothing of the like. Looking at her brought his childhood flooding back. What had hers been like? Had she been lonely at school? Had the other children treated her well, giving her the attention she'd never received from her family? It was disturbing to think she'd never known her mother. Fleetingly, he wondered about her father. But she was his kin. He should talk to her. He tried to remember what eight-year-olds thought about.

"What was the academy like?" he asked.

Emily stopped eating, set down her spoon and glanced from Miss Rose back to his face. "I enjoyed school, sir. I liked all the lessons, especially reading and history. I'm proficient with numbers and spelling."

"Did you have friends?"

"Yes, I had classmates, sir."

He'd expected her to mention other children, but she said nothing more. She watched him with uncertainty. Sometimes, during brief months of normalcy, he and Meriel had played and laughed together like other children. They'd gone fishing and made sailboats from twigs and leaves. The memories were poignant. "You look just like your mother."

"I do?"

He nodded. "Yes. Your eyes are like hers—dark and full

of mystery. When a person looks into your eyes, they wonder what you're thinking."

Emily returned his even gaze. "I was thinking about all the water we pumped today and wondering if I would have to go out to the trough in the dark to let enough water out to wash these dishes."

Taken aback by her practicality, Jules paused over his reply. "No," he said finally. "Wayland, the cook, will take care of the dishes."

She nodded. "I'm not afraid. I just don't much like the dark."

Jules glanced at Miss Rose, but she kept her gaze on her meal.

"Are there wolves and coyotes out there?" Emily asked.

"Not many this time of year," he answered. "In the spring, a mountain lion took a couple of the calves."

Emily's eyes widened.

Miss Rose lifted her head and cast him a pointed glance.

"It moved on, of course," he added quickly.

"It *killed* the calves?" Emily's voice rose in horror.

He had about as much tact talking to a kid as chickens had brains. He chastised himself. "Did you see my book on animal husbandry?" he asked quickly.

"What is that?" she asked.

Miss Rose cleared her throat this time.

Maybe the silence had been better. He went back to his meal, and Emily picked up her spoon again.

The quiet lasted another whole minute before a gunshot volleyed across the clearing and the echo reached them inside the cabin.

Emily dropped her spoon into her bowl with a clatter. She looked to Miss Rose in horror. "What's happening?"

Chapter Four

"It's no cause for concern," he told her, pushing back his chair with the backs of his knees as he stood. But his hand went instinctively to the .44 on his hip to draw it from its holster, and Emily's terrified eyes followed. "Stay put," he cautioned unnecessarily.

He headed for the door and loped toward the bunkhouse, where the side door stood open, illuminating a long rectangle of ground. "What's goin' on?"

"Judd shot hisself an elk!" Coonie called back, appearing from the darkness. "We won't be eatin' stringy squirrel meat tomorrow night."

"Ain't nothin' wrong with a good squirrel stew," Wayland grumbled from the bunkhouse doorway. "We need us some pheasants. Why don't you complainers shoot *pheasants?*"

Jules turned his back on the argument and headed back to the cabin. Emily had seated herself on the narrow bed under the window against the side wall. She put on a brave front, but fear was evident in her wide eyes and trembling lower lip. "Was it a mountain lion?"

Miss Rose looked at him as if to say, *Good job, terrifying the child with your story.*

"No, there aren't any mountain lions this time of year. There's plenty of food for them away from populated areas. One of the hands shot an elk."

"Was it attacking the ranch?"

He blinked. "No. Elk don't attack anything."

"Then why did he shoot it?"

"For tomorrow's supper."

She swallowed. Her large brown eyes moved to take in the table where they'd been eating and the bowls still sitting there. "What did we eat tonight?"

Miss Rose moved into action then, stacking the bowls on the tray. "Thank you for bringing our supper, Mr. Parrish."

"Jules," he said. "Call me Jules."

She nodded. "Jules. We will read for a few minutes and then retire. We've had an extremely long and tiring day."

Surely they had. They'd traveled quite a spell in the heat and then cleaned this entire cabin and did their laundry. They'd bathed, too, apparently, because Miss Rose's red-gold hair shone in the lantern light and her burnt face glistened with some sort of salve. "What did you put on that sunburn?"

"Glycerin."

"I have some salve that'll take out the sting." He rummaged in a coffee can on a shelf over the dry sink and located the small square tin.

She took it from him. "Thank you. Emily, let's apply it to your nose and cheeks, as well."

Emily approached Miss Rose and stood still beneath her touch as the woman dabbed the ointment on her skin. Then the girl's gaze rolled to Jules. "You're not leaving, are you?"

"I'm going to sleep in the bunkhouse."

"What if a mountain lion comes close?"

Apparently, his words hadn't convinced her that there was no danger, and reasonably, there always was an unpredictable element of concern. He briefly considered telling her his rifle in the trunk against the wall was loaded, but that might scare her more, and Miss Rose didn't seem the sort to know how to use a gun anyway.

"We're going to be safe here, Emily," Miss Rose assured her, raising a finger to her own nose to apply the salve.

Jules didn't have a mirror in the cabin. The only one was beside the bunkhouse where he and the hands shaved. He pointed to her nose. "You missed…"

She looked down her nose, and her eyes crossed.

He chuckled and took the tin from her, their fingers grazing. He dotted his index finger in the salve and dabbed it on the spot she'd missed. The rest of her face blazed so red he couldn't tell the difference between sunburn and embarrassment. He hadn't meant to mortify her with the simple touch. Taking a step back, he recapped the tin and set it on the edge of the table.

"What if a bear smells the dead elk and comes looking for food?" Emily asked.

Her teacher's gaze riveted on Jules for his reply, as well. Both females stared at him as if he was offering them up for lunch.

"Can't you stay here?" Emily asked. "Me and Miss Rose will sleep in one bed…or I will sleep on the floor."

"Miss Rose and I," the teacher corrected, but she didn't look either of them in the eye.

"Wouldn't be proper for me to stay in here with you two females," he said.

Emily went back to the bed, but not before he saw her lower lip quiver.

"I have a couple more things to take from the clothesline," Miss Rose told her. "Do you want to come with me?"

Emily shook her head. "I'm not afraid. I just don't want to go outside right now."

The child was terrified. Jules thought over the predicament. He sat down. "I'll sit here for a minute."

Miss Rose went out of doors, leaving him stewing.

When she returned, he said, "There's a lean-to on the side of the cabin."

The woman nodded curiously and folded the clothing.

"There's a pile of firewood in there, but I'll clean that out and sleep there."

"Tonight?" she asked.

He gestured to a small square window covered by wooden shutters. "I'll be sleeping right under that window." He turned to Emily. "Will that make you feel safer?"

She nodded, a look of relief lighting her features.

He grabbed a lantern from a hook and struck a match to light it. "That's my plan then."

Olivia experienced a rush of relief, not only for Emily's sake, but also for her own. Sometime later, as she and Emily read their separate books, the sounds of Jules laboring on the other side of the cabin wall were comforting. Scrapes and thumps and an occasional grunt reached their ears, reminding them that he was there, close enough to keep them safe.

Eventually, Olivia tucked Emily into bed and prepared the other bed for herself. She thought longingly about the small bag of tea leaves she had traded for apples in Oregon City. This would have been the perfect time for a relaxing cup of tea. Her thoughts wandered back to evenings at the academy before the war. The cook had always served afternoon and evening tea, often accompanied by cookies or a slice of fruit pie.

Olivia had always been lonely and isolated, but she'd been comfortable. She suffered a pang of guilt over her longing for indulgent comfort, when Emily was her foremost concern at the moment. *The Lord is my shepherd. I shall not want.*

She reassured herself with the words of the psalm that promised she would be provided for, fed and protected. She had a heavenly Father Who loved her and cared about her every need. He would tend to her and guide her steps as He always had.

The sounds from outside had stopped, so she assumed Jules had finished cleaning out the lean-to and had prepared himself a place to sleep. She changed into a cotton nightdress before checking on Emily, then lay on the wobbly bed and pulled a sheet over her legs. The cabin was still warm from the day's heat. One of the two shuttered windows was directly over where their host slept, but now that the light was extinguished, she got back up and opened both to allow a breeze to flow through.

Jules lay on his pallet with his hands stacked under his head. He'd dislodged a dozen spiders from their hiding places in the woodpile before sweeping the ground and walls and making his bed. He hoped none of them decided to come back and pay their old place a visit while he slept.

Above his head, the shutter opened. Either Olivia Rose was hot or she was as frightened as Emily and wanted the comfort of knowing he was only a shout away.

"Everything all right, Miss Rose?" he called.

"Perfectly all right," she replied. And then a moment later, "Thank you, Jules."

Her use of his name stirred something akin to embarrassment. But he'd liked the sound. "Sleep well," he replied.

Olivia woke with a start. She'd slept straight through the night and part of the morning. Getting up, she padded to the door and cracked it open to peer out.

A gray-haired man wearing trousers with suspenders over a union suit stood from where he'd been sitting on a chair outside the door. She'd never seen a union suit other than the artists' renditions in the Montgomery Ward catalogue, and she caught herself staring.

"Mornin', Mizz Rose." He held a partially carved wooden animal of some sort in one hand, a pocketknife in the other. "You ladies ready to pump water? Boss set me to waitin' for you to wake."

"Yes, water would be nice. Thank you."

He gave a nod. "Name's Wayland George, mizz."

"Pleased to meet you, Mr. George."

"After you're washed up and such, I'm t' bring you pans and supplies. Boss says you kin cook breakfast fer yerseff?"

"Yes, I can cook. Thank you."

He turned and walked toward the windmill.

Olivia got a pail, padded to the dry sink and raised and lowered the pump handle repeatedly until the pail was full. She moved to the window and waved to let Mr. George know she had enough water.

Emily woke, and after they had washed and dressed, the cook knocked on the door to present her with a basket of eggs and a slab of bacon, along with flour, sugar and other ingredients he'd carried in a crate. "This should get you started. Boss said I should take you into town for anythin' else you need."

"I don't think we need anything else."

"He said not to take no fer an answer, mizz. Said there'd be soap and the like you'd need. I'll have the wagon ready in a hour."

Olivia unpacked the supplies and prepared a quick meal of scrambled eggs and bacon. When Wayland came for them they were ready. He'd donned a plaid shirt, but rolled the sleeves back, so the forearm portions of his union suit were still visible. Wasn't he too warm in this weather?

This time the distance between the ranch and town didn't seem nearly as far. Mr. George was a chatty fellow, pointing out landmarks, wildlife and varieties of plants.

Olivia had already seen Corbin's Bend, but the town seemed less forbidding and the people more friendly when she showed up with Mr. George. She used her own money to make a few purchases in the mercantile, and then Emily accompanied her to the post office in the rear of the building, where she asked for pen and paper and wrote a brief note to Mrs. Hugh, letting her know she'd found Emily's uncle.

Afterward, Wayland delivered them back at the cabin.

"Do you suppose Mr. Wayland will make those biscuits again tonight?" Emily asked. She didn't look at Olivia as she asked the question. They'd eaten dry, heavy biscuits with each meal so far.

"I have supplies to make bread," she told her. "You can help, and then we'll work on your arithmetic while the dough rises."

Emily nodded eagerly.

The afternoon passed quickly with lessons and bread

making. She was determined to continue Emily's studies, no matter their location or lack of stability.

As the sun lowered on the horizon, a visitor arrived on the doorstep to introduce himself. The dusty dark-haired cowboy held his hat against his chest. "Lee Crandall, Miss Rose."

"Pleased to meet you," she said with a hesitant smile.

He gave her a broad grin and produced a bunch of lavender wildflowers he'd been hiding behind his hat. "For you and the little miss."

Hesitantly, she accepted the fragrant blooms. No one had ever given her flowers before. "Thank you, Mr. Crandall."

"Somethin' sure smells good."

She sent him away with three slices of her fresh bread.

The smells of her bread wafting on the summer air attracted more than one ranch hand. Before she knew it, she had a full bouquet on the table and the three loaves she'd baked had been whittled down to a few slices for their supper.

"It's a good thing Wayland left us plenty of flour," she told Emily. "I guess I'll make more bread tomorrow."

Expecting another ranch hand bearing flowers when a knock sounded, she was surprised to open the door to Jules. He held a covered pot by the handle. "Brought supper."

She gestured to the table she'd already set with three places. "You'll be joining us, won't you?"

He glanced at Emily. He'd washed and changed into clean clothing just in case. "I will."

This time, he'd left his revolver in his bedroll so as not to unduly frighten the girl. Jules remembered to wait while Miss Rose said the blessing. She was the most grateful woman he'd ever known, thankful for meals and provision and safety, when it appeared to him that she actually had very little.

The smell of fresh-baked bread was unmistakable in the

tiny cabin. He shot a gander at the slices on the cutting board. "Is that bread for our supper?"

Miss Rose got up to place the slices on a tin plate and set it on the table. "Help yourself."

He took a slice and bit into it while she served roast, potatoes and turnips from the kettle. After eating Wayland's drop biscuits for months, it was a treat to taste bread. Especially Miss Rose's bread. The yeasty taste and soft texture was delicious. "This is good."

"That seems to be the consensus. This is all that's left from three loaves."

Jules raised his eyebrows. "The hands were pestering you?"

"Not at all. Emily and I were pleased to make their acquaintance. They're all quite nice."

He scowled at the flowers in the pitcher on the table. "They're supposed to be minding their own business."

"I baked late in the day. The smell must have drawn them."

He'd smelled the bread baking, too, and it had set his mouth to watering. Even the most seasoned cowboy couldn't resist a woman's skill in the kitchen.

"Mr. George provided me with plenty of flour and salt, and I bought yeast in town today. I'll just make more tomorrow…if that's all right with you."

He nodded. "Did you get everything you needed, Miss Rose?"

"You may call me Olivia. Yes, thanks. We don't require much."

"Females need more paraphernalia than what I've got on hand. I know that much."

"Emily and I packed our own paraphernalia and brought it with us."

He slanted her a glance. Was she joking with him? Her expression was completely serious, and because it was, he wanted to laugh. She wouldn't appreciate that, so he held his amusement in check and ate his meal.

"We didn't bring anything to protect us from wild animals," Emily said unexpectedly.

Jules didn't know how to reply to that. He'd told Emily that she'd be safe in the cabin. Why didn't she believe him?

They ate several bites in silence. "When I was very small, I was afraid of snakes," Olivia told Emily. "There had never been a snake indoors at the academy, but I saw one while weeding the garden. The sight startled me so much that I was afraid to pull back my bedcovers at night for fear there would be a snake in my bed."

Emily stared at her. "In your bed?"

"It was a foolish fear, of course. Mrs. Hugh scolded me every night for a month because I wanted to sleep on top of the coverlet. She would pull down the bedding and prove to me there was no snake." She turned to Jules. "But that didn't convince me. The next night I'd be afraid to look under the covers all over again."

"Really, Miss Rose?" Emily's eyes widened. "I didn't think you were ever afraid of anything."

The teacher merely tilted her head in silent reply.

Jules imagined Olivia as a small girl with no parents, living in a house full of strangers. Her childhood fears disturbed him. He didn't like the mental images. When he glanced to observe Emily's reaction, her expression stopped his breath. She was a child living with strangers—well, Olivia wasn't a stranger, but she wasn't family—and her fear was real.

It didn't matter that her fear was unfounded, or that he'd assured her no bears had ever come near the cabin. It had been irrational for Olivia to think there was a snake in her bed, too, but she had. Young or old, real or imagined, fear was fear.

Jules had thought a lot about Meriel that day, and now he experienced anger toward his sister for leaving her baby. What had been so important that she couldn't care for her own child?

His sister's daughter sat at his table. The fact took some time to sink in. She'd never known a family, and now here he was, a man she'd never met—hadn't even known existed. No wonder she didn't trust him yet. They'd have to build that trust. Together. "Tell me more about your life at the academy, Emily."

She set down her fork and folded her hands in her lap politely. "Mrs. Hugh was the headmistress. She checked our rooms and our beds each morning before we went to the classroom."

"Checked for what?" he asked.

"To make sure the room was clean and the bed neatly made."

His gaze slid to two perfectly made beds across the room. Not a wrinkle in sight. "Go on."

"Class began at seven-thirty. Mrs. Pierce was my teacher when I was small, and Miss Rose became my teacher when I learned to read and write."

"Were your teachers good to you?"

Her blue gaze never left his. "Miss Rose taught me English and spelling and history. I did all my work on time, and I received high marks for my achievements."

"That wasn't what I meant. Were they *kind* to you?"

She appeared to think a moment. "Miss Rose is very kind, sir. Sometimes she came to our room and read to us at night. And she often took us out of doors for walks and nature adventures." She gave Olivia a fond yet timid smile. "And when the others all left on holidays, we celebrated, just the two of us. On Christmas we cut down a little tree for the tabletop and decorated it with berries and cut-paper figures. It was ever so much fun."

"Just the two of you? Where were the other students?"

"Their parents came for them, sir."

Thinking about the two of them alone together at Christmas, Jules's meal settled like a lump in his belly. He dared a glance at Olivia. She had set her fork down, as well, and now stared at her plate, her cheeks flushed.

"You don't remember your mother, Emily?" he asked.

"No."

He let that fact finally sink in.

"Miss Rose said I have a grandmother."

He nodded and studied her curious expression. "Her name is Lorena. I remember her as being very pretty, with dark wavy hair."

"Like mine?" Emily asked.

Jules's throat tightened. "Exactly like yours."

"Do you think she will want me?"

Her straightforward question caught him unprepared. His mother had loved her children, but she hadn't protected them the way a mother should. Maybe it had even been a mistake to contact her. If her current husband was anything like his father had been, their home wouldn't be a good place for Emily. "Well, I—I can't say. She has a life in Cincinnati."

"We brought a map," she told Jules. "I looked at Ohio."

He nodded.

"Miss Rose and I planned our trip here with the map. We figured out the miles and the trains to take."

"You must have been scared."

She thought for a moment. "Leaving the academy was scary."

He laced his fingers and rested his chin against them, with his elbows planted on the table.

"You're safe here," he told her earnestly. "I won't let anything happen to you, and I'll find somewhere for you to live."

"At another academy?" she asked.

He didn't want to agree with her now. He'd thought finding a school would be in her best interests…but hearing the way she talked about her life there… She took being alone for granted. There were times growing up when he'd believed being alone would have been better, but he knew differently now. He'd spent plenty of holidays alone or punching cattle, but Emily was a *child*. She deserved someone to look out for her best interests and provide a home.

His own father had never been a good provider, and Jules had made up his mind he would never do that to a wife or kids. He was going to have his ranch operating, build a home and be financially stable before he took on the responsibility of anyone other than himself.

Kids needed someone to love them.

So far, everything he'd seen told him Olivia Rose was that person for Emily. If things were different—if he'd had more time to fulfill his plans—he might be able to think about keeping the two of them on. But he wasn't ready, and anything less was unfair to the kid. No matter how hard it was, he had to keep Emily's best interests in mind.

And Lord help him, from the look of things now, sending his niece away was going to be plenty hard.

Chapter Five

The remainder of the week went much the same. Olivia planned each day with time to make six loaves of bread. Before supper, she sent five with Wayland for the hands.

On Friday he didn't show up in the afternoon, so she waited until she saw Coonie returning to the barn and carried out the basket.

When the cowboy spotted her, he swept his dusty hat from his head, revealing sweaty hair and a white forehead above his tanned face. He grinned ear to ear. "Miss Rose!"

"Good evening, Mr. Boles. I wanted to make sure the men had bread for their evening meal." She extended the basket.

"Thanks, Miss Rose. We never ate such good bread before you got here. Gotta say, supper's the highlight of my day."

"Baking it is my pleasure," she told him, and she meant it. The men were so appreciative that she enjoyed making the loaves for them. "I was wondering…"

"Yes, miss?"

"I can bake a fair pie, too."

His eyes lit up and a grin split his face.

"But I have no idea where to come by apples or peaches or any type of fruit."

"Don't give it another thought," he told her, cradling the basket in one arm. His mount flicked its tail and raised its head, but Coonie held the beast by the reins without loosening his grip on the basket. "You'll have fruit for pies."

She smiled and thanked him just as Jules rode toward the barn and reined his horse to a halt.

Coonie backed away and tucked his hat back on his head.

Jules swung his leg over and dismounted. "Evenin', Olivia. How did Emily's studies go today?"

"Quite well."

"I was thinking," he said. "Since tomorrow is Saturday, and the two of you have been cooped up all week long, we should go for an outing."

She used her hand as a shade to keep the setting sun from her eyes and looked up at him. "What sort of outing?"

"A ride. Into town. Or whatever Emily would like."

She agreed with a nod. "I'm sure she'll be delighted."

The next morning when Olivia and Emily exited the cabin dressed in their colorful day dresses, two bushels of apples sat on the ground a few feet from the door. Olivia smiled. "Look! I can make pies."

Emily helped her drag the baskets indoors out of the sun. Jules joined them then.

"Where are we going?" Emily asked.

"Thought we'd go for a ride, then have a meal in town. That sound okay by you, miss?"

She tied the ribbons of her bonnet under her chin. "Yes, certainly."

Olivia enjoyed the countryside more than she had during their trip to this place. At that time everything had seemed vast and dangerous and uncertain. But Jules knew this land and could protect them should trouble arise. His provision was exactly what she wanted for Emily. This was a safe place, and he was someone who could care for her. It was plain he wasn't immune to the child's needs.

"A lot of the state is prairie," he said to Emily as he guided the horses pulling the wagon to stop above a wide valley that overlooked a gently flowing azure river. "Which is what you mostly saw coming here. I picked this area to ranch because it's closer to the mountains, so there's more hunting, fishing and, of course, more trees available for lumber. The corrals you see are all made from lodgepole pine." He pointed west. "Those hills are covered with ponderosa pine, spruce, fir, birch, red cedar, ash and alder. This here river has some of the biggest trout I've ever clapped eyes on. Tasty, provided the right cook fries them up."

"Have I ever had trout, Miss Rose?" Emily asked.

"I don't believe so. I can't recall ever eating much fish at all."

"We had chickens," Emily told him. "How do you get the fish out of the water?" she asked a moment later.

Jules raised his eyebrows. "With a pole and a line with a hook on it."

"Can I try it?"

He glanced at Olivia. "Sure. I was wondering…about tomorrow."

"What about tomorrow?" Olivia asked.

"It's Sunday."

"Yes."

"Well, seeing as you're a God-fearing woman and all, I supposed you'd want to go to church."

In Pennsylvania, Olivia had only been able to attend

services on Easter. Mrs. Hugh had held a Sunday-morning class in their upstairs alcove, where the teachers and students had gathered to listen to Bible readings and have a silent prayer time. "Why, I'd love to attend church with you," she answered.

"With me? Well, I—I, uh…." He tilted his head and scratched his jaw, but then he turned to look at her. "All right then."

She smiled hesitantly at the prospect of a church service when it wasn't even a holiday.

"Care to get down and walk a spell?" he asked. "There are wildflowers along the banks that slope toward the river."

Emily and Olivia agreed they'd enjoy a walk, so he stopped the wagon. He reached up for Emily first, his hands spanning her tiny torso and delivering her safely to stand in the grass. He reached for Olivia next.

She took the hand he offered. It was strong and callused and warm—and unlike any touch she'd ever known. She leaped easily to the ground and he steadied her with a hand at her back. His attentiveness warmed her more than the summer sun.

"I'll walk ahead and you follow in my path," he said.

His touch had been brief, but when he released her fingers, she experienced an unexplainable sense of loss. They swiftly learned why he'd gone ahead. The prairie grass was far taller than Olivia's knees and would have swallowed Emily, but with him flattening broad areas with each step of his booted feet, they were able to follow easily. His gentlemanly consideration was a new and heady experience.

Just ahead, a sloping field of bright orange flowers took Olivia's breath away. Emily dashed out from behind Jules to venture into the midst of the colorful flowers. "Look at all these orange flowers, Miss Rose! Have you ever seen anything so pretty?"

Jules halted and turned for Olivia to catch up.

"I don't believe I ever have," she replied in breathless wonder. "What are they?"

"Poppies," he answered.

"The ones that aren't open look like they're bowing their heads," Emily observed.

Olivia had never seen Emily so animated or free. Her smile encompassed her entire countenance. Turning in a circle, the child opened her arms wide and lifted her face to the sun. The picture she made, surrounded by flowers and uninhibited in her enjoyment, gave Olivia a bursting sense of contentment.

Being here was everything she'd ever wanted for Emily…and for herself, but she couldn't let her thoughts go there.

If she had a child of her own, she would make her feel special every day. She would make a point of telling her child daily how loved and wanted she was. And she would never let her be lonely. If God ever blessed her with a family of her own, she would make sure there were days like this and she would make them as happy as Emily was at this moment.

Her throat tightened with the threat of tears, so she took a deep breath to compose herself.

"I think she likes the poppies," Jules said from beside her.

"How could she not?"

"And you?" he asked.

She sensed his gaze on her and avoided his eyes. "I've never seen anything so beautiful."

"Takes your breath away, doesn't it?"

She turned to find him gazing at her. "That's it exactly. And to think God created this out in the middle of nowhere, for His own pleasure more than anything else."

"I never thought about it like that," he said.

"How many people do you suppose have seen this field?"

He studied the landscape from beneath the brim of his hat. His jaw was lean and recently shaved, and his lips parted to reply, "Just this season…or in all the years since it's been here?"

He turned his gaze back to her as though her reply mattered.

"In forever." Was there was an occasional passerby or was Jules the only human to appreciate this beauty?

"Don't know," he said finally. "I've thought about building a house right here, just below the crest of this hill, facing the river. Then I'd see the poppies every summer."

Olivia couldn't even wrap her imagination around a home like the one he spoke of.

"Not a practical idea, though." He shrugged. "House should be protected from wind and storms, like nearer the foothills, where my barns are. And there are shade trees there. I suppose a person could plant a few trees here, but it would take years until they were sizable."

Olivia studied the bank of flowers. "You could always dig up some of these and plant them near your house."

He turned and looked at her with a grin. "That's a smarter idea."

Emily leaped through the grass to where they stood and waited politely for Olivia to acknowledge her.

"What is it, Emily?"

"Remember the story we read where the family packed their lunch in a basket and ate it in a field of clover?"

"I do recall that story."

"May we do that one day soon? May we pack our lunch and come eat here?"

"Well, I don't know." The idea took her by surprise. She didn't have the capability to maneuver a horse and wagon to a remote spot like this. She doubted she could even find it on her own.

"You've never been on a picnic?" Jules asked Emily.

"No, sir. But I'd like to try it this once."

He used his thumb to ease his hat brim up and away from his eyes. When the sunlight hit them, Olivia noted how startlingly blue they were. She had never looked directly into his eyes for any length of time because it seemed forward and made her uncomfortable, so now she studied him as if for the first time.

Men were an oddity. She'd rarely encountered them in Pennsylvania—secluded as she was at the academy—and most she'd seen on their way here had left her unimpressed. They'd been dirty, and some had downright smelled. The way many of them stared at her had been disturbing. She didn't feel the same revulsion when Jules Parrish looked at her or spoke to her. His voice had a calming effect, and his smile…she couldn't even put coherent thoughts to the effect of his smile.

"We'll pick up a lunch after church tomorrow and come here to eat it," he promised.

"What do you mean pick up a lunch?" Emily asked.

"Buy food at the café or the saloon," he replied.

"We bought food on our way here," Emily told him. "Those was the first times I ever ate anything 'cept what Cook or Miss Rose fixed."

"Those *were*," Olivia corrected.

"Did you hear that, Miss Rose?" Emily asked with a bright smile. "We're going to come back here for a picnic *tomorrow!*"

"I heard," she replied.

A little later, as Emily made her way up the hill ahead of them, Jules studied her, then turned to Olivia. "Emily has nice dresses and shoes. An adequate supply, would you say?"

"The academy had an enormous closet of outgrown clothing that the children could select from for their own wardrobes. Many of the students had wealthy parents, and they provided their own children's clothing and shoes, and then donated the items once they were outgrown."

"Good system." He nodded and settled his hat properly, but looked at her from the corner of his eye. "And yourself?"

"I've made all my own clothing since I was seventeen. Sewing is one of the many skills the academy taught."

"What *does* she need?"

He looked and sounded as though his interest was sincere, as though he cared about Emily's welfare, and the significance did her heart good. "She needs a family."

Chapter Six

His expression, which had been one of open concern, swiftly closed, and he drew his eyebrows down to fix her with a hard stare. "I'm a man alone out here. You can see plain as day that this isn't anyplace for a young girl to stay."

Unused to confrontation, or any dialogue with men, she had trouble meeting his direct gaze. She glanced away and back, and her heartbeat sped up. Uncomfortable as a discussion might be, it was her mission to see that Emily had family to care for her. "You said you're going to build a house."

"That will take time and a lot of work, and even if I had a house, she can't stay alone while I'm gone every hour of daylight."

"There's a school in town, is there not?"

He blinked before replying, "There's a school. But gettin' her there and back would take precious time. It's plain that the best place for her is at a school where she can live, where there are other girls around and someone to watch out for her."

"Perhaps it's plain to you, but it's not plain to me. If you ask Emily, I'd suppose it's not plain to her, either. I've never seen her like this." She turned her attention to watch Emily pluck a yellow flower and raise it to her nose. "She's happier than I've ever seen her. You might not believe so, but she's always been a quiet and reserved child."

"She's the best-mannered kid I've ever met," he answered. "Not that I've known many. Doesn't change the fact that she can't stay here."

Olivia's optimism threatened to deflate somewhat, but she bit her tongue. Arguing with him wasn't going to change his mind today. There was time before his mother replied or before Olivia really had to help him find a school, and she prayed that during that time he would experience a change of heart.

Their disagreement put a damper on conversation the rest of the afternoon, but Emily didn't seem to notice.

Jules drove to town, and showed Emily the notions counter in the mercantile. Olivia remained near the sewing items to deliberately give them time together, and watched unobtrusively. Jules pointed out hair combs and hand mirrors, gathering a small pile of items to purchase.

"Miss Rose?" Emily called.

Olivia joined her where she stood gazing into a flat wooden tray of small silk and velvet flowers.

Her face lit with fascination. "Did you ever see velvet violets, Miss Rose?"

"I never have," Olivia answered with a smile.

"What's this one?" Emily asked.

"Morning glory," Jules replied.

"What do you do with them?" Olivia asked.

"Wear 'em in your hair," he replied.

The mercantile owner's wife who'd been silent until

then spoke up. "The larger ones are worn pinned on your dress or collar, miss."

"Oh, I see."

"I'm getting the forget-me-nots." Emily showed her the blue flowers she'd selected. She glanced up at her uncle. "Miss Rose should have a rose, don't you think?"

He glanced over the tray as though considering. "What color?"

"This bunch is lovely." The store owner picked up a delicate pink fabric rose with two tiny buds on a stem. "The leaves are muslin, but they look real, don't they?"

"We'll take that one," Jules decided.

"No, I—"

"What?" Jules asked, turning to her. "Emily's picking it out for you."

But they both knew he was making the purchase.

"I don't need it, really," she objected.

"Well, nobody *needs* one." He gave the other woman a lopsided smile. "Females like frippery and the like, don't they?"

"Most do," she agreed with a warm smile, then introduced herself to Olivia. "We haven't met yet. I'm Hessie Bates."

"Olivia Rose," she replied. "Your husband helped me last time I was here."

"Henry is my brother. My husband passed on five years ago."

"Oh, I'm sorry."

"No need to worry, dear." She stepped around the counter with the silk rose and a straight pin in her hand. "Miss Rose, is it? No wonder the child thought a rose was fitting." She pinned the artificial flower to Olivia's collar. "And pink suits you. Fresh and sweet."

Olivia blushed.

Mrs. Bates chatted with her while Emily and Jules finished their shopping and later wished her goodbye at the door.

The day's outing had exhausted Emily. On the ride home, she leaned against Olivia's shoulder and fell asleep. Olivia maneuvered her arm around the girl's shoulders so she could hold her steady and comfortably, and Emily nestled against her.

Holding the child near was an unusual experience, foreign and yet pleasant. The sun remained hot overhead, but she didn't mind the additional warmth against her side.

As a girl, she'd occasionally held the few babies at the academy while taking her turn in the nursery. When she had, she'd wondered about her own care as an infant. Who had looked after her, changed her and fed her? Had anyone ever rocked her or sung to her? Seeing the minimal attention the babies received, she doubted so.

She vaguely remembered Emily as an infant, and thought it sad that no one had doted on her progress over those months. Her first true recollections of Emily came from the time when Olivia had begun teaching, and Emily had been in the class of beginners. Olivia had been only nineteen at the time, but she'd tried to give special attention to each of her students. She knew what it was like to be overlooked and shuffled about, and she knew, as well, that Emily had no parents to oversee her care.

Emily's trust was a sacred thing. Olivia had promised that she would take care of her, and she was determined to do her very best. *Emily needed her.*

The warm thought gave her a sense of belonging she'd never known. Even out here in the middle of an unfamil-

iar land, living with strangers, she and Emily were bound…
like family.

Tears smarted behind her eyelids, and she blinked them
away. Getting sentimental wouldn't prove sensible. Once
Emily was settled, and Olivia was certain the child would be
safe and loved, she would be finding her own way, taking a
position wherever she could find one. After that it was likely
she would never see Emily again. She wouldn't delude herself
into thinking she might be able to visit one day in the future.

She didn't want to dwell on the inevitable, so she enjoyed Emily's head resting under her chin and admired the
beautiful, wild countryside.

When they arrived at the cabin, Emily roused, and
Olivia helped her down. Jules carried the supplies indoors.
He removed items from a crate and handed each of them
an object wrapped in brown paper.

"What is this?" Olivia asked.

Emily opened hers to find a pair of hair combs studded
with seed pearls. "They are my favorites!" She grinned and
looked up at him. "Thank you, Uncle Jules."

He looked a little taken aback by her address, but he
recovered. "You're welcome. They're perfect for your
pretty, dark hair." He turned to Olivia and raised a brow
in expectation.

"Oh." She looked down at the object she held, and
slowly peeled away the wrapping, revealing a hand mirror
set in smooth polished walnut. The slender handle had
been shaped to fit her palm. She caught the reflection of
the rafters and lifted the mirror to see herself. Her cheeks
were flushed, and tendrils of hair escaped her bonnet. With
her other hand, she removed her hat and glanced at her disheveled hair. "Oh, my goodness."

She tucked a few strands into her upswept knot.

Slowly, she lifted her gaze to Jules. He didn't ogle her the same way those other men had, and right now there was no humor reflected. She couldn't identify the expression in his blue eyes, but her stomach dipped with disquiet.

"Only mirror on the place is out where the hands shave," he said. "Figured ladies should have a mirror."

Each year at Christmas, she had received a practical, impersonal gift, such as a book or a handkerchief, from Mrs. Hugh. No one had ever given her anything as thoughtful…and certainly never on a day that wasn't Christmas. She didn't know how to react. "I—I don't know what to say."

He grinned. "If you like it, say thank-you."

"I do like it. Thank you."

Her reactions puzzled Jules. Sometimes he thought her a snob of the highest sort, and other times—like this—she behaved like a child experiencing life for the first time. From her shock at that simple mirror and the way she'd touched its handle, one would have thought he'd given her a diamond mine.

"I suppose you'll want to bathe tonight." He emptied the rest of the crate and stored items away. "After supper, I'll bring water from the trough. Faster than pumping that much. I'll make sure you have enough wood to heat it on the stove."

Spurred into action by his words, she moved over to the stove. Since she'd been gone all day and hadn't baked bread, Olivia quickly measured cornmeal and baked corn bread. Wayland provided them with roasted wild turkey and boiled potatoes.

After bringing in water and asking Coonie to stack wood beside the door, Jules excused himself and carried the dirty dishes out to the cook. During the summer, Wayland set up his outdoor kitchen under a lean-to built against the bunkhouse. Unless it rained, the hands most often ate at a roughly hewn table, sitting on benches made from slabs of tree trunks. Tonight most of them remained at the table, talking over their plans for Sunday, their day off.

"Wanna join us, boss?" the other man asked Jules.

"I'll sit with you for a bit."

"We sorely missed Miss Rose's usual bread t'day," Lee Crandall told him. "Though the corn bread was mighty fine."

"She'll be occupied tomorrow, too," Jules replied.

Wayland stopped scrubbing and looked up from the washtub, where he stood with his arms in suds up to his elbows. "She stayin'?"

"No. She'll be leavin' after we find a place for Emily."

Lee glanced up from his whittling. "Miss Rose probably won't be goin' far once the fellas in town get a gander at her."

Jules leveled his gaze in the man. "What do you mean?"

"I mean she's the prettiest little gal Corbin's Bend has seen in a long while. Somebody's gonna offer to marry her."

"If I had my own spread, I'd offer for her," young Ham Stowe said with a grin.

"She wouldn't have your ugly puss," Judd said.

The men chuckled, all except Jules.

Coonie squinted at Jules through the curling smoke of his cigar. "Why is it *you're* not askin' for her hand?"

Jules picked at a splinter on the corner of the table. "Marriage doesn't fit into my plans yet. I don't even have the house built."

"Summer's slow around here." Lee scratched his stubbled chin. "We could work on that house and have it done afore winter."

Jules frowned. "When I need your advice on pickin' a wife, I'll let you know."

The men chuckled and their conversation picked up another thread. Jules swallowed his irritation, but after a few more minutes, he decided to call it a night. He had enough on his plate without suggestions on how to make his life more complicated. There was nothing wrong with taking things slow and easy, accomplishing the things he'd set out to do in the sensible order.

That night, disturbing dreams of Meriel calling for help interrupted his sleep. He was wrapped in some sort of cocoon that kept him from going to her, and her voice grew farther and farther away, until he couldn't hear her at all. The next sound he heard was a child crying. *Emily?*

Jules woke with a start and blinked into the darkness. His arm had gone to sleep, so he sat and rubbed feeling back into it. He paused.

There it was again. The crying hadn't been part of his dream. He stood and crept to the window. Surely Olivia would hear Emily and comfort her. If that happened, Jules wouldn't want to intrude.

Stretching upward, he peered into the room. A shaft of moonlight laid an arrow of light across Emily's peacefully sleeping face. She hadn't been crying after all. The noise had been so real, he'd been sure he'd heard it.

He'd almost moved away, when he heard the sound again. A soft muffled sob. But the weeping hadn't come from Emily.

Olivia.

The realization burned through his awareness and stabbed him with empathy. She was of a delicate gender and tender age, a gently bred young woman doing her best to look out for her young charge, yet she had no stability or security of her own. Her composure and confidence had all been for show.

Softly spoken words drifted to him then, and he strained to make them out. Who was Olivia speaking to? She and Emily were the only two in there, and Emily was sound asleep.

"...I shall not want," she said. "You make me to lie down in green pastures. You lead me beside still waters. You restore my soul. You lead me in the paths of righteousness for Your name's sake. Even when I walk through the valley of the shadow of death, I will fear no evil..."

Jules had never heard anyone personalize a verse of Scripture and say it to God as though God was a person right there in the room with them. But that's what Olivia was doing.

"Lord, Your goodness and Your mercy followed me all the way to Montana," she continued. "And now I'm trusting Jules to do the right thing."

He got a hitch in his chest, a sensation more uncomfortable than his prickling arm. Lowering himself away from the window, he moved back to his pallet. Olivia's talking stopped and so did the crying. Apparently, she'd been comforted by that psalm.

The night's silence closed around him. The only sounds were the ordinary ones of the livestock, the wind and the creaking windmill, but he couldn't forget what he'd heard. And he couldn't go back to sleep. After lying awake until first light, he got up and started chores.

Sunday morning. Olivia was as pretty as a picture in a pale green striped dress, with the velvet rose pinned to her collar. She wore green silk ribbons threaded through her hair, the ends dangling from the shiny golden knot. She topped her head with a straw hat, hiding most of those shiny curls, and Jules disguised disappointment he shouldn't have felt.

Emily wore a shade of blue that reminded him of the bluebells he'd seen in Texas, and he told her so.

She thanked him politely. "Will you stay beside me in church?"

"Of course." He reached for her hand.

She looked at their clasped hands in surprise and then offered him a shy smile. "I won't know anyone there."

"You'll make friends."

She shook her head. "I don't think so."

"Why not?"

"I'm not from around here like they are. And besides, Miss Rose says I'm leaving to attend another school. I don't want to make friends and then leave." Remorse stabbed his conscience. He pushed it away by telling himself that sending Emily away was the right thing to do.

Yet in spite of his reassurances, Olivia's prayer the previous night still hadn't left his thoughts. *And now I'm trusting Jules to do the right thing.*

She had more faith in him than he had in himself.

Chapter Seven

Emily's practical reasoning about avoiding new friendships rubbed him wrong all through the drive to town. A child shouldn't plan to hold herself in check. A little girl should just…be a child. But that was another argument for sending her away, wasn't it? No child would be safe all alone in his cabin every day. He wasn't going to feel guilty about looking out for her best interests.

His presence at the First United Fellowship of Christ Church was an oddity in itself, but arriving with two unfamiliar females in tow caused a stir that morning. The women gathered around, eager to learn about his guests and introduce themselves.

Emily participated in the singing with enthusiasm, while Olivia held herself more in reserve. Both showed interest in Reverend Vaughn's sermon, and both placed a coin in the offering basket as it passed. After the service, it appeared as though Lee Crandall's prediction might be correct. Half a dozen single men—cowhands, ranchers and the barber's son—all asked for introductions.

Obviously embarrassed by the attention, Olivia offered polite greetings, but it was plain she only wanted to escape the building and their interest. She was more vulnerable than he'd first thought, and his inconvenient need to protect her grew each day. Jules couldn't help recalling the sounds of her soft crying the night before or her voice as she turned a psalm into her heartfelt prayer for comfort. He'd overheard something so intimate that it embarrassed him to have eavesdropped.

A slender woman who hadn't been among the throng of fancily dressed churchgoers who first greeted them approached, carrying a baby on her hip. "Hello, Miss Rose. I'm Tanis Roland. My husband is one of Jules's hands. We live in the wagon and tent down by the pasture. You've probably seen it."

Two small children clung to her skirt. "This here's Abner," she said, referring to the baby she held. "And the older ones are Charlie and Noreen."

"It's a pleasure to meet you," Olivia said with a warm smile. "This is Emily Sadler, Mr. Parrish's niece."

"Except for your dark eyes, you look like him around the eyes and mouth," Tanis told Emily. "I could've picked you from a crowd."

Emily's pleasure at the remark touched Olivia. The woman had no idea how gratifying her words had been to a child who'd never had a family connection. Olivia studied the youngsters, fascinated by their resemblance to their mother. Their eyes, however, were brown while hers were pale green.

A man no taller than Tanis came up beside her and offered Olivia his hand. "Will Roland, miss."

The children had his warm brown eyes.

"Do you already have plans for dinner?" Tanis asked.

Jules glanced at his niece. "Emily wants to have a picnic, so we're picking up a meal on our way out of town. You're welcome to join us."

Tanis and her husband exchanged a look. He nodded.

"We'd like that," Tanis said with a smile. "I don't have anything fancy, but we'll share what we have. Where?"

"Let's combine our dinners and eat whatever shows up," Jules told her. "You can follow us."

Jules led his two guests outdoors and across the lawn to where the wagons and buggies waited. At the café, he purchased a crateful of food, along with wrapped jars of milk and lemonade, and stored them securely in the wagon bed.

They stopped by the ranch first so the Rolands could pack supplies, and then the family followed as Jules directed the horses. This time, he navigated along the river, so they approached the location from below, rather than above, and had the shade of the trees along the bank in which to leave the wagons and set up their picnic area.

He had planned ahead, packing tarps and blankets. Will helped him create a shelter with canvas and poles. Then Jules spread the blankets on the ground, while Will took the baby from his wife so she could unpack food and dishes.

Olivia assisted her, enjoying all the new experiences and the company of another young woman.

Once everything was arranged, they sat in a circle on the blankets, and Tanis nodded at Will.

He doffed his hat, and Jules did the same. "We're almighty grateful for this food, Lord," Will prayed. "And the company. We'd be obliged if You'd bless it now and watch over us this fine day. Amen."

"Amen," the children chorused.

Tanis gave her husband a smile so warm, a person would

think he'd just recited the most eloquent prayer in history. He placed the baby on the blanket, where the little guy sat up on his own, stuck one finger in his mouth and blinked at the strangers.

"That fried chicken sure smells good," Will remarked.

"I got plenty," Jules told him.

Tanis had sliced ham and cheese and bread. "How did you bake bread?" Olivia asked, wondering how the other woman managed, living out of a wagon.

"Will bought me a stove," the woman replied. "It sits out of doors until we have a place, but it works fine, all the same."

"Come winter, I think you should take the cabin," Jules said as they ate.

"But that's your place," Will replied.

"Can't have your children sleepin' in a wagon during a Montana winter," Jules argued. "I can stay in the bunkhouse, same as the other men."

"Or we could get your house built this summer, like Lee suggested."

Jules didn't reply, nor did he look to see if Olivia or Emily glanced at him. He gave Will a silencing glare, and the other man grinned and looked away.

Tanis poured drinks into jars. "Where are you from back East, Miss Rose?"

Her question and the attention caught Olivia off guard. She gave Tanis and her husband a self-conscious glance. "Pennsylvania."

"Did you grow up there?"

She nodded. "Yes."

"Will's family is in Illinois," the woman told her. "We met a year or so after he came West. I've been in Montana my whole life. Never seen an eastern city. My pa runs a stage station to the north. I grew up mucking stalls and trimming hooves."

"Tanis knows how to cure what ails a horse," Jules added. "Her doctoring has come in handy more than once."

"I don't know anything about horses," Olivia said.

"You're a teacher, is that right?" Tanis asked. At Olivia's confirmation, she glanced at her husband. "My kids are going to learn to read and figure," she said and blushed. "I can barely sign my name."

Olivia sensed her embarrassment. "If I'm here long enough, I'll be glad to teach you to read and write."

The other woman got tears in her eyes. "You would? You would really do that for me? I'd be grateful, miss. Then my younguns wouldn't have to be ashamed of their ma."

"They don't have reason to be ashamed of you now," Olivia assured her. "But, yes, of course I will."

"I can't pay you much," Tanis added.

"I couldn't take anything. It would be—"

"A gift?" Emily asked.

Olivia glanced at her. "Yes, I guess so. A gift."

"Miss Rose and I got gifts from Uncle Jules." Emily raised her hand to touch the ornament in her dark hair. "He gave me these hair combs, and Miss Rose got a hand mirror."

"I noticed your combs," Tanis said. "They're so pretty."

"I never got a gift when it wasn't Christmas or my birthday," Emily added.

"When *is* your birthday?" Jules asked.

Emily told him the date in October, and he nodded.

If her uncle had his way, Olivia would be gone by then, as would Emily. She would think of a gift to leave with Emily before they had to part.

Leaving her anywhere, whether it was at a new school

or even here with her uncle, would break Olivia's heart. If she had her wish they would remain together. But wishes weren't for people like Olivia. She had to think practically and without sentimentality, because dreaming did no good. This was the life she'd been given, and she had to make the best of it. She trusted that when the time came, God would heal her broken heart. As long as Emily was safe and happy, Olivia would find a way to be content.

Thank You, Lord, for this time with Emily. Let me be a blessing to her and make a difference in making her life better.

They finished eating, and Jules shooed Tanis away to play with the children while he and Olivia cleaned up. She carried their plates and forks to the river's edge to swish them in the cool clear water. A swarm of tiny fish darted away, startling her. As the children ran along the bank, frogs leaped from hiding places in the long grasses into the river.

Olivia had never been this close to a river or seen frogs or live fish. She discovered all her new surroundings with acute fascination.

Turning, she found Emily and Noreen, hand in hand, wading through the orange field of poppies. The ocean of flowers swallowed Noreen all the way to her midriff, but she laughed with Emily.

Previously, Olivia had observed that Emily was good with younger children. Had she stayed at the academy, she would have made a good teacher one day. She still might choose that path. Secretly, however, Emily hoped she would find a man to love and raise a family of her own.

Arresting her thoughts before they took her on another road to their parting days, she finished rinsing the dishes and set them out to dry. Jules had stretched out on the blanket and lay with his hat over his face, his hands folded on his chest. She seated herself, careful not to disturb his rest, and watched the Rolands playing with their two younger children.

She wondered what it was like to be a wife and a mother, how it would feel to have people who were your family, your flesh and blood. Will and Tanis had a history—with their parents, with each other, and were creating future stories for their offspring.

"Kind of you to offer to teach Tanis."

She'd thought Jules was sleeping, so his remark surprised her. "It's something I can do."

He reached to remove his hat and set it away. "Checked with the town council, but we don't need a teacher in Corbin's Bend."

"I'm sure I'll find a position." She had no other skills, so she had to utilize her education. "Someone will need a teacher."

A moment later, he sat up and glanced absently toward the river. She wondered what he thought when he looked out across the landscape. He probably didn't feel as small and alone as she did. He seemed confident with himself and his abilities. Confident about the future that lay ahead of him. She admired his ambition and drive. What must it be like to take control over one's own life and manage situations?

People looked up to him and respected him. The hands listened to him direct their tasks and often came to him with questions and concerns about the way a job should be done. She'd seen the way he'd been welcomed by community members at church that morning.

"When's *your* birthday?" he asked.

That wound still raw, she hesitated. "I'm not sure."

He glanced at her with a question in his expression.

Olivia raised her chin and studied the sun sparkling on the rippling river. "I always believed it was in May, but recently I learned that one of the teachers selected that date because the academy had no idea when I was born. Seems one day a delivery boy just showed up with me at the door. He turned over money, but no note or names or dates. The same teacher who chose my birthday gave me a name."

Jules didn't say anything for a moment. Finally, he said, "She picked a good name. Suits you."

She turned to catch him studying her, his expression soft, like the way he looked at Emily sometimes. "Miss Porter said I had a mouth like a rosebud."

She hadn't intended to seat herself so close to him, and he'd inched even closer. His eyes were vivid against his tanned skin and the backdrop of blue sky.

Being close to him flustered her, but when his gaze dropped to her lips, her stomach filled with butterflies. This *definitely* wasn't the same look he gave Emily.

Chapter Eight

The moment stretched out. The sounds of the river and the children faded into the distant background. Olivia's vision blurred around the edges and then came into focus again. She'd never experienced anything like this. His riveted gaze and her reaction confused her.

Attention of any sort was out of her experience, and his was doubly startling. Not because she didn't like it—but because she did.

He leaned toward her. She moved, as well, unintentionally, but forward all the same, until their faces were mere inches apart.

She had a life-altering moment, in which she realized what was going to happen. The anticipation caught her by surprise.

He kissed her then, closing his eyes and touching his lips to hers in a tentative greeting. Caught up in the idyllic moment, Olivia let her eyelids drift shut. Nothing had prepared her for his kiss, for this moment or the experience.

Mrs. Hugh had taught them deportment, manners and

etiquette, but the subject of kissing had been omitted from her education. Had anyone told her it would happen to her, she might have been interested. Had anyone told her she would like it, she would have been doubtful.

But she enjoyed Jules Parrish's kiss more than was likely proper. Without a doubt, she could grow overly fond of kissing him.

He moved back, and she opened her eyes.

"I didn't mean to do that." He looked away.

Should she be embarrassed? Ashamed? Olivia didn't know how to react. His attention was flattering. The kiss had taken her breath away. But then he'd ended it.

Perhaps he found her lacking.

She straightened and gathered her wits. A man like Jules wasn't looking for a nobody like her. She lacked the attributes a man wanted in a wife. She didn't have a good background or family connections—or a dowry.

Emily and Noreen joined them then, each holding out a fistful of wildflowers. Olivia peeled her attention from Jules and her thoughts from what had just transpired to take the blooms and thank the girls. Noreen backed right into Olivia's lap and sat, turning up her liquid brown gaze and a bashful smile.

Olivia couldn't resist grinning back at her, while appreciating the beauty of the child's confidence in her welcome and her lack of inhibition in seeking affection. Noreen knew she was loved and wanted. She had no reason to believe anyone would turn her aside. By the time Tanis and Will returned, Noreen was sound asleep in Olivia's arms and Emily had plopped down on a blanket to rest.

Tanis separated from the rest of them to sit apart and nurse Abner in private, while Jules and Will spoke in low voices and the children napped. Olivia had never over-heard a conversation between two men, and their talk fascinated her. They were absorbed in their topic—something about horse breeds—and the rise and fall of their deep voices mesmerized her.

Olivia tucked every beautiful moment of this incredible day into her memory.

Attending church on a Sunday that wasn't a holiday had been a treat. Adding her voice to those of all the worshippers and singing the words to hymns had been pure, heartfelt joy. In some ways she felt as though she'd been released from a cage and given her freedom for the first time. Everything was more clear and brighter. Smiles and sunshine and ordinary conversation held new meaning.

In the months and years to come, she would take out these moments and savor their perfection and splendor. And she would always remember that she'd spent a liberating day under the wide Montana sky, sharing food and smiles and the wonder of life. She would never forget that a handsome man had kissed her.

Even once she was far from here, she would always have the memories.

The following day, Olivia set to work peeling and slicing apples. By midmorning, half a dozen pies cooled on the worn tabletop.

She changed her clothing and brushed her hair, checking it in her hand mirror. Emily sat on a chair with a book in hand. "Are we having class now?"

"Since it's not too hot today, let's venture over to Mrs. Roland's and see if she wants to start her lessons."

As they passed, Judd waved to them from the corner of

the corral where he was mending the lodgepole fence. "I was up at the barn, Mizz Rose. Smelled something mighty good comin' from that cabin."

"You'll have your apple pie for supper," she called back.

He grinned and went back to his task.

Tanis was delighted to see them. She had just made noodles, and they hung drying on a line strung inside their wagon.

She and Olivia set chairs and a table under the shade of a canvas tarp and set to their task.

The youngsters played quietly with their wooden horses while Olivia taught the other woman the first few letters of the alphabet. Glad she'd saved and packed not only primers, but slates and chalk, Olivia used the aids for instruction.

Later, they rested in the shade.

"I'll bet most of the children you teach catch on quicker than I do," Tanis said.

"Not at all. You're a clever pupil. You'll be reading in no time."

"You're a good teacher," Tanis told her. "Do you have plans to teach again?"

"It's what I know how to do," she answered. "Once Emily is settled and I know she's all right, I'll have to find employment somewhere. I have a little money left, but I can take work anywhere to earn train fare."

"Can you cook?" Tanis asked.

"I'm a pretty fair cook," she replied. "I used to roast chicken when it was my turn in the kitchen." Olivia glanced toward the barns. "There's a chicken house back there. Wayland brings me eggs, but never a chicken."

Tanis fanned herself with a handkerchief. "Sure would

be nice to have chicken and noodles, instead of game, wouldn't it?"

They looked at each other.

"Someone always brought them to me. Have you ever killed a chicken?" Olivia asked.

"A hundred times."

"I'll grab two if you'll clean them."

Tanis nodded. "Jules won't mind."

Heading for the coop, Olivia questioned her impulsive decision. Even as she drew closer, the creatures squawked and scattered. She thought over the dilemma and rummaged through a couple of storage bins behind the cabin, finding a gunnysack for capture and a denim jacket that could protect her arms and shirtwaist.

Determined, she donned the jacket and set off for the area behind the enormous stable. The chickens were fenced inside a wire enclosure with a wood-and-wire gate. She entered, and the hens clucked and ran in a dozen directions. Olivia stood still and waited until the creatures went back to pecking at the ground. The feathered fowl intimidated her, but she focused on how badly she wanted chicken with those noodles. Each time she approached, the birds skittered away. Finally, she crouched on the ground with the bag in hand, waiting for one to come near. When it did, she placed the bag over it and scooped it up. Now what? She had one bird in the sack and couldn't use the bag the same way again for another.

She exited the gate and carried the fluttering chicken all the way back to Tanis's camp. "I got one."

Reaching into the bag, Tanis pulled the bird out by the feet and handed the bag back to Olivia. "Grab it by the feet and hang it upside down. It'll just hang there and not fight."

That would have been useful knowledge the first time she'd gone to the henhouse. And Tanis had been right. She caught the next chicken by the feet, and as soon as she flipped the bird over, it hung motionless. She didn't even need the bag. Grinning, she proudly carried back her catch.

Much later, she delivered pies to Wayland and told him he didn't need to send food for them that evening. Smelling his bubbling pot of brown stew confirmed that her supper would be far more appealing. Not that she didn't appreciate his efforts, because she did, but she didn't share his fondness for cooking small, wild creatures.

Minutes later, Jules entered the cabin with his hair still wet and smelling of soap. He stopped and inhaled. "What is that wonderful smell?"

"Chicken and noodles with apple pie."

His eyes widened. "You made chicken and noodles?"

"Tanis made the noodles and shared them. I caught the chickens and she cleaned them. But we cooked them together."

He chuckled and seated himself. "I would've liked to have seen you catching chickens."

"I did quite well, actually."

"Obviously."

"Emily, why don't you say the blessing this evening," Olivia suggested.

Obediently, Emily nodded and bowed her head. "Thank You for this food, Lord. God bless those fat chickens in Uncle Jules's pen. God bless my new family and my new friends. And God, please bless Miss Rose real good and don't let her find a job too far away. Amen."

Jules couldn't make himself look up at Olivia. He was Emily's family. Her heartfelt prayer touched him with regret and guilt and made him feel as though he was tearing the two females apart by not allowing them both to stay here. Even if he let Emily stay, her teacher needed to find employment. They wouldn't end up together.

The kiss he'd shared with Olivia had been on his mind all day. He'd overstepped a boundary, and her surprise had been plain, but he couldn't bring himself to regret it. Olivia Rose had the prettiest mouth he'd ever seen—or kissed.

He took control over his thoughts and swung them back to the meal she'd prepared. He couldn't remember the last time he'd tasted anything as delicious as the savory chicken and noodles. "Perfect."

Olivia's pink cheeks showed she was unaccustomed to praise, but she grinned and thanked him.

When she served slices of flaky-crusted apple pie, he closed his eyes and let the sweet cinnamon flavor melt on his tongue. "Where did you learn to bake like this?"

"We shared kitchen duty at the academy. All of the young ladies were instructed in cooking and baking." She glanced at Emily. "Emily can make a fine pound cake on her own."

The girl nodded. "And biscuits," she added.

He had a thought. "What did you do with the seeds from the apples?"

"I gave the cores and peels to the chickens."

"Are there more apples?"

"Oh, yes. The men left two bushels."

"Save seeds next time. I'll plant 'em and maybe get a few trees started."

She studied him for a moment, then got up and grabbed the tin pot to refill his coffee cup. "You're a forward thinker."

"Because?"

"Because you think of planting trees and you lay plans for things that will come to pass in the future."

He stirred in sugar and then sipped his coffee. "You don't?"

She resumed her seat and sat thoughtfully for a moment. "My future is as uncertain as my past. I have to focus on today."

He'd never considered planning ahead a luxury before, but for someone living from day to day as Olivia had been, he supposed it was. He looked at Emily. He didn't want her to feel insecure about her future. He hadn't been able to shake his growing concern about being solely responsible for her or the possibility that he wasn't going to have any help from his mother. The more he learned about Olivia and her lack of family connections and life experience, the less inclined he was to lay the same fate on his niece.

Maybe he should go ahead and build the house. If Emily was still here by winter, the two of them could move into the new place, and the Rolands could have the cabin. He couldn't let himself be affected by Emily's concern that her teacher not get a job too far away, however. He might feel bad about the uncertainty that ruled Olivia's life, but it wasn't his problem to fix. Nor was it the problem of all the men who'd swarmed around at church, seeking introductions. He pushed the thought away.

While Olivia and Emily cleaned up after the meal, he went out to the bunkhouse. Summer was slow for the men, but he kept them on because he didn't want them finding jobs elsewhere when he'd need them again in the fall to bale hay and ready the ranch for winter. He found the bunkhouse empty, so he moved on, discovering them gathered at the table under the stars.

"Hey, boss. Need a hand with something?"

"Nope. Came to let you know we'll be startin' on the house."

Coonie cackled. "Thinkin' you might need yoursef a wife, after all?"

"I'm thinkin' Will needs a place for his family come winter, and it might as well be the cabin."

No one questioned his reasoning, but when he told them to show up early the next morning, Lee and Wayland grinned.

Over the next two weeks, the men worked long hours, clearing the land and laying the framework for the house. Every day after her morning baking and Emily's and Tanis's lessons, Olivia helped Wayland prepare lunch and deliver it to the site. The house was being constructed several hundred feet from the other ranch buildings, on a flat strip of land nearer the wooded foothills to the west. Tanis explained that the location would provide protection from wind and snow.

The men planed and notched logs so they fit together snugly to create walls. Olivia joined the men in gathering stones. She and Emily couldn't lift the biggest rocks, but they carried and stacked the smaller ones.

Two fireplaces—an enormous one for the main room and a smaller version for a bedroom—were constructed and the mortar left to set. Olivia enjoyed watching the walls go up and appreciated the way the men worked together. Sharing outdoor work was yet another new experience. Every morning, she prayed for the workers' safety. While Jules created window frames, Will worked on building heavy shutters, and together the two men hung them.

Eventually, Jules directed the construction of six stone pillars ten feet away from the front wall.

"What are those for?" Emily asked.

"They'll hold up the roof that extends from the house and give us a porch," Jules explained.

That night they ate a late supper with the Rolands.

"We're going to have a porch!" Emily told Tanis.

Will covered his wife's hand with his own and gave her a tender look. "I'm going to build a place like that for my family soon."

"Moving out of the wagon will be an improvement," his wife told him.

Will squeezed her hand. "You deserve better."

She smiled at him in return, her fondness for her husband no secret.

Their exchange fascinated Olivia. Having grown up in a houseful of women and little girls, she'd never seen a husband-and-wife relationship. She noted that Jules had overheard, as well, but he kept his gaze averted.

When they headed back to the cabin, Emily ran ahead. "I'm going to get ready for bed and read," she called back to them.

A single figure broke away from the shadows of the bunkhouse and approached at a quick pace.

Olivia had the impression that Jules didn't recognize the person approaching, because he stepped between her and the man, and his posture tensed.

"It's Marcus Stone," the man identified himself, sweeping his hat from his head.

"Marcus, what brings you out so late?" Jules asked.

Olivia moved around him to see the man paused four feet away.

"I arrived earlier in the evening, but you weren't here, so I waited with Lee and the fellas."

Jules turned to nod at Olivia. "Miss Rose, this is Marcus Stone. He has a spread east of here. Marcus, Olivia Rose."

"Pleasure to meet you, Miss Rose." Marcus stood expectantly. She couldn't see him well in the moonlight, but she could tell he was tall and broad shouldered and that he'd combed his hair with a part. A spicy scent in the air suggested he'd bathed recently or doused himself with whatever men used after shaving.

"It's a pleasure," she said. Olivia belatedly remembered it was up to the lady to extend a hand, and she'd probably offended Jules's friend by neglecting the courtesy. Embarrassed by her inexperience, she hoped she could slip inside and leave them to their business.

"What can I do for you?" The man hadn't answered Jules the first time.

"Actually, I came to see Miss Rose," he replied.

Jules glanced at Olivia and back. "Oh? About what?"

Marcus held his hat by the brim and gave it a half turn. "I came *calling,* Jules."

Chapter Nine

Olivia had read extensively, and she knew the term meant seeking a woman with the purpose of courtship, but hearing it used regarding her caught her by complete surprise.

Jules recovered his composure first. "Excuse me then, while I read with my niece before her bedtime."

He headed into the cabin and closed the door. Emily glanced up at him from where she sat at the table. She'd lit a lamp and sat with a book open. "Where's Miss Rose?"

"She has a visitor."

Her eyebrows rose in curiosity. "A visitor?"

"Yes, a rancher from a spread nearby."

Emily got up and started for the door, but Jules stopped her by saying, "Give 'em privacy."

Emily paused and turned wide brown eyes up at him. "Is she safe?"

He nodded. "I know the man well. If I had any doubts, I wouldn't have left her out there with him."

"What does he want?"

"Apparently, he came calling."

"What does calling mean?"

"It means—" He had to force out the explanation. "He needs a wife, and he came to see if your teacher would make a suitable one."

Emily scurried over to stand right beside him. Worry creased her forehead. "Would she?"

"No doubt she'd make any man a fine wife."

"But she doesn't know him."

Recognizing her concern, he sat and explained. "Many people marry for practical reasons, Emily. Men out here sometimes send for a bride by mail and get one sight unseen."

She absorbed that information in silence, moved back to her chair and perched. Jules wanted to get up and go look out the door, too, but restraining himself, he remained seated.

After a moment, Emily spoke again. "Why don't *you* marry Miss Rose? Then we'd all be able to stay together."

Her suggestion wasn't a terrible one, and he wasn't completely loath to the idea.

In fact, it was a simple solution. But easy didn't always mean best. What if he wasn't ready for marriage? Marrying for the wrong reasons could be disastrous and end up making everyone involved miserable.

Marriage hadn't been in his plan just yet, but then neither had Emily or the new house. His plans had been knocked askew by the arrival of these females, and he wouldn't be getting his life back in proper order anytime soon.

He'd seen a lot of things during the war that made him question people and not take anything or anyone at face value. He'd believed he needed more time between himself and those experiences before he started looking at being capable of love and trust.

But what was there about Olivia not to trust?

No. It was her vulnerability that frightened him. He didn't know if he was ready to be the man she needed.

Had it been Lee who'd suggested the nearby men would soon be making efforts to snag her? He'd been right. Marcus had only just heard about Olivia, hadn't set eyes on her beforehand, but he'd come calling. *Calling.* What did that entail, anyhow? And how long was it supposed to take? Shouldn't she be coming in by now?

Jules had been pushed off center by Marcus's pronouncement. Had he done the right thing in leaving them standing out there alone? Olivia was in his care while she was staying here, after all. He was responsible for her.

He got up, strode to the door and opened it.

The two of them stood pretty much where he'd left them. Marcus was still worrying the brim of his hat, but he was smiling.

Olivia spoke first. "It's been a pleasure, Mr. Stone. I'll look forward to our ride."

"'Night, Miss Rose." Marcus settled his hat on his head and headed back toward the bunkhouse.

Olivia stepped past Jules to enter the cabin.

"Your ride?" he asked.

"He's taking me for a carriage ride on Saturday morning."

Jules didn't know why that announcement irritated him, but childishly, he wanted to go out there and tell Marcus Stone to take a long walk off a short cliff. Pretty pushy of the man to come over here and plan outings with Jules's guests.

"Does he want you to marry him, Miss Rose?" Emily asked.

Olivia flushed bright pink and turned away to tidy the dry sink and nearby cupboard. "That's certainly jumping to a conclusion. I've only just met the man."

"Uncle Jules said calling means a man needs a wife, and he said you'd make a good one."

Olivia turned a startled blue gaze on Jules.

He hoped she didn't think he approved of Marcus's bold intent. Not that he disapproved entirely.

"I think Uncle Jules should marry you, Miss Rose. Then you could stay here, and we'd all be together."

Olivia spun to gape at her young student. "Emily!"

"Well, I do think so. What's wrong with saying so?"

Olivia couldn't even meet Jules's eyes. She headed for the door and escaped back out into the night and the blessed darkness, where she pressed her palms to her heated cheeks.

Behind her the door opened and closed, and Jules's boots swished through the grass. She didn't turn around. "Please. Just don't say anything."

Of course Emily's idea had been ludicrous, but she couldn't bear hearing that he didn't want her. His lack of interest was understood without additional humiliation.

"I'll just stand here, then."

The silence grew louder than anything he might have said. Finally securing a sense of composure, she turned. "You don't have to mention that I'm ill prepared for this life or that I'm not skilled at handling myself. I'm aware of my shortcomings. And I realize that men out here aren't entirely discriminating when it comes to selecting wives. But I'm going to keep my options open, in the event that I'm unable to secure a position that pays well enough to support myself in a respectable fashion."

"I have nothing critical to say about your choices," he replied. "You're the smartest woman I've ever met."

His compliment brought no comfort. She had an excellent education, yes. She used perfect diction and knew appropriate deportment. She could set a table for tea and recite poetry, but she would trade everything she knew for a home where someone loved her. She yearned to hear someone say she looked like her mother or reminded him of her grandmother.

"Your lack of experience makes you vulnerable," he continued. "For now, it's my responsibility to protect you."

Everything had become so confusing. Sometimes Olivia wished she could fall asleep and wake up to find her life was uncomplicated and safe the way it had once been. She may have been unwanted, but she'd known how to be useful and she'd always known what to expect from one day to the next. Now the uncertainty wore her composure to a frazzle.

"You've been around children your whole life, and Emily is my first," he said. "Do younguns always say what they're thinking?"

"If they're confident with the person they're speaking to," she replied. "Emily took to you from the first day."

He reached for her wrist and caught her before she could turn away. "Let's not let a little discomfort keep us from the tasks at hand," he said. "We both have Emily's welfare at heart. Can we just focus on that?"

Could he detect the rapid increase of her pulse in her wrist? Standing this close, experiencing his intense attention flustered her. "Yes, of course."

"Olivia."

She liked the way he said her name in a low rasp that sent a shiver up her spine. Liked it too much, in fact. And then he did something entirely unexpected and used her wrist to urge her toward him, where he wrapped an arm around her shoulders and planted a toe-curling kiss on her lips. Olivia suspected she enjoyed the embrace a bit too much for it to be proper, so she eased away slightly.

Jules released her shoulders, but held the kiss as long as he dared. He recognized the petty jealousy he'd felt over Marcus's visit and her agreement to accompany the man on a ride. If he wasn't interested in her himself, he wouldn't care that she had made plans with the other rancher. So much for deluding himself about his attraction to her.

Separating them, she took a step back and stared at him in the darkness. It wasn't fair to kiss her while he expected her to leave after helping him with Emily, and now he'd done it twice. What was he afraid of?

Thunder rumbled in the distance. The sound seemed to shake Olivia into action. She headed for the door. "Good night."

He stood in mute confusion as she closed herself inside. Eventually, he forced himself to put one foot in front of the other and head for the barn to check on the animals before turning in.

His uncertainty angered him. He didn't like not being in control. He liked order and simplicity. He liked having a plan and sticking with it. Nothing about Olivia Rose had been in his plan.

And he certainly wasn't being fair to her. He expected her to be looking for a job, but didn't want her to take a husband? And thinking of Marcus as a husband was jumping the gun, but without a doubt marriage was the man's intent.

And then *kissing* her again?

He filled water buckets and closed the latch on the last stall. Yes, his behavior had to be confusing her and was definitely unfair. She was trusting God for her safety and provision. Jules should be helping her, or maybe even praying for her instead of kissing her.

He stood with his hand on a beam and dropped his head back to look up at the shadowy dark rafters. He wasn't much good at praying. He knew God loved him, but he'd never held much confidence that a God so busy with important things had time to listen to his trivial concerns. And he never knew what to say anyway.

He remembered Olivia's prayers, the way she spoke to God as though He was right there listening, caring. She used psalms as her own prayers. Jules doused the hanging lanterns and lit one in the tack room. Lifting the lid of a wooden box, he pulled out a worn Bible and sat on a saddle propped over a sawhorse, opening the book in the center and thumbing back to the psalm he sought. After glancing over a couple chapters, he honed in on the hundred and sixteenth.

I love the Lord because He hath heard my voice and my supplications. Because He hath inclined his ear unto me, therefore I will call upon Him as long as I live.

Remembering Olivia's personalization, he read aloud, "I offer to Thee the sacrifice of thanksgiving, and I call upon Your name, Lord."

Many of the verses spoke of God hearing David's prayers. Jules knew enough about David to know that he hadn't always done the right thing or listened to God's direction, but he had always repented and God had always loved and forgiven him.

"Thank You for loving and forgiving me, Father. I'm callin' on Your name for direction and wisdom. I don't know what to do about Emily—or Olivia, but I'm going to put my confidence and trust in You to show me."

Lightning didn't strike, nor did he have a flash of realization. But what he did experience was a peace that hadn't been part of him before. "Trust and confidence," he reminded himself, and closed his Bible.

Work on the house had been under way for a couple of hours the following morning, when Coonie pointed out a dust trail moving in their direction. Jules removed his gloves and got a drink from the bucket that was shaded by a tarp over a wagon bed before he loped out to meet the approaching buggy.

His first thought was that if it was another suitor for Olivia, he would send the fellow packing.

Instead, he recognized the driver as Corbin Bend's *married* liveryman. His fare was a woman dressed in a dove-gray traveling suit, with a plumed hat set on her head at a jaunty angle. He squinted in puzzlement. He didn't know any women who would dress like that to come calling out here.

Olivia and Emily, who had been studying under the branches of the hemlock tree, stood and walked toward the front of the cabin, where the buggy met all three of them.

"Jules," the driver said, and tipped his hat at Olivia. He tied the reins and moved around to help the woman to the ground.

She was small of stature and slender, wearing pristine white gloves and polished kid boots. Jules's gaze moved upward from her feet as they reached the ground.

She raised her head, angling the sweeping hat brim upward, so her face came into view. It took him a good thirty seconds to find his voice. *"Mother?"*

Chapter Ten

"You are breathtakingly handsome, Jules," she said with a catch in her voice. Pressing a gloved hand against her cheek, she blinked rapidly as though fighting tears. She turned her shimmering gaze downward with a sweep of dark lashes. "And this is Emily?"

"Yes," he managed to reply. "This is Emily. And her teacher, Miss Rose."

She knelt without a care for the hem of her skirt that puddled in the dust, and placed her hand under Emily's chin to tilt her face. "You look just like your mother, child."

Jules gathered his wits. "This is your grandmother, Lorena."

"How do you do?" Emily said, doing her teacher proud with the polite greeting in such a startling moment.

Lorena drew the child into a tender hug and closed her eyes.

Olivia's chest hitched with the swift emotion she experienced watching the woman's loving acceptance of the grandchild she hadn't known existed. Tears prickled behind her lids, and her throat stung with happiness for Emily. "Oh, thank You, Lord," she breathed.

She could almost feel those arms around her. She imagined the warmth and softness of that motherly embrace, and her heart sang. At last, a woman to give Emily all the affection she so needed and deserved. The affection Olivia wished she knew how to give.

Lorena stroked Emily's arm through her sleeve and released her as though she regretted having to do so. Self-consciously dabbing her eyes with a lace-edged hankie, she sat back on her heels. "We have a lot to talk about."

Glancing up then, her soft, dark eyes lit on Olivia. She stood. "Miss Rose. How can I ever repay you for looking after Emily and keeping her safe?" She took Olivia's hand, surprising her with the unexpected touch. "I've been traveling, and I returned to find the telegram from Jules. I came as quickly as I could. You poor dears, what you must have suffered through these past months."

She released Olivia's hand and wrapped her in an impulsive hug. She smelled like the lilac bushes that had lined the perimeter of the academy's side garden and bloomed in profusion each spring. The soft embrace surprised Olivia. The older woman's slender frame trembled with emotion. The only other embrace Olivia had to compare was Jules's the night before, and there was no similarity.

"Thank you," Lorena said and leaned back, cupping Olivia's cheek in her gloved palm. She released her and turned to gaze up at her son. "It's been a long time, Jules. You look well."

"I'm good, Mother. Didn't know you were coming."

Olivia sensed a discomfort she hadn't suspected until

Lorena held herself in check and didn't reach for her son as she had Emily and Olivia. Olivia sensed she wanted to.

"I barely had time to pack fresh clothing while Stuart secured a railroad ticket for my journey. Unfortunately, I unpacked and slept a night before reading mail and telegrams, or I'd have been here yesterday." She turned and surveyed the barn and outbuildings before her dark gaze lit on the cabin. "Is this your home?"

Jules bent and picked up two satchels the driver had set nearby. "You're probably hot and tired from your trip. Let's get you inside."

Once inside the cabin, Lorena removed her feathered hat, revealing lustrous dark hair shot with silver and swept into an elegant chignon, with sausage curls trailing the back of her neck. She didn't appear as though she'd traveled hundreds of miles in the heat.

"I brought tea," she said, and rummaged in one of her bags to produce a tin.

Olivia accepted the offering with a grateful smile. She hadn't tasted tea in a long time.

"I'll go get mugs from the bunkhouse. And then I'll bring in the tub and pump water so you can bathe." Jules headed out.

Olivia and Emily resumed studying their vocabulary words out of doors. Jules went back to the house site, while Lorena enjoyed a bath and dressed in fresh clothing.

Before full dark, they came together once again for supper. "We have so much to talk about. I want to hear all about your school and your trip here," Jules's mother said. "And I'm sure you want to hear about your mother."

Emily nodded solemnly.

Lorena grew subdued while they ate, finally setting

down her fork and waiting for the others to finish. "I'm afraid I have some very bad news."

All eyes focused on her.

Emily was seated beside her, and Lorena reached for the girl's hand. "Among the letters and telegrams I received was one from a man named Roman Terlesky."

Olivia knew that name. He'd sent the banker's notes that had paid Emily's tuition for the previous eight years. A sinking feeling settled in her stomach and increased when Lorena pursed her lips in a straight line and blotted tears.

"Your mother was aboard a ship that met with a storm at sea. She drowned, dear. Mr. Terlesky was traveling with her on a return trip from Ireland, and the two of them were separated. He was Meriel's close friend for many years and sent me his regrets."

Emily's face showed bitter disappointment. No doubt she'd been imagining that her grandmother's arrival meant she would be united with her mother. However, no sign of grief darkened her features, unlike Jules, who sat with his elbows on the tabletop, the lower portion of his face hidden by his tautly laced fingers.

Olivia didn't have any experience with losing a loved one, but she could imagine how much his loss hurt. If losing a family member was anything like yearning for a loved one, she empathized. She wished she could go to him and comfort him. Once again her inadequacy to reach out with the most simple of human touches gnawed a painful cavity in her heart. She pictured herself touching his shoulder, his hair, and she ached at her pathetic incapability.

Emily had never known her mother, so grief wasn't an emotion she could be expected to feel, though the pain of finality had to be a crushing blow. Just as it had been to

Olivia the day she'd learned she had nothing—no mother, no father, no birthday, no history. Not the same as the death of a person, but the demise of a dream and the end of all hope of ever being loved or accepted were heartbreaking all the same.

Olivia yearned to jump from her chair and take Emily in her arms and comfort her. The glaring inability to do so proved her a disappointingly poor candidate for a mother.

She hurt for Emily, but she held in the pain, not knowing how to express her empathy and concern. *Holy Spirit, You are the Comforter. Show me how to connect and love,* she prayed.

Lorena moved from her chair to kneel beside Emily's, where she placed her hand on the girl's shoulder. "It's okay to be sad, darling."

What a perfect thing to say. Emily looked up at the woman, a world of questions in her eyes. Olivia knew each one. *Why didn't she want me? What is wrong with me that she didn't love me?* But as sad as the questions were, Olivia knew that the hardest trial of her mother's abandonment had already passed for the girl.

Emily was only eight years old, and now she had a family. These people loved her and cared about her, and she was still young enough that she would soon be able to ask those questions and be reassured that they cherished her, regardless of what her mother had done.

At Lorena's urging, Emily slid off the chair and into her embrace. Olivia closed her eyes and swallowed hard against the wall of emotion that threatened to tumble her composure.

She opened her eyes and looked instinctively at Jules. The pity she read in his expression shamed her. Her soul had been laid bare to his gaze, all her glaring inadequacies exposed to scrutiny.

She was the one who'd been with Emily all these years, yet she was incapable of comforting her while a woman Emily had only just met today held her and tenderly kissed her cheek. She felt more insignificant and useless than ever. She stood and gathered plates.

While Olivia cleaned up the table and the dishes, Lorena took Emily to a chair and pulled her into her lap, where she kissed her temple and smoothed her hair and spoke to her in a soothing voice. Olivia could barely tear away her gaze to perform her tasks. Her chest ached with longing to be the one doing those things and comforting the child she loved.

Much later, Olivia tucked Emily into bed. Lorena kissed her good-night, and the three adults went out of doors. Jules led the way toward the new house in the darkness. The building was another cabin, Olivia had noted somewhere along the line, constructed of logs and beams with stone fireplaces, and rafters in place for a roof and a loft. But it was five or six times the size of the small cabin.

Jules gestured for the women to sit on a platform constructed beside the new well. "Who is Roman Terlesky?" he asked. "Is he Emily's father?"

"No, but as I understand it, he was your sister's gentleman friend for many years."

"He paid Emily's tuition," Olivia supplied. "It's recorded in her file. That's how I know."

"Did you keep in touch with Meriel?" Jules asked.

"I had an address for her in London," his mother replied. "I wrote her occasionally, and she wrote me once or twice, but I hadn't heard from her for many years. I didn't know about Emily. If I had, I'd have gone for her and taken her back to Cincinnati."

"Your husband would have approved?" he asked.

"Stuart is a kind and generous man," Lorena assured him. "He encourages me to keep inviting you for holidays, even though you've never replied."

"Never had much time for holidays."

Even in the dark, Olivia could tell Lorena had more she wanted to say. She wasn't sure if it was her presence preventing the woman from speaking or the palpable barrier Jules had erected.

"I want to take Emily home with me," Lorena declared. "She needs to be somewhere safe, where she can get the best education possible and be with people who love her."

Jules had been in a fog since his mother's arrival, but instantly the fog cleared and he felt as though he'd been slammed in the gut with a two-by-four. "You think your home is better than a boarding school?"

"Of course it is! I *want* her. She's my granddaughter." She studied his rigid posture in the moonlight. "Victor is a good man, Jules. He's *nothing* like your father. Nothing. I can assure you he will welcome Emily and provide for her. He's also wealthy. I've never wanted for anything, and I've never regretted marrying him."

Jules didn't harbor ill feelings toward his mother. She'd been trapped in an ugly situation with an unstable man, and she'd done what she thought was best at the time to retain peace and keep people safe. And, God help him, he believed her about her stable life and her kind husband. She had never lied to him and she had no reason to start now.

She was a good woman. A loving woman.

Olivia was embarrassed to be included in their personal discussion. Of course, she cared about the outcome, but she wasn't part of their family. "Excuse me. I'm going to go get the bed ready for you, ma'am."

"You don't have to go," Lorena told her.

"Yes, I do." She hurried toward the cabin, her thoughts in a whirl. Jules's mother could be the answer to her prayers for Emily. She was without a doubt exactly what the child needed—someone kind and loving and affectionate—someone who wanted Emily and could provide a loving home. Being wanted had to be the best feeling of all. If Emily went to Cincinnati, Olivia would, in all likelihood, never see her again, but she could live with that as long as she knew the girl was happy.

She paused in front of the cabin and stared up at the broad expanse of star-studded heavens. "Lord, help me be happy for Emily. You know how much I want a family of my own and how much I would have loved to be able to care for her and be a mother to her, but You have her best interests at heart. I trust You to provide for her. I don't know anything about being a mother, and I certainly don't have a home or a husband or the means to support her. Lorena has all those things, and she's kind and loving, besides."

Lorena's tender concern and warm affection stabbed Olivia with a sense of inferiority and unworthiness that settled on her chest like a weight. She took a shaky breath. "Help me to let go."

"Do you doubt I can care for her?" his mother asked.

Jules shook his head. "No."

His mother sighed. "I know you and Meriel had a hard childhood. Those years weren't easy for me, either."

"I know."

"I regret that I never stood up to your father. I was weak and went along with his whims, and in doing so, I wasn't a good mother to my children."

"You were always a good mother," he disagreed.

She shook her head. "I feel responsible for Meriel leaving at such a young age, and for you leaving, too. I can't ever make it up to her now. Or to you. But I am asking you to forgive me."

"You don't need my forgiveness, Mother. I never held anything against you or blamed you."

"But I need your forgiveness, Jules. I need you to acknowledge my regret."

"Then I forgive you. Of course, I forgive you."

She wept silently into her hankie. Jules hadn't realized how much she regretted and blamed herself for the life they'd led while she'd been married to his father. Thinking of how long she'd carried this burden, his heart ached for her. He stepped forward to pull her close and comfort her. "You did the best you knew how. That's all any of us can expect of ourselves."

"Thank you," she whispered.

"Don't thank me."

A moment later, she inched away and dried her tears with her handkerchief. "I can't change the past. But I can do everything in my power to give Emily a good life. I want to take responsibility for her. I want to start over and do it right this time, raise her in a stable home and provide for her."

Lorena taking Emily was the perfect solution. Even better than a boarding school, because Emily would be with her doting grandmother. Lorena could do everything he couldn't. She could provide a better education. She could provide constant companionship. And one day Emily would have the opportunity to marry well.

The child yearned for family and affection, though she hid it well. She and Miss Rose were very much alike in their self-sufficiency. They'd learned to protect themselves from hurt and rejection, and breaking through those walls would never be easy. Lorena had already shown she was going to give it her best, and Emily had responded to her.

"I can't fault your reasoning," he said at last, though his chest ached through and through at the admission.

"Then you agree she should come home with me?"

"Yes." His nose itched and he rubbed it. "It'll be best for her to go with you."

Chapter Eleven

In her grief over Jules's announcement that Emily would be going to Cincinnati with his mother, Olivia's Saturday engagement slipped her mind. Jules hadn't forgotten, however, and reminded her as they ate breakfast.

"Suppose Marcus will be here soon."

His remark sunk in, and Olivia remembered the rancher who'd asked to call on her.

Lorena's eyebrows shot upward. "A caller, young Olivia? How exciting. We'd better get you ready to receive him." She turned to her son. "Is he a respectable young man?"

"Has a respectable spread," he replied.

"Is he handsome, Olivia?"

She hadn't given the man's appearance much thought. "I suppose so."

Jules stood. "I'll leave you women to dresses and the like."

He strode from the room.

By the time Marcus arrived, Olivia was dressed in a peach-and-cream organza dress with a gusseted bodice and lace at the neckline and wrists. It was a well-made dress she'd inherited from a teacher who'd resigned and married, and Olivia had altered it and added the lace. The style was a little too fancy for the schoolroom, so she'd only worn the garment once before.

Lorena had fashioned Olivia's hair into sleek curls that draped the back of her neck. "Your hair is as fair and shiny as an angel's. Meriel's hair was dark and wavy like Emily's."

Emily came to stand and listen.

"She was beautiful," Lorena added with a wistful catch in her voice. She turned and caught her granddaughter's expression. "Just as you are, my darling."

Emily smiled, and Lorena gave her a quick squeeze.

Olivia watched their exchange with a hollow emptiness aching inside. She was delighted for Emily, though, so she smiled.

The sound of a horse and buggy filtered through the open window. Olivia met Lorena's smiling gaze. "I won't know what to say."

"Don't be silly. You'll talk about the mountains and the sunshine. You will simply enjoy yourself."

"I don't think I will." Her breakfast had rolled into a knot in her stomach.

Lorena handed her a gauzy parasol. "Protect your lovely fair skin from the sun, dear. And enjoy yourself."

Olivia greeted Marcus with a nervous smile. He swept his hat from his head and ushered her up to a seat before climbing up beside her and urging the single horse forward.

From his position on the roof of the new house, Jules watched Marcus Stone's sleek black Bavarian warmblood pull the buggy past the corral, then squinted at the trail of dust. He was going to pair his Cleveland mare with Marcus's stud in the spring and have some fine-looking warmbloods like that, too. Likely even sturdier.

Marcus didn't have a barn like Jules's. None of the other ranchers had a barn that could hold a candle to it, either.

He hammered a shingle into place with unnecessary force. If his mother hadn't shown up when she had, he would have asked Olivia to stay and help him take care of Emily. He would've needed a teacher for his niece and, in a couple of years, for the Roland children. Having the two of them here would have worked out.

He didn't want to think about Emily leaving. And it made his gut ache to think of Olivia marrying Marcus— or anyone else. But he wanted what was best for both of them. Emily would have a better chance for a good life and a future marriage in Cincinnati.

Still, he wouldn't be such a bad choice for Olivia. He nearly had a fine house finished. With Tanis nearby, she'd have companionship. And eventually…they'd have children.

Marcus already had a house, he recalled with a sick feeling. He'd ordered lumber from somewhere up north and built a wood-frame structure with a porch along two sides. At the time, Jules had thought the man should be focusing on his spread and his barns. Their priorities had been different.

Jules caught himself daydreaming. He hadn't hammered a nail for ten minutes. He glanced down at the pile of remaining lumber on the ground. Probably enough to make a couple of chairs for the porch. Definitely enough to keep his hands occupied, if not his mind.

Supper was more festive than usual. Lorena used one of her shawls for a tablecloth, and they ate quail with stuffing made from Olivia's bread. Lorena had managed to talk Wayland out of carrots, which she baked with a maple glaze. Dessert was a golden-crusted pie made from a jar of blackberries Tanis had offered.

"Emily and I will leave next Monday," Lorena told them as they ate. "Once we reach Cincinnati, I will take you to my seamstress," she said to the girl. "We'll have you fitted for dresses for school and church."

"But I have dresses," Emily told her.

"I know, dear, but won't you be excited to have all new?"

Emily nodded, though her expression showed her uncertainty.

"We'll make you something from velvet for the holidays. A deep green perhaps. Have you ever had a velvet dress? There's nothing like the feel of the luxurious fabric. You will love Christmas in the city. There are holiday parties and Christmas programs. You will likely sing with the children's choir. We'll bake pumpkin and mince pies and shop for gifts. We will find a special tree this year. One as high as the ceiling in the parlor, and we'll decorate it with beads and glass ornaments. Doesn't that sound like fun?"

The girl glanced at Olivia, who gave her an encouraging smile. Olivia imagined the holiday the woman described, a holiday unlike any they'd ever celebrated. Everything they'd ever dreamed of would now belong to Emily.

Lorena had seen the look pass between them. She folded her napkin. "The two of you have been together for many Christmases, haven't you?"

Olivia fought back a flood of emotion to nod. She did feel joy in her heart for the new life and experiences Emily would enjoy. The child's happiness was all that mattered. "Your plans sound lovely. Emily will enjoy herself."

Lorena reached across the table to place her hand over Olivia's. "Why don't you come with us?"

Olivia raised her gaze in surprise. "For Christmas?"

"No. For good. We have a big home, with plenty of space. You would have your own room. Emily will need a teacher, and who better than the one she already knows and loves?" Lorena's enthusiasm for the idea snowballed. "The two of you have a special connection and a history. I would feel terrible tearing you apart. When Emily is older, you can remain my companion, if you wish. Or you could be her chaperone at university."

Olivia struggled to comprehend the incredibly generous offer. "You want to hire me as Emily's teacher? Have me come live with you in Ohio?"

"Yes." Lorena gave her a broad smile. "What do you say?"

Olivia glanced at Jules, who stared at his empty plate. "Well, I don't know," she said slowly. "You've caught me by surprise. It's a completely generous offer."

"You have a week to think it over," Lorena said. "I hope you know I'm sincere and that I would truly love for you to join us."

"Yes. Thank you."

Olivia couldn't even wrap her thoughts around the idea. No searching for a job or a safe place to live? No worry about the future or Emily's welfare? And she and Emily would be together. Emily beamed and cast her a hopeful glance.

It all sounded too good to be true.

Lorena and Emily left together to take the scraps to the compost pile.

Jules hadn't touched his coffee. Olivia stood and picked up his cup. "I'll get you a hot cup. This is cold."

She poured a fresh cup and placed the mug in front of him.

Their eyes met, and she gazed into the blue depths of his, wondering what he was thinking. "What do you think, Jules?"

He touched the rim of the cup, but didn't pick it up. "I think it's the best opportunity Emily will ever have. She'll have everything she needs."

She'd actually been wondering what he thought about his mother's offer to give *her* a home, as well. "Your mother is generous."

"She is." He seemed to think a minute before he spoke. "If you went with her, you'd have a job you love."

So he had considered it. "And I'd be near Emily."

"There's that."

She'd only known him a few weeks. She couldn't expect he'd developed any particular fondness for her over that time. He'd kissed her, yes, but kisses weren't promises or security. She had to go where someone needed her and wanted her. Lorena's home sounded like that place.

"What about Marcus?" he asked.

"We shared a buggy ride," she answered. "That's hardly grounds on which to base a future. Your mother's offer is right here and now—and it's a choice that involves being with Emily." She didn't know if he could understand. "She's the closest thing I have to family. I feel as though she's my own."

"I believe she is…in all the ways that count," he said.

Tears welled in her eyes. She turned away and shaved soap into the dishpan. She may never have another opportunity like this one. She'd been trusting God to provide for both of them, so why not believe this was her answer?

That night she lay on her pallet on the floor, feeling small and unimportant. Lorena was a warm and kind-hearted woman. She would be a good influence on Emily.

She would show Emily how to express love the way Olivia never could. Just thinking of the way Lorena touched Emily, smoothing her hair and holding her close, made Olivia's throat constrict painfully with inadequacy.

Emily would learn and respond—and she would transfer her feelings of devotion and trust to the woman whose expressions of love came easily. Olivia's chest ached with selfish, empty longing. She prayed for the Lord to take away feelings of jealousy that would undermine her ability to appreciate Lorena.

She cast through her memory for a verse of Scripture to hold on to, and it came to her: "Charity suffers long and is kind," she whispered. "Charity envieth not. Charity vaunteth not itself." She'd looked up that word, and it meant lifting up oneself. "Charity doesn't seek her own, nor is it easily provoked." She thought ahead. "Charity believes all things, hopes all things, and endures all things."

She already loved Emily with all her heart, and she could love Lorena with Christian love. The Godly kind of love that would never envy what the child and her grandmother shared. Olivia already believed Lorena's offer was the best for Emily, and she would never give up desiring the best for her. She didn't want to take away what Emily had discovered. But would God ever give her a chance at a happy, loving home? She didn't see any way that could happen. She was a grown woman, not a child.

Olivia wiped tears from her cheek and rolled over. She was nearly asleep when the same words she'd spoken to Emily before their trip West came to her. *Even as He cares for and feeds the sparrows, He cares for us even more. We are valuable and special to the Lord.*

She was special to God. She closed her eyes and rested peacefully.

She woke before the others the following morning and opened her Bible to the Book of Matthew. *Are not five sparrows sold for two farthings, and not one of them is forgotten before God? But even the very hairs of your head are all numbered. Fear not therefore: ye are of more value than many sparrows.*

She had no reason to fear. Her Heavenly Father cared about her. She was not forgotten, as it had seemed over the years.

The rest of the week went too quickly. Since Emily was leaving, Jules suspended work on the house. It looked as though Olivia would be going with them. He'd have plenty of time after they were gone to finish up the details. For now he wanted to spend all the time he could with them.

He had promised to take Emily fishing, so the women packed a lunch.

"We'll need a spade," Olivia told him. "And several buckets."

"How many worms do you think we'll need?"

"You'll see," she answered mysteriously.

He grabbed a spade from the barn and laid it in the wagon bed beside a stack of empty pails. They traveled to a stream where Olivia chose to rest in the shade rather than fish. She had something else she wanted to do. After digging for worms, Jules baited Lorena and Emily's lines and showed them how to cast into the water and wait for a bite.

Their lunch consisted of Olivia's mouthwatering bread sliced for ham sandwiches and a watermelon Jules had picked from Wayland's small garden.

Jules, his mother and Emily went back to the stream to check their lines. A long time later, they returned, and packed up to head home.

He stopped and stared into the bed of the wagon.

All the pails he'd brought along were lined along the side rail and brimming with drooping poppies. The sight gave him a strange feeling. Turning, he sought her out.

Olivia stood to the side of the wagon. Her face was flushed, her pretty, blue dress damp with perspiration. Her bonnet had fallen back, and tendrils of hair clung to her neck and cheeks. She was the prettiest thing he'd ever seen. And she'd dug up poppies to plant in his front yard.

He didn't want to think about the following summer or the ones to come if she was gone and all he had to remember her by were those blooming flowers.

That night they ate crisp-fried trout for supper, along with fried parsnips and boiled greens.

Olivia and Lorena shared duties in the compact area, which proved they were compatible and lessened one area of Olivia's doubts about being in the way if she accompanied her to Ohio. Lorena was nothing but generous and good-hearted.

Olivia had every confidence in Lorena to be a good mother to Emily. Her own presence, however, would likely add confusion. She would always be a reminder of where Emily had come from. She would be known in Lorena's social circles as the poor young woman with no family of her own. Her dilemma remained.

When they arrived at church Sunday morning, the local newspaperman introduced himself. "Will you join me for dinner here in town one night this coming week?" he asked.

Olivia glanced at Emily, who stood nearby, listening.

Olivia hadn't yet made up her mind about the trip, so she couldn't answer. "May we speak privately after church?" she asked.

Mr. Saxton's toothy grin showed his pleasure with her request.

Jules gestured for Olivia to lead them to one of the pews. She did so, and he gave her a sidelong glance. She had to make up her mind today and give Lorena time to purchase her ticket if she decided to go.

After church, she explained to Mr. Saxton that she wasn't sure if she would still be in town. She assured him she would contact him if she stayed. Jules took them to the café for a meal of sliced beef, creamy potatoes and gravy.

"Why aren't there roasts like this on your dinner table?" his mother asked. "We haven't eaten beef once since I've been here."

"Beef is my living," he told her. "Every head I sell buys breeding stock or lumber. Until my herd is established, we only eat a cow if it has to be put down because of an injury."

"And when will your herd be established to your satisfaction?" she asked. "I saw a lot of cattle on those hills."

He seemed to consider her question, but didn't give her a reply.

Emily didn't finish her meal, and she was especially quiet.

"Are you feeling well?" Olivia asked her.

"I feel fine."

But she continued to hang back and not participate after Jules drove them home and suggested another fishing expedition that afternoon.

Lorena sat on the bank, wearing one of her wide-brimmed hats and dangling a line in the water. Jules encouraged Emily to join them, but she said she was tired and laid on the faded blanket in the shade of a rustling cotton-wood. She watched the shimmering leaves overhead, her hand tucked under her cheek.

"Are you going to tell me what's wrong?" Olivia asked. "You're not acting like yourself."

Emily sat up and glanced toward the stream, where her uncle and grandmother fished.

"Are you worried about something?" Olivia prompted.

"I don't want to leave!" Emily burst into tears.

Chapter Twelve

The child sobbed brokenheartedly.

Taken aback by Emily's uncharacteristic display of emotion, Olivia's heart leaped. She looked at her helplessly, knowing she needed to do something, but not sure what.

Remembering Lorena's loving example, she crawled forward and reached a tentative hand toward Emily. She drew the hand back once, but then scooted right beside her and drew the child onto her lap.

Emily trembled, but her warm slender body fit right into Olivia's arms and against her chest. Olivia rocked her gently and threaded her fingers into her dark, silky hair. "Shush, now, dear one. Everything's going to be just fine."

After several minutes, Emily's tears subsided. Without releasing her, Olivia reached for a napkin and dabbed at the child's eyes and nose. Emily sat up to look into Olivia's eyes. "Grandmother is kind, and I like her ever so much, but I want to stay with Uncle Jules. I don't want to go to Ohio. I like it here."

Olivia couldn't have been more surprised. She found her

voice. "Are you certain? Your grandmother has the means to take care of you and buy you things. You'd live in a big city and never want for anything if you went with her."

"We lived in the city before," she answered. "Back in Pennsylvania. It's better here."

"The way we lived wasn't a good example of living in the city," Olivia told her. "We didn't have any interaction with others outside the academy. And we weren't shown love. Your grandmother loves you."

"Uncle Jules loves me, too. And I love him back. I feel safe here. I don't want to leave."

Olivia couldn't argue with the child wanting to cling to the sense of security she'd experienced with her uncle. She certainly understood. And agreed. "If it's what you really want, then you have to tell them. Both of them only want your happiness."

Emily nodded. "But I don't want to hurt Grandmother's feelings."

"That's kind of you. But even if telling the truth hurts her feelings, it's still the right thing to do. You're not intending to hurt her. Let's pray for her first."

Emily nodded. Olivia asked God to help Emily be strong and to also be a comfort to Lorena.

"I'll tell them at supper," Emily decided.

She joined Jules and her grandmother then, taking over a fishing pole and enjoying the rest of her afternoon.

At supper, Olivia recognized her hesitation and gave her a warm smile of encouragement. "Emily has something to say."

Emily hadn't yet picked up her fork. She sat with her hands folded in her lap, wearing a look of distress.

"Whatever is it, child?" Lorena asked.

"I don't want to go to Ohio." Her voice trembled. "Not because I don't love Grandmother, but because I want to stay here with Uncle Jules." She swallowed, and Olivia felt her fear and hesitation as if it were her own. "Unless you don't want me." Her dark pleading gaze lifted to her uncle. "It will be all right if you don't, though. Then I'll go with Grandmother."

The courage those words took were more rewarding to Olivia than anything she could imagine. She couldn't have been more proud of Emily if the child was her flesh and blood and had flown to the moon and back.

Even at the risk of his rejection, Emily had spoken her feelings. If only she had the courage to ask the same thing. But she wasn't his family. Olivia's heart pounded in anticipation of his reaction. If he turned her away, Olivia would feel solely responsible for encouraging Emily to do something she hadn't the daring to do herself.

Lorena appeared taken aback, but she simply rested her hands on either side of her plate and waited for Jules to reply.

Jules had raised his eyebrows as though the expression helped him sort out his thinking. He sat like that for a full minute, and then finally cocked his head to the side as if shaking off confusion. "You sure about this, Emily? Your grandmother has a nice house in the city and can afford fancy dresses and the like."

"I'm sure," Emily replied. "If you want me, I'll stay here and live with you."

Jules didn't know what had prompted his niece's surprising pronouncement, but his sharp sense of relief told him he'd wished for this all along. He would never have asked her to stay, because he sure didn't think he was her best option, but he was mighty glad she didn't agree. "I want you, Emily."

She jumped down from her chair and ran around the end of the table to fling herself at him.

He scooted back his chair in time to envelop her in a hug. She was the sweetest little thing that had ever come along. Knowing his sister's child—and now making a difference in her life—was going to change everything. He hadn't thought he was ready for this, but he would never have been ready to say goodbye.

Over Emily's shoulder, he looked up to gauge his mother's reaction and then meet Olivia's tear-filled eyes.

Emily extricated herself and turned in his embrace to look at her grandmother. "I'm sorry."

"Don't you be sorry for a moment, darling. I want you to be happy. And I want your uncle to be happy, too. If the two of you find that together, I won't feel bad at all. Not at all."

Eventually, they dried their eyes and resumed their meal. Emily even asked for second helpings. Olivia served apple cobbler she'd made with the last of the apples.

She resumed her seat while Lorena poured coffee. The older woman rested her hand on Olivia's shoulder. "My invitation is still open to you, dear. You are welcome to join me in Ohio."

Emily staying did change the situation back to the way it had been before. She needed a job. There was nothing nearby. She could take her chances here in hopes of a marriage proposal, or she could go with Lorena. "Thank you, Lorena."

There were drawbacks to all her options. Staying here might reveal no prospects—or an invitation to marry a man she didn't know or care about just to find a home. Leaving on her own might or might not gain her employment nearby, and she would have to struggle to fend for herself. Leaving with Lorena meant she'd likely never see

Emily—or Jules—again, or if she did, the meetings would be seldom. Emily would grow away from her.

Even if she stayed and married, she wouldn't be able to be as close. It was time to face facts and decide on the least difficult route. "I'll pack and join you in the morning."

At Emily's stricken expression, she added, "It's what we planned, Emily. Ever since we made our plans to come to Montana, we knew that once you found your family, I would have to take a position elsewhere."

Emily broke into sobs and threw herself against Jules's shirtfront. He patted her back helplessly.

Olivia got up and went out of doors.

The air flowing down from the mountains was cool this evening, and it felt good against her heated cheeks. She walked all the way out to the hemlock tree and stood with its bark biting through her shirtwaist against her back. An owl hooted, startling her. She glanced upward, her vision blurred with tears. "Thank You, Lord."

Two people wanted Emily, and she was counting on God to provide her with that same wonderful acceptance. Perhaps her answers were waiting for her in Cincinnati. She chose to believe that they were.

Jules had never been so confused. His life had been simple, just rolling along smoothly—until all these women had converged and set his well-laid, sensible plans spinning.

What he knew about kids and women he could store under his hatband. He'd thought Emily had everything all settled in her mind and was pleased as a cat with a fat field mouse to go along with his mother, but apparently that hadn't been the case.

He'd never seen so many tears. Didn't they run out?

Emily brought him a book from the pile on the shelf he'd made her. He took it and looked at the cover absently. "I'm going to build you a whole case for your books in the new house."

She gave him a soft smile, but her eyes were red from crying. She turned around and eased onto his lap. Being an uncle had grown on him. He'd thought about a wife and kids, of course, but children had only been an idea until now. Now that he knew a few, he appreciated their innocence and inquisitiveness. Emily was incredibly bright and obviously sensitive.

He read aloud. She pointed to a word, spelling and repeating it. "You're a smart girl," he said.

"Miss Rose taught me."

"I know."

"When we stayed at the hotel in Oregon City, I was scared at night. Our trunks were at the train station, so we didn't have any books. Miss Rose made up stories at night." She looked up at him. "Sometimes we heard guns."

He'd already been mortified at the thought of their journey alone. "What kind of stories?"

"She told a story about a girl who took a train all by herself. She was scared, but she prayed and God kept her safe. And she told stories from the Bible, like the one about Jonah and the whale."

Jules found a marker for the book and tucked Emily into bed. Olivia still hadn't returned. Lorena joined him then and stood on tiptoe so he'd bend for a peck on the cheek.

"'Night, Mother."

Out of doors, he let his eyes adjust to the dark. He'd taken a few steps when the woman he sought walked toward him on her way to the cabin. "Good night, Jules."

She moved past, opening the door and disappearing inside. He looked at the door for a moment, and then headed for the barn.

He didn't join them for breakfast the following morning. He had a lot to plan and think about. He was going to have to get help to care for Emily. Perhaps Tanis would be willing to have her during the day.

He hadn't slept more than an hour or so all night. He was dreading this day. He kept telling himself it was for Emily's sake that he was fretting about Olivia leaving, but he wasn't convinced. He didn't want Olivia to leave any more than he wanted her to marry Marcus or anybody else. But he didn't want her to feel obligated to stay.

The time to head out to the train depot drew close, and he walked toward the cabin. Emily waited out front, a bonnet shading her eyes. It was the same one she'd worn the first time he'd seen her. The first time he'd looked into those coffee-dark eyes and recognized his sister's child. He would be forever grateful to Olivia for risking everything to find him and bring her to Montana. Had he told her how much he appreciated that? He'd neglected to tell her he appreciated everything about her.

The door opened and she came out, wearing a pale green dress and a straw hat. She took note of him standing there with a nod.

"Don't think I ever said how grateful I am that you traveled here to bring Emily to me. It was a brave thing to do."

"I'm glad it all worked out," she replied. She gestured back toward the cabin. "My trunks are still in there."

He moved past her and found her trunks and his mother's satchels inside the doorway. His mother tied the ribbons on one of her sweeping hats and greeted him. "We're all ready."

He loaded their belongings into the back of the wagon, but looking at Olivia's things gave him a sick feeling in the pit of his belly.

Climbing up to the seat beside the women, he picked up the reins and sat there.

He didn't want her to go.

A vivid memory of the night before washed over him. Emily hadn't wanted to leave. Without any assurance that he would accept her, she'd been brave enough to come out and say it. Emily had risked everything to ask him if he wanted her.

Olivia had risked her life traveling to a strange land so he and Emily could be together. Even his mother had been brave enough to ask his forgiveness.

He was the only coward on this wagon.

"Jules?" his mother questioned.

If Emily could take the risk, he could. He turned to look at the two women.

"Is everything all right?" his mother asked from beside him.

"Are we going, Uncle Jules?" Emily questioned from her seat behind him.

"No."

"What?" Lorena asked. "The train leaves in forty-five minutes."

"I'm not all right." He tied the reins to the brake handle, stood and jumped down. Striding around to the other side of the wagon, he extended a hand. "I need to say something."

Beneath the brim of her hat and his mother's lacy

parasol, Olivia's face registered confusion. She glanced at Lorena, but his mother only smiled and waved her forward.

Olivia reached for his hand, but instead of taking it, he reached up to bracket her waist and lower her to the ground.

"What are they doing, Grandmother?" Emily asked.

"I think your uncle is finally coming to his senses."

He took Olivia's white-gloved hand and led her away from the wagon to the shade at the corner of the cabin.

His behavior had Olivia's nerves in a frazzle. She barely had control of her emotions and needed to carry on with her plan before they unraveled.

"I don't want you to go," he said.

Had she heard him correctly? "I beg your pardon?"

"I don't want you to leave and live in Ohio. I want you to stay right here."

She shook her head to clear it. "I've thought it all through. A clean break will be better for Emily."

"No. It won't. Won't be better for us, either. I've just been too pigheaded to see that. I thought I had to follow some sort of logical plan and do everything in order. But love isn't logical. I was being stubborn and blind, not listening to my heart. Emily showed me how to do that."

"Love?" she questioned, singling out that word above all the others. Her heart skittered erratically, and she flattened her palm against her chest. "What is it you're saying, Jules?"

"I'm sayin' I love you. The idea of you with Marcus Stone ate a hole in my gut. I don't want you to marry anybody else. Ever. Except me. Marry me."

He hadn't said anything about her staying for Emily's sake or staying to be a teacher. He'd said he *loved* her. Her pounding heart recognized before her head did just what that meant. "Marry you?"

"Marry me. I love you."

No one had ever spoken those words to her before. "You want me?"

"If it's what you want, Olivia." He ran a hand over his eyes. "I know how Emily felt when she told me she wanted to stay. I feel like I'm standin' on the edge of a cliff, waiting for the ground to drop out from under me."

Olivia took a step back and then another to ground herself in reality. She turned in a circle, taking in the cabin, the wagon, the outbuildings, without really seeing anything. And then she looked back at Jules. "You want me. You want to be together. Make a family." She gestured toward the new structure. "Live in that house up there. With poppies in the yard."

He nodded. "Yes. For goodness' sake, Olivia, yes!"

"I just want to hold on to it a minute longer." She closed her eyes. Took a deep breath. Opened them. And then she crossed the distance between them, without a thought for anything except the sheer joy of his acceptance and love. She threw herself into his arms. He caught her in an embrace, knocking her hat to the ground and kissing her soundly.

"I love you, too," she told him between kisses. "I think I fell in love with you the day I met you."

"I've wasted so much time," he murmured against her lips.

"We have plenty left."

"I'm going to make you a good husband," he promised her. "I'll listen with my heart from now on."

"What's your heart telling you right now?"

"That I scare you, but you're brave enough to take a chance on me."

She smiled and returned another kiss.

"What does all this kissing mean?" Lorena called from the wagon.

They separated, looked into each other's eyes with their hearts welling, and then grasped hands to walk toward the wagon. "That your son is done being stupid and is going to marry this beautiful woman before she gets away," he called.

Olivia shot her gaze to his. "Beautiful?"

"Forgot that, too, didn't I? You're the most beautiful woman I've ever seen, Olivia Rose."

"You're *staying?*" Emily screeched.

Lorena leaned forward to protect her ears.

"I'm staying."

Lorena stood. "Well, then I'm staying longer. Come help me down. I'm not going to leave now and miss my son's wedding."

Jules released Olivia's hand long enough to help his mother and niece to the ground. Lorena hugged both of them, as did Emily.

Joy filled Olivia to overflowing at their generous acceptance and love. She was indeed special to God. And at long last she was special in the eyes and hearts of people she loved and who loved her in return.

Jules had shown her that looking forward held more promise than looking back. She was going to be Jules's wife and Emily's mother. From here on out, it didn't matter where'd she'd come from or who she'd been. All that mattered was where she was going and who she'd become.

"Thank You, Lord, for my family."

* * * * *

Dear Reader,

I loved every moment writing *Mountain Rose*. Olivia Rose and young Emily are two characters who deserved to find a home and a family who wanted them. There's something deeply satisfying about devising ways for story people to find fulfillment in relationships and in their walk with our Heavenly Father.

Mother's Day is a special holiday for many of us, a time when we express our appreciation for the women who have shaped our lives and reflect upon those who have loved us and sacrificed on our behalf. I wish those of you with children a lovely Mother's Day. May you take time to reflect on your blessings and perhaps even indulge in a little chocolate. You are special, after all.

Blessings,

Cheryl St. John

QUESTIONS FOR DISCUSSION

1. Because of her lack of family, Olivia encouraged herself with the knowledge that God loved her. We must know who we are in Christ and appreciate what Jesus has done for us in Heaven in order to understand our significance to God. What does the Bible say about your importance to Him?

2. In order to find Emily's family, Olivia put her trust in Isaiah 41:10, a verse that tells us God is always with us. Can you remember a time when your situation looked impossible, but when you placed your confidence in God's Word? When God was faithful to His promise, what did that do for your faith in Him?

3. Have you ever had to start over in a new community or school where no one knew you and everything was unfamiliar? What advice about making new friends would you offer someone like Olivia or Emily?

4. Jules had the impression that God had more important things to do than concern Himself with his trivial issues. John 14:14, Matthew 18:19, John 16:24 and I John 5:14 are only a few of the verses that tell us we can ask anything of God and He hears us. What do you believe the Bible tells us about God's concern for our daily lives?

5. Jules picks up on the way Olivia finds comfort and strength in Scripture, and reads Psalm 116 for himself.

Are there any particular verses that encourage you when you're seeking guidance?

6. Even though Jules had a forgiving nature and never held his mother to blame for his unpleasant childhood, she needed to apologize and know his forgiveness. Sometimes it's easier to forgive another person than yourself. If there's something you've been holding on to, would this be a good time to allow God's mercy and grace to heal those wounds?

7. Sometimes it's difficult to be genuinely happy for another's good fortune. When Olivia sees Emily being embraced by a loving uncle and grandmother, her own lack of family is a painful wound, but she is filled with joy over the child's good fortune. What is the difference between desiring something and being jealous?

8. Do you remember a holiday during which you had very little material wealth, but when you were grateful for God's abundant love and the blessings of health and family?

A FAMILY OF HER OWN
Ruth Axtell Morren

To the hardy people of coastal Maine, who haven't changed so much over the years....

He maketh the barren woman to keep house, and to be a joyful mother of children. Praise ye the Lord.
—*Psalms* 113:9

Chapter One

Wood's Harbor, Maine
1870

Noah Samuels walked past the crumbling stone wall, noting the wild rose creeping over everything. He kicked at a shoot growing across the paving stones. Tenacious stuff once it got going, almost impossible to get rid of, its roots spreading everywhere.

"Papa, why don't we live here?" He glanced over at his daughter, who held his hand as they walked to the house he'd grown up in.

"It's been sitting empty too long." He remembered the place in his grandparents' day. The lawn kept short by the grazing cow, the stone wall neatly stacked to form a boundary along the road, the walkway free of invading grass…

He dismissed the memory. No point in reminiscing about things long past. He was here to check on the storm damage from a few nights ago.

"Papa, who's that?"

His gaze followed Melanie's pointing finger to the meadow beyond the dilapidated house and was arrested by the figure of a woman. She stood amid the tawny, uncut hay, staring out at the indigo bay beyond.

Noah stopped, sensing something familiar in that straight, lithe figure. "I don't know, sweetie." Abruptly, he changed course, Melanie's small hand clutching his. The closer he got to the woman, the stronger his impression grew.

His memory didn't picture the black dress, however. It remembered a light-colored frock and auburn hair held back with a big bow. Now, a full, black skirt disappeared into the sea of high grass. The dress was tightly cinched at the waist, emphasizing a small waist and slim torso. She held a straw hat in one hand, as if she couldn't abide anything that prevented her from feeling the sea air across her face. The hat's black ribbon danced in the breeze at her side.

Her hair no longer hung down her back. It had been tamed into a thick knot, but its color hadn't changed. Noah would never forget that rich auburn, which, like burning embers, didn't reveal its fire until disturbed.

He'd been sweet on her once. It was but a vague memory now, that last year of his youth. Oh, he'd been full of dreams then, too. Not for the wide world, as she. His gaze drifted past the woman to the inky-blue bay beyond. Who needed to travel far from home, when he had the best of the world right here at his fingertips? He'd been itching to be a fisherman full-time since the day he was old enough to be taken out in his father's boat.

The woman hadn't moved. Noah cleared his throat.

She turned.

Noah stared.

She no longer had the fresh-faced look of a schoolgirl. Yet the expectancy of the girl remained, in the slightly widened eyes and half-parted lips. Her light brown eyes, the color of cider, he used to think, traveled from him to Melanie. There her gaze lingered, before coming back to his, a question in her eyes.

She made a small sound, between a cough and a laugh. "I believe I'm on your land." Not an apology exactly, yet an acknowledgment of the facts.

He ignored her words, saying only, "Hello, Rianna."

She touched her hair, before quickly returning her hand to its place.

"I'm surprised you recognized me. It's been a few years."

He didn't return her smile. "The years have treated you well."

She shrugged. "I can't complain." She looked at Melanie again and smiled. "Hello."

Melanie took a step closer to him and gave a quick bob of her head.

"This is my daughter, Melanie."

"Your daughter." Rianna breathed the word, as if in awe. Then her smile returned and she extended her hand. "How do you do, Melanie? My name is Rianna Bruce. I used to live here in Wood's Harbor."

The two shook hands, Melanie's gaze solemn.

Rianna turned back to the bay, taking a deep breath. "It revives me." She glanced over her shoulder at them, smiling. "Do you smell it?"

Melanie sniffed the air, looking puzzled. Noah inhaled, smelling only the sea mingled with the sweet hay.

"I call it sea and roses. It brings everything right back again, as if I'd never been away."

Melanie's mouth broke into a wide smile. "I can smell it!" She turned to him with a triumphant look. "It's the roses, Papa."

Rianna took another breath before walking toward the old house. Noah followed her, Melanie skipping along beside him.

When Rianna reached the house, she touched its weathered shingle exterior. "It's yours now, is it not?"

His reply was more a grunt than a word, but she took it as an affirmative.

"We used to have such amusing times here. I always remember the parties."

"You came to my great-grammie and -grampie's?" Melanie asked with childish wonder.

Rianna gave another laugh, a sound so clear and sparkling, Noah was startled for an instant, thinking he was back at one of those socials over a decade ago, hearing her laughter above the crowd of young people gathered. "Yes, dear, I certainly did. Your papa can tell you all about it."

Melanie glanced up at him, a question in her deep brown eyes.

"It was a long time ago."

Rianna's eyes held a familiar twinkle. "I remember the way your papa's grandfather would roll back the carpets and pick up his fiddle. His gnarled finger would pluck a few strings and we knew the music was coming. Everyone would stand up and form lines." She smiled in reminiscence. "How his bow would fly over that fiddle and how we'd dance."

Noah couldn't help being caught back to that time—a time he hadn't thought about in an age. Melanie seemed captivated, as well, her attention riveted on Rianna.

"Then your great-grandmother would bring out a tray of lemonade or mulled cider, depending on the season, and warm molasses cookies, so large and soft. Mmm-mmm. She made the best cookies."

"Mrs. Avery has taught me how to make sugar cookies."

Rianna smiled at his daughter. "Has she, dear? That's a very useful thing to know." Rianna turned her attention back to the house. "Do you have any plans for it?" Her question was brisk and matter-of-fact, as if relegating all talk of the past firmly to its place.

With effort, he shook aside the thoughts of those bygone times and looked at the house. The house that held those memories…memories he'd firmly stamped out to the last dying ember.

It was his turn to touch the old dwelling, reaching out to tug at a vine growing over the pine-green door, its paint badly chipped. He yanked at the vine with his fingers, pulling it off and tossing it to the ground. "It'd take a lot to make this place livable again. Stood empty too long." *By his own choice.*

She tilted back her head to glance at the eaves. "Oh, I don't know. It all depends on how sound the foundation is."

"I wish we could live here."

Noah eyed his daughter. She'd never expressed such a desire before. She'd barely been to the house.

He turned away from it. Best not let Rianna fill his daughter with illusions. "What brings you back to these parts?" he asked Rianna, curious despite himself.

"Mother. She's been ailing, and I came up to help out until she's back on her feet again."

He knew Rianna had become a nurse. "Of course. I heard your mother wasn't doing well. How is she now?"

"She's better." Her smile widened. "She enjoys having me back. We've spent hours catching up on everything. I think there's nothing I don't know about what's happened in Wood's Harbor in the last ten years." Her amused glance encompassed Melanie. "Somehow, I missed your arrival, young lady. When did you come along?"

Melanie returned her smile. "I just turned eight last month, ma'am."

"Oh, my, you'll soon be a young lady." She turned to Noah, her smile fading. "I'm sorry about Charlotte," she said softly.

He stared hard at her, as if suspicious of her sympathy then glanced at her widow's weeds. "You've suffered your own loss."

She only nodded, her eyes studying him. Gradually her smile returned.

He felt exposed somehow. "What's so funny?"

She blinked as if startled. "Was I smiling? I wasn't aware." She clasped her hands in front of her, and instead of answering, said, "Well, I'd best get back now. Mother will wonder what's keeping me. She shooed me out, telling me to enjoy this fine weather. I promised to bring her back a little of it. I remembered the roses here and thought I'd pick her some. They have such a delightful scent." She filled in her lungs again and smiled. "You caught me trespassing. I'm sorry."

Melanie's eyes rounded at the mention of trespassing and she glanced up at him.

"Sorry you trespassed? Or sorry I caught you?"

Rianna's eyes widened for an instant, and then she dissolved into laughter. Melanie giggled.

"I'm not sure. I'll let you know when I do. It was very nice to meet you, Melanie. I hope we meet again while I'm here."

"It was nice to meet you, too, Mrs. Bruce." The two shook hands.

Rianna gave a wave. "Bye-bye." She began walking toward the road.

"You didn't get what you came for," he said without thinking.

She turned midpath. "Oh, the roses!" She shrugged. "Well, now that the owner is here—"

"Come, I'll pick you some." For some reason, he wanted to prolong her stay.

He walked around the house to the backyard, its wide expanse overlooking the rocky bay. There against a crumbling stone wall grew the high shrubs of *Rosa rugosa,* that hardy species that endured every sort of buffeting, salt-laden wind. Taking a jackknife out of his pocket, he cut off a few stalks heavily laden with the deep pink, fragrant roses and deftly removed the thorns from the base with a flick of the sharp knife.

"Here." He presented the bouquet to her with no flourish, no pretty words, and yet the moment she reached out her hand, the thought crossed his mind that he hadn't picked flowers for a woman since he'd first courted his wife.

"Thank you, Noah," she replied softly, taking the lush bouquet, careful to grasp it with her fingertips just where he held it, where the thorns had been removed. Their cool fingers touched briefly, but in that instant, a shock ran through him.

Her eyes shot up to his, as if she'd felt it, too. A second later, she stepped back from him, her gaze fixed on the roses, frustrating his attempt to read her expression.

"Oh, how pretty," Melanie said, eyeing the flowers.

* * *

They were perfect, just as Rianna remembered—deep fuchsia, velvety-soft petals with yellow centers, their heady fragrance already touching her nostrils. Her mother would enjoy them. Of course, that was why Noah had been so considerate. He'd remembered her mother. She looked up at him gratefully, composed now that she was on sure footing again. For a second, when his fingers had touched her, she'd felt shaken.

Almost as badly as the moment she'd beheld his daughter.

Noah with a daughter. A daughter just a little younger than hers would have been. The thought had shot through her lightning swift, leaving a sense of pain, regret and loss in its wake.

Why hadn't she heard about Melanie? Why hadn't her mother told her in all these years?

"I'll pick you a bouquet, too, sweetie," Noah told his daughter, his voice softening as he addressed the girl.

Rianna watched him cut the stems. "You've grown a beard since I left." It made him look older, more rugged. But no less handsome. He had been the handsomest young man in Wood's Harbor. So handsome, she'd been in danger of losing her heart. It had made her run. Had she made the wrong decision back then? "But I still recognized you."

Melanie answered for him. "Papa always grows a beard in summer."

He rubbed his chin. "I let it grow in the summer and shave it off in winter."

"I would think you'd need the warmth in winter."

"In winter I don't take the boat out before dawn and have time to shave every morning."

"I see." She looked away, her gaze caught by the black-eyed Susan, clover and daisies bobbing in the breeze. "I've worked so hard on Mother's garden, and look at these."

Stretching out her arm toward the meadow, she quoted, "'Consider the lilies of the field, how they grow; they toil not, neither do they spin: and yet I say unto you, that even Solomon in all his glory was not arrayed like one of these.'"

She turned in time to catch the frown on Noah's face. "What's the matter?"

He shook his head. "I never thought to hear you spouting Scripture."

She burst into laughter. "Well, you know what they say." She gave no further explanation, but with a half wave of her bouquet, she moved away. "So long, you two. Thank you again for the flowers. Mother will be touched."

"Come pick roses whenever you want," he called after her.

She glanced back briefly. He hadn't moved, but stood with his daughter, the two looking at her. She nodded acknowledgment. "Thank you. I shall." What a nice pair they made, father and daughter. The image gave her another pang.

She quickly dismissed it, reminding herself she had dealt with her loss long ago. As she walked away from them, she had to resist the urge to turn around again, although she could feel Noah's hard stare on her back all the way down the rutted, dirt road.

Chapter Two

"What can I do to help you, dear?" Mrs. Devon asked, looking around at Rianna's supper preparations.

"Oh, Mother, you didn't have to get up." Rianna straightened from the woodstove, shoving a strand of hair from her damp forehead.

"Nonsense. You can't expect me to lie around all the time, just because I feel a little weaker than normal." She took a few slow steps to the kitchen table.

"Here, sit down." Rianna pulled out the wooden chair for her.

Mrs. Devon reached for a large metal colander filled with lima beans. "I can shell these for you."

"Sure. I'll get you a saucepan." When she'd settled her mother at her task, Rianna stood a moment, watching her mother's once-nimble fingers now slowly taking apart each pod to extract the beans. Rianna frowned, but refrained from saying anything or offering a helping hand. Instead, she turned back to the kitchen counter and continued her supper preparations.

"I hope you had a nice walk today. The roses were lovely. I smelled them as soon as I awoke."

Rianna thought once more of her encounter… Perhaps her mother could shed some light on Noah's brusque, forbidding manner. And the existence of his daughter. "I thought you'd like them. I walked over to the old Samuels place. I remembered the nice bushes they had there."

Mrs. Devon clucked her tongue. "It's a shame to see that place go. Every winter storm does a little more damage. Pretty soon the house or barn will cave in."

"Oh, no." The idea shocked her. "It's not that far gone. A little fresh paint, a few new shingles, the grass cut…" She pictured how tidy it used to look when Noah's grandparents had been alive.

As the two worked together silently, Rianna puzzled awhile more over Noah's reaction to seeing her. Although she had turned him down, that was long ago. She'd heard he married shortly after she'd left Wood's Harbor, so Rianna had assumed his feelings for her hadn't been too deep. She took out a wooden board and brought out a chunk of salt pork from the pantry. With a sharp knife she began slicing it. "I ran into its owner this afternoon."

"Whose owner?"

"The Samuels place."

Her mother dropped a handful of lima beans into the pan. "Oh, you mean Noah. I haven't seen him lately. What was he doing out there?"

"I don't know. I never did get around to asking him. He caught me trespassing."

"Nonsense. I shouldn't think anything of it. I'm sure he was glad to see you."

Rianna pursed her lips, hesitant to say anything to her

mother, but certain that *glad* was not Noah's reaction to the encounter. She put aside the meat to dredge in flour later and went back to the pantry to get some of the new potatoes her father had dug up that day.

"I also met someone else."

Her mother lifted her eyebrows. "Oh?"

"Noah's daughter."

Her mother looked at her, her expression almost… guilty.

"You never mentioned her."

"Didn't I?" Her mother picked up another bean and concentrated on shelling it. "I suppose with the war…so many other things going on…it slipped my mind. She's quite a big girl now."

"Yes, she told me she'd just turned eight."

"My, my, how time flies." Her mother's hands fell idle as she sat back in the wooden chair, her expression troubled. "I'm sorry, dear, I should have told you, but at the time, your own loss so fresh…"

Rianna nodded. "I understand."

Her mother sighed. "Yes, Noah and Charlotte had a daughter, about a year or so before he was drafted. He was one of the last to go. Nice-looking little girl, takes after him with her dark hair and eyes."

"He hasn't remarried?" Rianna asked as she set the potatoes on the table and sat across from her mother.

Her mother shook her head and picked up another bean. "He pretty much sticks to himself, ever since he came back from the war and found himself a widower. Awful shame about Charlotte, being all alone here when she died. And with a baby. Her own folks passed away in that awful epidemic we had the year before." She clucked, her fingers stilling on the bean pod. "The neighbors did what they could, but it wasn't the same as having family close by."

Her mother sighed. "I haven't been out to the Samuels place in ages. It would have made a lovely home for him and Charlotte, but he doesn't take any interest in it now."

"Where does he live?" Rianna asked, wondering how someone could pass up the chance to live in such a lovely house overlooking the sea, especially with a child of his own. A home of one's own for oneself and one's offspring. A cozy picture presented itself to her.

"He boards over at Mrs. Avery's. Can't think that must be very nice for a man his age, no real home. He must be thirty-one now. All he does is work. I imagine he must have saved up quite a bit by now. But of course, Melanie needs someone to look after her."

Rianna's paring knife stopped. "Mrs. Avery does that?"

Her mother nodded. "He told you?"

Rianna smiled. "Actually, Melanie did. Noah wasn't too talkative."

"He has grown so reserved since coming back from the war. I don't see him much anymore."

Rianna could only nod, taking it all in. The image of Noah—so harsh and dour—with a smiling young girl so like him physically, was still hard to square. "How sad that they don't have a home of their own, especially when the old Samuels place is sitting there empty."

"Yes, everyone thinks it's a shame, but of course, Mrs. Avery is a kind soul."

"Still, it's not like having a home and mother of her own." The thought of a little girl without her mother wrung her heart. A child without a mother and she without children…how strange life could be. If she'd been asked at seventeen where she'd be at twenty-seven, would she have pictured a husband and a child at her side? She had dreamed of seeing the world, but that hadn't meant she didn't want to someday fall in love and have a family of her own. "I wonder why he hasn't remarried."

Her mother only shook her head.

"He doesn't seem anything like the boy I remember," Rianna said at last, tossing the peeled potato that was beginning to turn brown in her hand into the pot of water. "But that was quite a while ago."

Her mother looked shrewdly at her daughter. "Seems to me he had his eye on you once."

For a second, Rianna relived the sensation she'd experienced when her fingertips had brushed Noah's—a sensation she hadn't allowed herself to dwell on. As soon as the memory rose now, she dismissed it with the same firmness she used to push aside the growing mound of potato peelings. "He only danced with me a few times. I hardly think that's enough to constitute a courtship."

Her mother smiled at her. "Still, he wouldn't make a bad catch for some woman. He does well with his fishing. His grandparents left him that house. He's got a few acres of timberland besides. What does he spend money on? He has no family but Melanie, and she's a dear thing." Her mother let another handful of lima beans fall from her hand. "Then again, he might not be so easy to live with. The war and widowhood changed him." She sighed. "He was such a fine young man, a bit serious, but always polite and helping others out." Her mother rose with effort to take the filled pot of beans to the sink.

"Here, let me—"

Her mother waved her back down. She filled the pan

with water and set it on the stove. "I never hear anything but good about Noah from Mrs. Avery though," she said, returning to the topic of conversation as she sat back down. "He's away at first light in his boat. In the winter he helps her around the place. And he's a good father. Mrs. Avery says he shows a gentle side to his nature around Melanie, and the girl adores her father."

Rianna thought how his tone had softened whenever he'd addressed his daughter.

Her mother looked into the distance, her smile dreamy. "You were sixteen when you left, and he was just a few years older, I recall."

Rianna couldn't help a smile of her own, remembering that time Noah had first asked her to dance, when she'd been only fifteen and he nineteen. Although they had grown up in the same town, she had never really known him. "Yes, but to me he seemed all grown-up." That evening, she'd discovered a young man dedicated to his own dream, patiently helping out his grandparents as if he'd been their son, while keeping his eye fixed on his goal.

Rianna looked down at the potato in her hand, seeing Noah's dark, unsmiling eyes fixed on her. "Noah certainly seems to need a little joy in his life."

"That's for sure." Mrs. Devon took up a potato and knife. "Well, I daresay there are plenty of widows just waiting for the chance to comfort a man like that."

Rianna shook her head, forcing herself to laugh. "I daresay." With a determined effort, she put away thoughts of the brooding widower. "It would do you good to get out the way I did today. Why don't we drive out together to the Samuels place. There were so many flowers in bloom. There's also a bit of blueberry land around there, as I recall. I could collect a pail for a pie. Papa would enjoy that." She warmed to the idea. "We could take a picnic. The sunshine would be beneficial. You're looking far too pale."

"As long as it's not too much work for you, dear." Mrs. Devon sighed. "It's so frustrating, not to have the strength to do what I want."

"I know." Rianna reached out her hand. "Don't fret. You're going to get better."

Her mother smiled. "It would be nice to have an outing."

"Then we shall go tomorrow." Rianna picked up another potato, telling herself the Samuels place was the perfect spot for an outing by the sea. No matter that there were plenty of other places offering wildflowers and blueberries.

Why did Noah's old homestead draw her as nowhere else in Wood's Harbor had since her return? His daughter's tone of longing when she'd expressed a wish to live there tugged at her heart. Poor child, both homeless and motherless.

The following afternoon, Rianna turned to her mother, brushing the remaining crumbs off her skirt. "Now, wasn't that a good idea?"

Her mother smiled from under the brim of her straw bonnet. "I'll have to admit it was. Too bad your father couldn't come—but summer is such a busy time for him. It's been a delightful afternoon."

The two women looked at the bay before them from the high ridge where they sat. The tide was out. Far out on the mudflats a few clam diggers bent over their rakes. Some, already finished, loaded their bushels of shellfish onto their wagons and guided their horses toward the clamshell-strewn road leading off the flats.

Rianna glanced down at the pail beside her. Its empty insides chided her. She turned back to the seashore. "I should have picked those berries before lunch."

Her mother looked at her in understanding. "Forget about them. Why don't you go and take a walk along the beach instead. You've been so busy with me you haven't had a chance to enjoy the beautiful weather. Before you know it, it will be over."

"What about you, Mother?"

"I think it's a good time for a nap." She lay back, resting her head on her folded shawl.

Rianna opened her parasol and placed it beside her mother to shade her from the direct sunlight. "I'll walk down to the beach then and see if there are any treasures."

Her mother smiled, her eyes closed. "Scavenging? You used to spend hours down there as a child. Are you going to fill the house again with bits of broken glass and shells?"

Rianna laughed. "I'll try to restrict myself to only the choicest objects." As she spoke, she unlaced her boots and removed her garters. Wriggling her toes, she felt the years fall away from her as quickly as the stockings from her legs.

"I won't be long," she told her mother as she stood and looked for the path that used to lead down to the beach. It was still there, though hidden by the long grass. The earth was packed down, as smooth and hard as stone, with only an occasional root protruding to hinder her progress. She clambered down until she reached the round pebbles and wide swath of rockweed edging the top of the shore.

She shaded her eyes and looked over the curve of the beach. Her mouth curled upward as she recognized Melanie sitting on a rock in the distance. Quickly, she picked up her pace, curious to know more about Noah's little girl.

She waved as she neared the child. "Fancy meeting you out here."

Melanie greeted her with a wide smile, which made her stop short. What would it be like to have a child greet one so each day? The pain she'd thought she'd gotten over so many years ago hit her so forcefully that she had to clutch her heart a moment.

An adult front tooth was halfway grown in, the space beside it still empty. "I'm waiting for Papa." Melanie pointed far out to the mudflats. "See, he's clamming."

Rianna looked at the distant figures. "Yes, though I can't tell from here which one he is."

"What are you doing here, Mrs. Bruce?"

Rianna smiled, putting her sadness away from her. "I'm scavenging for treasure."

Melanie's brow furrowed. "You are?"

"Would you like to help me look for treasure?"

The girl scampered down from her perch. "Is there really treasure here?"

Rianna widened her eyes in mock surprise. "You mean you've never hunted for treasure on the beach?"

She shook her head.

"Goodness, then we have a lot of work to do. I haven't hunted on this beach since I was about your age, so there must be oodles washed up. Come along, I'll show you what to look for."

Suddenly, Rianna got into the spirit of the task. In her work as a private nurse in the last decade, often she would meet a family's children and had to reassure them in the face of serious illness. By being away from home so long, she'd missed getting to know her own nieces and nephews. At the time, it had helped ease the pain of her own loss, but now she wondered if perhaps she'd deprived herself of something precious.

Over the next hour, she and Melanie examined wet clumps of rockweed and kelp strewn along the beach and peered into tidal pools formed in the undulations of sand.

Rianna straightened, easing the kinks from her back, amazed at how much fun she was having.

Is this what motherhood would have been like? She stopped a moment, unsure if she wanted to pursue the thought. For so long, she'd resigned herself to her childless, widowed state, content with her calling to be a nurse.

Farther out, the sand turned into mud pockmarked by clam holes. Their feet sank into the warm, wet clay. "It feels warm and squishy!"

Rianna laughed at the mud oozing between the girl's toes. Seeing no one close by, she hiked up her skirts into the waist of her apron. Everywhere sharp edges of clam shells stuck out, so they turned back toward the sand, picking up empty mussel shells, their interiors pearly pink, and sticking them into their apron pockets.

"Here's one for you." She handed an especially pretty one to Melanie. How delightful it was to be with a child, so filled with curiosity and enthusiasm about the simplest things. While she'd always wonder what it would have been like with her own son or daughter—the little one she'd been destined never to know—the happiness she found in today's encounter helped her to disregard the pain.

"Oh!" Melanie stooped down. Rianna came to look over her shoulder. A perfectly formed crab, desiccated by sun and sea, lay in a crevice between two stones. She picked it up carefully and set it in the palm of Melanie's hand.

"It's so tiny," exclaimed the girl.

"Yes, not more than an inch and a half across, I'd say. Let me put it in your other pocket. If you're careful, it shouldn't get broken."

"I can show it to Tad and Robbie."

Rianna glanced at her as they resumed walking. "Who are they?"

"Mrs. Avery's grandsons. They're visiting with their mother, Mrs. Johnson, over the summer."

Rianna nodded, remembering Mrs. Avery's daughter, Amelia, from her girlhood. "Oh, yes, I think I saw her in town the other day, but I wasn't sure if it was she.

"Let's see if we can find some beach glass," she suggested to Melanie. Together, they trod the rounded stones carefully, keeping an eye out for the colorful fragments worn smooth by sand and surf.

"I found a blue piece!" Melanie pounced on the colorful shard as if it were the most valuable jewel.

"I think it's time to wash our feet off and take a rest," Rianna suggested. She led Melanie toward a brook, which meandered from the meadow above down to the beach in a snakelike pattern to the sea. Offering Melanie a strand of goose grass to nibble on and taking one for herself, she explored the murky edges of the brook. The grass's salty crunch took her back many years. She remembered so many summers scampering around with her sisters, not having a care in the world.

She wondered Melanie hadn't done the things she'd taken for granted as a child. "Doesn't your papa ever take you out on the beach?"

Melanie shook her head. "He's very busy in the summertime fishing. He usually doesn't take me like today, when he goes clamming. But I kept asking him, until he finally said yes. He told me to be careful and wait for him."

Rianna glanced back out toward the men bending over their clam holes, wondering which one was Noah.

"Well, we shall have to find a way to remedy things. There is still so much to explore." Why had she stayed away so long? First, there had been the war. Then she'd used the excuse of work to her family, but deep down she knew it wasn't the reason. Was it fear?

She shook aside the ugly word. Today was too beautiful a day to dwell on dark thoughts. Instead, she and Melanie waded in the fresh water as they followed the brook seaward, searching for seashells in the wet sand. On the other side of the brook, large boulders sat strewn upon the sand as if haphazardly thrown down there.

"Here's a good resting spot." Rianna climbed up one slate-colored one and Melanie chose a granite one.

They examined their treasures as the sun warmed them.

"Ahoy there!"

Rianna straightened at the sound of the masculine voice.

"Papa!" Melanie called out joyfully.

Rianna shaded her eyes, spotting the tall, lean man heading toward their rocks.

She swallowed, thinking of her disheveled appearance and bare legs. If he'd sounded disapproving before, what would he think of her now?

Bringing a hand to her mouth, she stifled a giggle. Nothing to be done for it but to put on a brave face. As he drew closer, she joined Melanie in waving to him.

Noah reached them quickly with his long stride. He was wearing high leather thigh boots folded down at the top.

Melanie quickly slid down the rock. "Papa, look who's here—Mrs. Bruce."

"Hi, sweetie." His glance went to Rianna and he nodded. "Hello, Rianna."

"Hello, Noah. I came down to the beach and found Melanie."

"I hope she hasn't held you up."

"Oh, no, we've been having a grand time."

"We've been hunting for treasure, Papa. Come, see."

He looked at the pebbles and seashells she'd spread out on the boulder. "Very pretty."

Then he approached Rianna's perch.

He stood at eye level with her where she knelt. She studied his sun-bronzed face framed by dark hair and beard. Under the brim of his straw hat, his gaze was as steady and penetrating as it had been the day before.

"You seemed rather absorbed in what you were doing."

"I haven't done this since I was Melanie's age."

"Any luck?"

She patted her bulging pockets, which rattled with the sound of shells and pebbles.

"Look at my best treasure." Melanie pulled open her pocket and carefully extracted her little crab. "See?" She held it out to him. "I found him myself."

Noah bent down, examining the tiny pink crab. "That's quite a nice treasure. Tad and Robert will be jealous."

His daughter smiled. "Will they really? I'm going to see if I can find another one!" With those words she ran off.

"Don't wander too far," he said. "We'll be heading back soon."

His gaze turned toward the shoreline where his old house stood high above the fields. "You came back for more roses?"

Rianna's cheeks reddened and she laughed. "No, blue-berries this time! Actually, Mother and I came for a picnic.

"I thought an outing would do her good. I saw so many blueberries the other day, I brought a pail with me today to pick for a pie." She paused as she realized she was trying too hard to explain her appearance.

She shrugged and smiled shamefacedly. "The seashore beckoned me, so I'm afraid Papa will have no pie. The month is going by, and I haven't had a chance to pick any berries at all. I'm sorry, I should have asked permission."

He shook his head. "Pick all you want. I don't use that field by the house. I rake another one."

She nodded, wondering where the conversation would proceed. In the silence she became conscious of her bare legs, hidden at the moment by her kneeling position. Before she could figure out how to release her skirts in a natural way, Noah spoke up. "I wouldn't think such simple pleasures as combing the seashore would appeal to you after having been away."

His tone sounded almost accusatory. "On the contrary, I appreciate them all the more." She sighed in contentment, resting her hands in her lap. "It's wonderful to be back. It's almost as if I'd never been away. All my old friends remember me. I've been invited everywhere. The people I was close to before I left Wood's Harbor have just opened their arms to welcome me back into their circle."

"It sounds as if you expected otherwise."

She blinked at the words. He was the first person to have guessed her uncertainty at coming home. Gazing down at her hands, she hesitated. "It was just…that I'd been away so long." She opened her hands, palms up, her fingers splayed as she searched for words to explain her doubts.

"It has been over a decade, after all. People change, circumstances change. And the longer I stayed away, the harder it got to return." Her voice ended in a whisper as she stared at him. Would those deep brown eyes, so dark it was hard to distinguish pupil from iris, condemn her?

He nodded slowly, as if digesting the words. "I still find it hard to believe you'd find enjoyment in any of the things Wood's Harbor has to offer."

Rianna made a face at his skeptical tone. "Oh, yes, after the places I've seen?" She shook her head with a bittersweet laugh, seeing again the young girl she'd been when she'd first set out to conquer the world. "Let's see, where should I begin? First was the life of a city girl working from dawn to dusk at the mill. I sometimes think the slaves in the South had it easier. The only difference was we girls got paid. Of course, we had to live off what we made."

He seemed to be listening intently, so she continued. "Days and days over a loom, doing the same task time and again until I thought I'd expire of the boredom, but my hands would continue performing the task long after I had left it.

"Then we'd arrive home—" she snorted "—a boardinghouse run by a dragon lady—merely to eat and sleep. I admit, at first it was nice to earn my keep, and I felt proud to be able to send my earnings to help the folks, knowing Mother could buy my sisters a few nice extras. But as far as enjoying the independence I'd craved so much—" She shook her head. "I had less freedom there than here. Our landlady guarded our virtue jealously." She laughed. "With no real cause. There was no opportunity to get into trouble, since it was early to work and early to bed."

"You must have had some opportunity to meet young men."

"Oh, yes, there were opportunities to meet factory workers, farmers, the butcher, the baker, the candlestick maker…" She trailed off in amusement. "All eyeing those young lasses, fresh from the country, with honorable and dishonorable intentions alike." She made another face. "Even those with the best intentions were only looking for a young workhorse to hitch up with and take back to the farm. I wanted none of that!"

"So you disdained them all, just as you did the honest young laborers in these parts?"

Rianna peered at Noah, surprised at the censure in his tone. Did he think she had turned him down because he was a fisherman? It hadn't had anything to do with that, but with her own yearnings to be away, and to do and see things for herself. So she smiled a bit sadly, and nodded. "I suppose I did." Her gaze took on a faraway look as she remembered those days. "Until Ralph. Dear, sweet Ralph." She gave a dreamy sigh.

"Your husband." His tone was flat.

"Yes." The two were silent for a while. Rianna wasn't ready to tell him about the husband of her youth. The way Noah had been staring at her made her feel he'd seen more than she had intended to reveal. She'd grown accustomed over the years to having no one take an interest in her life beyond the sickroom.

Her gaze strayed to Melanie, bent over the sand. "You've been blessed with your daughter. She's a delightful child."

"Thank you." His dark eyes continued watching her until again she felt self-conscious.

"I imagine it must be difficult raising her by yourself."

He shrugged. "Mrs. Avery is a big help."

"I remember her as a nice woman." When he offered nothing more, she turned to look back at the shoreline, wondering if her mother was waiting for her.

"You haven't any children of your own?"

She stiffened at the sudden question then forced herself to relax. It was a natural question, even if people never asked it of her on her nursing jobs. She was just Mrs. Bruce then, or Nurse Bruce—a woman who was always at a patient's side, with no life of her own outside the sickroom. Was that one reason she'd feared coming back home, knowing it was a question she'd have to get used to answering over and over? "No…no, I haven't any." She began to say something—anything—to fill the awkward silence, when they both began to speak at once.

She motioned with her hand. "You first. I wasn't going to say anything important. I just thought I'd better go see if Mother is ready to go home. I left her napping…on your property," she finished with a strained smile.

Noah shifted his feet, not quite meeting her eyes. "Would you like a mess of clams to take back with you? Seeing as how you didn't get your blueberries?"

She let out a silent breath, relieved at the change in topic. "That would be lovely." She giggled, glad the awkward moment had passed. "Papa will get a chowder instead of his pie."

A sudden joy surged through her as she saw the smile tugging at his lips. "You haven't forgotten!"

The humor disappeared from his face. "Forgotten what?"

"How to smile." She sat back on her perch and beamed in satisfaction.

He coughed again and looked away from her. "I'll get the clams."

"Wait, I'll come with you." Rianna jumped down from the rock, quickly letting down her skirt as she moved, and hoping he hadn't noticed. Noah's hand came up to steady her.

"Thank you," she said, flustered. "May I accompany you?" she asked quietly, wondering what he was thinking.

"Better not. That mud'll be hard on your bare feet."

His tone sounded so matter-of-fact, she thought she must have imagined the tension in the air. "I don't mind. Come on, show me the way." She turned to Melanie, who was kneeling in the sand. "Come, dear, it's time to go."

"You'd best stay here," he told his daughter when she looked up. "I'll bring the buckboard."

Rianna started walking seaward.

Noah quickly passed her and led the way out to the flats.

The going got harder, as the mud became deeper and softer and broken shells less visible.

"Ouch!" she cried, picking up her foot from an ankle-deep pool and rubbing her heel, almost slipping in the process.

Noah quickly stopped and looked back at her. "Wait there. I'll bring the wagon to you."

She did as he said, watching him reach the buckboard and put away his things. He climbed aboard and guided the horse toward her.

When he reached her, he climbed back down to help her up to the seat, but before she could swing her legs inward, he stopped her. "Better wash your feet off here."

She followed his gaze to her two bare feet hanging over the side of the wagon. They were covered in the gray, claylike mud. "Yes." She made to get down again, but Noah reached for her wrist, stopping her.

"I'll bring you a bucket of water." He reached into the back of the wagon and took out a pail, wading farther out to sea to fill it. When he returned, he grasped one of her feet in his hand and poured water over it, rubbing off the worst of the mud. He repeated the procedure with her other foot.

Rianna sat perfectly still, watching his rough hands wash her feet. Although the water was icy cold, numbing her feet and turning her skin red, his hands felt warm and gentle.

Her mind thought of all the sick and wounded men she'd nursed, the many limbs and feet she'd washed.

This was the first time in her memory someone was washing hers.

Chapter Three

Noah bent over the field of blueberry bushes, the long even strokes of his rake turning to jerky whacks the more he thought about Rianna Bruce.

The fact that he couldn't stand there talking with a woman who'd scorned him more than a decade ago and not be swept in by her charm once again was a bad sign.

She still talked with the same lilting voice, the same enthusiasm of the young girl he'd known. But now the attraction was made fatal by tones tempered with the maturity of self-knowledge.

The worst thing was she seemed to be exercising that same charm on his daughter. Melanie was his only child, the only thing he had left. She was the one bright spot in his life, his reason for getting up before dawn and coming home in the late afternoon.

She'd shown more animation around Rianna than she had since she was a toddler. By the time they'd parted, Rianna had invited her to tea and Melanie had accepted with a wide grin.

What if she hurt his little girl the way she had—

Noah stopped his thoughts cold. That was in the past, dead and buried.

He shook his head in disbelief as he remembered how Rianna had just smiled at his comment about disdaining all the young men of these parts, and acknowledged it as the truth! How many women would have answered so honestly and brazenly?

And yet balancing her childlike frankness, there was something besides mere maturity, something deeper, more attractive than anything he'd ever seen in her before. He couldn't define it except as some radiance that lit up every word she spoke.

He'd attributed it immediately to her husband. Ralph. The way she'd said his name—almost in reverence— showed the depth of her affection. But that didn't make sense—the man had been dead longer than Charlotte.

Had Rianna found the kind of once-in-a-lifetime love the poets wrote about? The notion shook him, causing his rake to snag in the low-lying bushes. Clearly, he hadn't awoken that depth of sentiment in her, no matter how much he'd thought to the contrary. The time they had spent talking about anything and everything after dancing at his grandparents' socials—he'd never opened up like that to anyone. He'd known then that she was the only woman he'd ever want. Noah sat back on his haunches and wiped the sweat off his brow with his bandanna. From his vantage, he could see the sinking sun across the bay. There had been a sadness in Rianna, too, he realized. He'd noticed it as soon as he'd asked her about children. He wondered what had happened. Had she been unable to have any?

He shook away thoughts of Rianna. She was none of his

business. She was here to nurse her mother and soon she'd be off to greener pastures again.

But his mind refused to dismiss her image. Had she found what she'd been looking for in the big city? With her youthful, romantic notions, she'd probably been swept off her feet by some handsome man who could fulfill her every dream. A poor fisherman could never have competed with that.

With an impatient sigh, Noah continued down the row of blueberry bushes, emptying his rake every few strokes. His basket was only half-full. He'd better get his mind on the task, or he'd spend the greater part of the evening picking through it to clean out all the bits of leaves and branches he was getting with his uneven strokes.

When he finished the task of raking blueberries, he sat awhile by his wagon, cleaning the berries and dividing them up. One bushel into a good-size basket, the other to take back with him to Mrs. Avery.

On his way through town, he stopped his horse in front of the Devon place. No one was on the front porch. He glanced at the gardens edging the white picket fence, remembering Rianna's remark about toiling away at it. It certainly seemed a whole lot more attractive than the field of hay and wildflowers she'd found so pretty on his property.

Hating himself for his quick, furtive movements, he swung the basket down from the wagon, glanced up and down the street, and seeing no one, made his way toward the back of the house. There, he quickly set the bushel basket down by the kitchen door, then turned on his heel and walked to his wagon, not breathing easy until he was well on his way home.

Why couldn't he stay away from Rianna? No sooner did

he see her than he had to hike on over to her, drawn like a fly to flypaper.

Back at Mrs. Avery's, the screen door banged behind him as he entered the kitchen.

"Papa!" Melanie turned in her chair, her face beaming. "You're finally home!"

He leaned down, squeezing her shoulder, and gave her cheek a quick peck. "What are you up to?" Her cheeks and hands were dusted with flour.

"I'm helping Mrs. Avery make the biscuits for supper." She patted down the rolled-out dough with her hand.

"Oh, my," he said, glancing over his daughter's head and winking at Mrs. Avery, who stood at the stove. "I'll bet that's a big help, isn't it, ma'am?"

"Goodness, yes. Soon, she'll be making them all by herself."

He gave Melanie's thin shoulder a final squeeze and stepped back. "I'm sure they'll be the best biscuits I've ever had."

Melanie used the biscuit cutter and carefully cut another round, then laid it on the greased baking sheet.

Noah stepped toward his landlady. "I brought you some berries. Where would you like me to set them?"

"How thoughtful of you. Just leave them by the door for now. We'll pick over them after supper." She looked toward the doorway to the dining room. "Look, Amelia, at what Noah's brought home."

Mrs. Avery's married daughter stepped into the kitchen. "Good afternoon, Mr. Samuels." The stately woman, looking as cool and refreshed as if she'd just stepped out of her bath, walked toward the basket and eyed it. "How lovely. We don't get blueberries like this down in Massachusetts."

She picked a berry off the top of the pile and popped it into her mouth. "Mmm." She smiled at Noah, making him feel as if she were a queen bestowing her approval on a subject.

He gave a brief nod of his head. "Evenin', Mrs. Johnson." Before he could say anything, two pairs of running feet came crashing through the outside door. "Mr. Samuels! Mr. Samuels! You're home!" Two boys lunged at Noah.

Noah grabbed them both under their arms and swung them around. The boys shouted with glee.

"Robert! Thaddeus!" their mother admonished, "Not in here! Some decorum, please!"

The boys paid her no mind, their attention on Noah. "When're you going to take us out on your boat? Didya know we went fishin' up t'the pond today? Caught us a mess o' trout. I got the biggest one, didn't I, Tad?" The oldest boy wriggled around Noah to ask the younger.

Tad nodded. "And Grammie's fryin' 'em tonight for our supper."

Noah smiled over their brown heads at his landlady, who nodded confirmation. "Think you'll have a frying pan big enough, ma'am?"

Mrs. Avery pursed her lips and shook her gray curls. "Oh, I was worried for a minute there. I thought I'd have to borrow one from the neighbor, but luckily the trout just fit one of mine." She nodded toward the pan on the stove.

Noah dismissed the idea of sitting in an easy chair and reading the paper for the few minutes before supper. "Why don't we go outside and toss a ball around until your grammie calls us in to supper."

The boys both shouted their assent, and kept on shouting as they dragged him by the arms toward the door. He glanced back at Melanie, who was looking at him with longing. "Why don't you come along, too, Melanie. That is, if Mrs. Avery can spare her main cook." He waited for the older lady's permission.

Mrs. Avery inspected Melanie's tray of biscuits. "Why, these are ready to go into the oven. You did a fine job, dear. Run along with your papa."

Melanie scooted off her chair and hurriedly rinsed her hands. Noah opened the back door and held back Tad by the shoulders. "You know the rule, ladies first."

As soon as Melanie had stepped through the doorway, the boys raced outside, their shouts carrying back to the kitchen. Noah nodded to the two ladies. "I'll bring them back in a few moments."

"Thank you, Noah. You're always such a help," Mrs. Avery told him.

When they were called back inside to the table, the boys stood behind their chairs, their wet hair slicked back, hands scrubbed, until Mrs. Avery gave the nod to be seated.

As soon as she'd said the blessing, Noah and the boys dug into their food. Melanie whispered to him, "Papa, did you try one of the biscuits yet?"

Noah looked up from his plate. "What—? Oh, no, not yet, Mellie. I'm going to right now." He picked up the warm biscuit and split it open. "Sure feels light." He took a bite. "Mmm-mmm. That's about the lightest biscuit I ever tasted, no disrespect to yours, ma'am," he assured Mrs. Avery.

His landlady chuckled. "None taken. I feel complimented that she's learned so well. And only eight years old!"

Noah turned his attention back to his food, hardly listening to the two ladies' conversation.

"I saw Mrs. Miller today," Mrs. Johnson began as she took a steaming bowl of potatoes from her mother. "She invited us to a clambake. I told her the boys would enjoy that."

"Oh, dear me, yes. When is it to be?"

"On Saturday." Mrs. Johnson turned to Noah. "Would you like to accompany us, Mr. Samuels?"

Noah looked up from his plate, swallowing hastily. "Uh, no, thank you just the same, ma'am."

"The boys would love to have you. You're always such a help with them."

He wiped his mouth with the napkin. "I don't go in much for socializing."

Mrs. Johnson held up a dish. "More greens?" As he took it from her and helped himself, she continued. "An occasional outing would do you good. Mr. Johnson always takes us on an outing at least once a week."

"When do you think he can come up from Boston to join us?" Mrs. Avery asked.

Noah turned back to his food, relieved to have Mrs. Johnson's attention temporarily diverted from him.

"The town swells to twice its size this time of year with so many family members coming from far and near to visit," Mrs. Avery said.

Mrs. Johnson buttered a biscuit. "That's one of the reasons I'm looking forward to the clambake. It will be a good opportunity to see everyone." She bit into the biscuit, brushing the crumbs from her fingertips without commenting on its texture. "I bet I know one person sure to be there."

"Who is that, dear?" Mrs. Avery paused at her daughter's significant tone.

Mrs. Johnson contemplated her biscuit before answering. "Rianna Devon, or I should say, Rianna *Bruce*."

Mrs. Avery nodded. "I'd heard she was back."

Noah's glance flicked to the younger woman, wondering at her peculiar tone. When her gaze crossed his, he quickly looked back down at his plate, but his ears remained alert.

"I couldn't believe it myself. I passed her on my way to the store. Goodness, I stood there openmouthed, thinking I was seeing an apparition. She smiled at me as if we'd only just seen each other yesterday and wished me a good morning before walking right on by."

Mrs. Avery's eyes widened. "You don't say."

"I haven't seen her since…let me see…" Mrs. Johnson paused, calculating. "Why, since we were both in grammar school. I remember she was in such a hurry to leave Wood's Harbor."

Noah had stopped eating altogether, though he kept his head bent over his plate.

Mrs. Avery sat back with a reminiscent smile. "They were such nice girls, the Devon girls. They all married well to local boys, except, of course, Rianna. I don't know much about her, only that she was widowed. The others come by and see their folks regularly. All except Rianna." Mrs. Avery clucked her tongue. "I never could understand why she didn't come home. During the war, of course, it was impossible, but it's been five years since the peace. What's kept her away so long?"

Mrs. Johnson picked up her fork and knife. "I heard she became a nurse during the war and that she's continued with it. Except now, it's *private* patients." With that pronouncement she calmly brought a forkful of trout to her lips and began chewing. When no one said anything, she looked around at them, her gaze coming to rest on Noah. "Wealthy old-men patients."

Mrs. Avery's mouth made a little circle of wonder.

As the silence drew out, Noah brought his knife and fork to rest at the sides of his plate. "What's wrong with nursing old men?"

Mrs. Johnson took her time wiping her mouth. "Wealthy old men can grow attached to their attractive young nurses." With a glance toward the boys, who were talking to Melanie about their fishing trip, she lowered her voice, "I've heard of cases where an aging man will suddenly up and change his will. His heirs will be out every penny, and away walks the nurse, a wealthy woman." She gave a decided nod of her head.

Noah eased back in his chair, his food forgotten. "Just what are you trying to say?"

Mrs. Johnson blinked. "Say? Why, nothing at all. I just wonder what would bring Rianna back home now."

"I think if you have anything on your mind, you'd better spell it out, preferably to Rianna's face."

"Now, Mr. Samuels, don't get upset. Amelia didn't mean anything against Rianna. She was just talking of *some* people," Mrs. Avery hurried on. "I'm sure our Rianna wouldn't be capable of such things. Now, have some more potatoes."

Noah took the dish from her, but didn't serve himself any. He set the bowl down. The remains on his plate no longer held any appeal. His stomach felt as if a piece of lead had just settled in it.

Mrs. Johnson spoke up sharply. "Of course, I wasn't implying anything. I was just pleased to see that Rianna is back to help with her mother. About time, too," she added, though now she addressed her mother exclusively. "The poor woman's been ailing a long time, the way I hear it…"

Noah stood, throwing down his napkin. "As far as I know, Rianna Bruce has never done you any injury, and I would suggest you don't start harming her reputation now."

The two women stared at each other in shock.

With a sharp nod, he excused himself to Mrs. Avery and left the dining room, ignoring the boys' cries asking where he was going. The last thing he saw was Melanie's wide-eyed look, but he didn't stop.

Feeling too restless to sit down and read the newspaper, Noah left the house, preferring to walk off his anger. Although his instincts would have taken him toward the harbor to check on his boat, he avoided that locale altogether since it would mean passing the Devon house. Instead, he took a brisk walk in the opposite direction, leading out of town. He ended up back at his grandparents' homestead. Rather than calming him, the place only agitated him the more.

Fool women, gossiping about someone they knew nothing about. And Rianna, why'd she have to come back now and have people talking about her? Why did she have the ability to get under his skin as no other woman ever had? With Charlotte, it had been a nice comfortable affection. With Rianna, even after all these years, he felt stretched taut one moment, snapped loose the next.

Noah looked out into the bay. Dusk was falling. The peace of the water beckoned, and he decided in that instant he'd take the boat out next morning for a few days. Usually he came in with his catch daily, but he needed to put things back into their proper perspective, and only the sea had the ability to do that. He'd have to reassure Melanie that he wouldn't be gone long. Thankfully, he could depend on Mrs.

Avery to take good care of his daughter. Once again, he remembered Melanie's tea with Rianna. His jaw hardened.
He'd just have to trust that one visit wouldn't do any harm.

Taking a deep breath of the salt air, Noah already felt
better…until he caught the heady perfume of rugosa roses
on its perimeter, and he was back where he'd begun.

Would he find no peace! He whirled around, heading
back to town, to let young Joe, his first mate, know they'd
be going out at dawn.

Chapter Four

Rianna put a frilly tablecloth on the front-porch table and placed a bouquet of pinks in the center, wanting to make the occasion into a real tea party.

She'd run into Mrs. Avery with Melanie in the store the day before and had asked the older lady if she could bring Melanie over for tea.

"How pretty it looks," her mother said, coming to sit on the cushioned rocker.

Rianna smiled. "I thought it would be nice for Melanie. I remember when I was that age liking to pretend I was at a real tea party."

"How thoughtful of you. I sometimes think Melanie is a lonely child with no brothers or sisters and Noah with no close family around."

They had no more time for conversation as the gate opened and Mrs. Avery came up the walk with Melanie.

Rianna went to the head of the porch steps to meet them. "I'm so glad you could come by."

Melanie held out a covered basket. "We brought you something, ma'am."

"Oh, my goodness, what is this?" she asked with exaggerated wonder as she took the shallow basket by the handle. She lifted the gingham napkin covering it. Inside was a pie.

"Blueberry pie, baked this morning."

"It looks absolutely perfect."

"Melanie has been helping me bake. She rolled out the pie crust herself."

"How lovely," Mrs. Devon said. "I'm sure we shall all enjoy it. Blueberry is my husband's favorite pie. He'll be a happy man tonight. We just received a bushel basket of fresh blueberries last evening."

Rianna glanced from the pie in her hands to the platter of blueberry cupcakes she'd set out. Someone had clearly been out picking blueberries. Could it be—?

"Come and have a seat," her mother said to their visitors. "Rianna made some blueberry cupcakes this morning in honor of the occasion."

When they had sat down, Rianna poured the tea and offered them the cakes.

Mrs. Avery set her silver spoon on her saucer and sat back. "Tell me what you've been up to all these years. I heard you'd become a nurse."

Rianna set down the pot carefully, bracing herself for the curious looks and gentle questions that followed every new encounter at Wood's Harbor. "Yes, I trained during the war."

Mrs. Avery tsk-tsked. "Oh, you must have seen some awful things."

Rianna nodded. "Yes. It was a terrible time. So many wounded men." She slowly stirred her own tea and set down the spoon. "I feel blessed that I was able to nurse my own husband and be at his side at the…end." She looked across at the older lady. "It is how I decided to remain a nurse. There was too much suffering going on around me to dwell on my own sorrow at the time."

Mrs. Avery shook her head. "Oh, dear, what you must have gone through."

Rianna glanced at the young girl beside her, who seemed to be drinking in every word she said. "Anyway, let's not dwell on such sad thoughts," she said with a friendly firmness, not liking to recall that time when she'd first gone to Washington to nurse Ralph. "Not on such a beautiful day and with such nice company. Tell me, Melanie, what do you like to do?"

The little girl swallowed the bit of cupcake she'd taken. "I like to play with my dolls and help Mrs. Avery in the kitchen."

Rianna smiled, remembering her own girlhood. "Do you have a favorite doll?"

She nodded. "Her name is Annabelle. She was my mama's doll when she was young."

"Oh, how nice to have your mother's doll. I had a favorite doll, too, when I was your age. Her name was Esther. She had dark painted hair and pink cheeks. I made clothes for her."

"Annabelle has two pinafores, but only one dress."

"Well, she clearly needs a seamstress to sew her up a few more. Do you know, I'm making myself a new gown. Perhaps you'd like some of the remnants to make Annabelle a fashionable outfit."

The girl smiled. "Oh, yes, I'd like that very much. And so would Annabelle."

"I'll show you the material before you go. Is your papa out fishing today?"

Melanie nodded. "He's staying away three days."

"Oh." Why did the news disconcert her? He hadn't mentioned anything to her about going away. But then, why should he? She gave herself a mental shake. She thought again about the bushel basket of blueberries left on her doorstep and couldn't help smiling.

The girl finished her cupcake then said, "Sometimes Papa takes me out on his boat and I like that. Right now, Tad and Robbie are here, so Papa usually takes them along wherever we go."

Rianna turned to Mrs. Avery. "It must be nice having your grandsons visiting you."

She smiled. "Oh, my, yes. Though they are a rambunctious pair. Noah is such a help with them. Poor Amelia has her hands full. Do you remember my daughter?"

"Yes, of course." Rianna drew her eyebrows together. "Didn't I see her the other day? I think I hurried by her before realizing who it was. I hope she didn't think me rude."

"She did mention that she had seen you. Goodness, she was surprised."

Rianna smiled faintly. "As everyone is, I suppose."

"It's just that we haven't seen you in so long, and suddenly you appear as if out of nowhere." She turned to Rianna's mother. "You didn't say a thing about your daughter's return."

Mrs. Devon gave a helpless shrug and small laugh. "She surprised us, as well." She looked at Rianna. "She knew I wouldn't want her giving up her position just to come take care of me, so she decided to come without warning."

Mrs. Avery chuckled. "Well, we are all glad you are back. Are you here for good?"

Rianna took a sip of tea, unsure how to reply, since she didn't know the answer herself. "I was tending a patient, an older gentleman. He is such a dear. When he heard

Mother was doing poorly, he insisted I come back and help her. But I don't like to leave him alone for long." She sighed, still feeling torn.

Mrs. Avery's smile disappeared. "An older gentleman?"

"Yes, my patients usually are."

Abruptly, Mrs. Avery turned back to Rianna's mother. "It's been a busy summer, you know, with Amelia and the boys home. We're expecting Mr. Johnson in a week's time."

Rianna frowned, wondering at the woman's sudden change of demeanor. With a sigh, she turned to Melanie. "I bet you have fun on the boat when your father takes you out. He always did love the sea."

Melanie nodded and continued studying Rianna's face until Rianna wondered what was on the girl's mind.

"What was it like when you used to go to my great-grammie and -grampie's house?"

Rianna rested her chin in her hand and smiled. "It was lots of fun. I have three sisters, and Mama would send us over there to help Mrs. Samuels with her baking or if she needed heavy housework done. But we had so much fun, especially when we got older. They'd always invite lots of young people over."

Melanie listened with the same intentness Noah had. Rianna extended the cake platter toward the girl. "Would you like another cupcake?"

"Yes, please." Carefully she took one. "They're delicious."

"Thank you. Would you like to learn to make them?"

The girl's eyes lit up. "Oh, yes. May I?"

Rianna smiled at her eagerness. The child seemed starved for attention. "Of course. At the moment, we have lots of blueberries to use up. Perhaps if Mrs. Avery would let you come by tomorrow or the next day, we could make blueberry cake." She turned to the older lady for permission.

"I suppose so. If it wouldn't be too much trouble for you to have her."

"Oh, no, not at all. I'd love to have your company, Melanie."

The grateful smile the girl gave her warmed Rianna. The child was so very dear, and reminded her strongly that her own baby would have been just a year older...

Noah threw the last bucket of water over the deck, and watched as Joe swabbed it down. Then he turned around to stow his gear.

He and Joe climbed aboard the painter tied alongside the twenty-five-foot sloop and rowed back to the harbor. Earlier they'd unloaded their three-day catch and had returned to the boat to leave everything tidy for the night. Now, it was late afternoon, and they both felt tired. Even the usually exuberant fifteen-year-old Joe was subdued. But it was a good tired. Noah stretched his aching muscles. He hadn't felt so good since... Well, he wasn't going to dwell on that anymore.

He and Joe made their way up the wharf to the street. "We'll take a rest tomorrow," he told the boy. "Have to re-plenish our bait, anyhow."

"Sure."

Noah noticed the look of relief on the youth's face. "Any special plans for tomorrow?"

"Well, kind of." The boy's sunburned face deepened in color. "There's going to be a clambake on Wilson's Beach. I had a mind to go."

"I see. Well, you go and have a good time."

"Ain't you goin', Noah?"

"No."

The boy shook his head, but said no more.

The town's main street climbed upward at a gentle slope. They were approaching the Devon place. Noah looked straight ahead, determined nothing was going to affect his newfound peace of mind. He'd just walk by, the way he had for the countless years he'd lived in Wood's Harbor. He swung his jacket over his shoulder and stepped up his pace.

Then he heard the humming, and his steps slowed. It was more than humming. An occasional phrase floated over to him from the high flowers. *"How great Thou art. Then sings my soul—"*

He couldn't help glancing sideways along the white picket fence. A profusion of flowers grew along it.

Before Noah could command his legs to resume their pace, Rianna straightened from where she was kneeling at the edge of a garden border, and their gazes met. Instantly, a large smile broke over her face.

Noah stopped, unable to resume his movement.

"Hello, Noah. Back from the sea?" Rianna looked up from under a wide-brimmed hat and sat back on her heels. A flat, open basket lay on the grass at her side, a pile of cut flowers scattered upon it.

"Yes. Just back." He couldn't do anything but stare at her. He felt like a man who hadn't eaten in three days and was suddenly presented with a feast.

"Good catch, I hope?" She held a pair of clippers in her gloved hands.

"Fair enough."

"Hello, there." Rianna looked past him, and it was then

he remembered Joe's presence. Before he could dismiss his first mate, Rianna stood and came to lean across the picket fence. "I don't believe we've met." She removed one of her gloves and held out her hand. "Rianna Bruce."

Joe stepped forward shyly, sticking out his own hand. "Joe MacDonald."

Rianna smiled. "Pleased to meet you, Mr. MacDonald."

Noah watched Rianna's charm take hold of the boy. His chest expanded a fraction with the pride of being referred to as "mister." "Oh, just call me Joe. Everyone does."

"Very well. Joe." She removed her hand. "May I interest you two men in a cup of tea after your journey?"

"Thanks, ma'am," Joe answered at once. "I'd love to stay, but I'm expected back home."

"Of course. Some other time, perhaps."

"Sure. I'd like that. Well, be seein' you." He touched his hand to his hat and set off down the road, whistling.

Rianna turned her gaze to Noah. "How about you, Mr. Samuels? Are you expected home right away?"

He could see the playfulness in her amber eyes. At the moment, they awaited his reply, her two finely drawn eyebrows raised above them.

Before he could formulate words of refusal, she continued. "The offer of tea comes with blueberry cake." She swung her clippers back and forth over the fence. "You know, I've been up to my neck in blueberries for the last three days. Uh-huh," she said with a nod. "Thanks to a mysterious benefactor, my family will enjoy blueberries this winter."

Noah could feel his own neck redden, and an unwilling smile tug at his lips. Rianna just kept looking at him archly until his smile widened.

"Now, how about that tea?"

Although tempted, he suddenly remembered how he must look—and smell. He made a futile gesture toward his garments. "I'm not too presentable."

"Fiddlesticks. You should have seen me this morning covered in flour and blueberries." She opened the gap in the gate wider. "Come on, Mother will be glad of the company."

With that final reasoning, Noah argued no further, but followed her up the path to the front porch. Her black dress brushed against the bright flowers and foliage lining the path. She carried her basket of cut flowers on one arm. "Mother, look whom I've invited to have tea with us."

Mrs. Devon was sitting in a wicker rocker in the recesses of the porch. She smiled in welcome. "Hello, Noah. How are you?"

He walked over to her. "Fine, thank you, ma'am. Hope you don't mind my stopping by. I'm really not fit to be seen in company. I've just gotten off the boat and was heading back to Mrs. Avery's."

"Nonsense. Come, sit a spell."

He glanced at Rianna. "Perhaps if I could wash up a bit first?"

"Certainly," Mrs. Devon answered for her daughter. "Just follow Rianna out to the kitchen."

"Come along." Rianna beckoned. "I've got to put these flowers in water before they wilt in this heat."

Once in the kitchen, she showed him to the sink and fetched him a clean towel. He heard her bustling about as he washed his face and hands.

"It's been warm, hasn't it?" she asked as she arranged the flowers in a vase. "Of course, you probably don't notice on the ocean. It must be nice to be out there, only you and the sea and the Lord."

He made no reply, content to hear her talk as she turned to get the tea things ready. He took the linen towel and rubbed his face and hands in it. It smelled clean and fresh.

"Is Joe your helper?"

"Mmm-hmm, first mate," he answered absently.

"He seems like a nice young man." Rianna placed cups and saucers, creamer and sugar bowl on the tray then glanced at him with a smile, which caught him up short.

"I had my own young helper with my baking this morning."

He paused, looking at her with a question.

"Melanie."

Noah frowned, wondering at the sense of disquiet he felt. "Melanie was here while I was gone?"

She smiled. "Twice. Once for tea, and then again this morning to help me bake a cake." Almost as if she could read his thoughts, her face sobered. "I hope you don't mind. I thought with the two boys visiting at your place, she might want a little female companionship. I did ask Mrs. Avery's permission."

Noah shook his head, his worry replaced by confusion. "That wasn't necessary, I'm sure. I—I hope Melanie didn't make a nuisance of herself."

Rianna drew her eyebrows together. "Nuisance? Goodness, no. She's a delightful child, a credit to both you and Mrs. Avery."

He stopped drying his hands, his mind too mesmerized by her proximity and the warm tenor of her voice to think about his uneasiness over Melanie getting too attached to her. He knew from experience that Rianna wouldn't stay.

He didn't want his daughter to be the one to get hurt this time when she left.

"What's the matter?" Her soft voice finally broke through his thoughts.

Noah set down the towel. "Uh—nothing."

Rianna turned back to the kitchen counter. "Anyway, Melanie was a big help." She lifted a cover and held a cake aloft with a flourish. "Blueberry cake." She set it on the tray then poured water from the kettle into the pot and set it beside the cake.

"She takes after you."

He started. "What—? Yes, so I've been told."

Rianna took up the vase and inhaled the flowers' fragrance.

"Mmm." She held the bouquet out before him. "Have you ever seen anything lovelier?"

Not noticing that he was looking at her and not the flowers as he shook his head, she continued. "Except for those roses on your property, of course." She turned her attention back to the laden tray. "Would you carry the tray for me, please?"

He jumped to attention. When he was ready to lift it, Rianna stopped him with a gasp. "Your hands!"

He looked at them and knew they mustn't be a pretty sight to a lady.

"They're full of cuts. Do you get those from fishing?"

"Yes."

She set down the vase and took one of his hands in both of hers, turning it around. "Don't you put anything on them?"

Her voice had taken on the professional tone of nurse.

He made a sound of amusement. "Salt water."

She continued examining his hand, and he had an urge to take it back and stuff it in his pocket. His skin was red and rough, marked by old scars and fresh wounds. His fingernails were not taken care of, his palms and fingertips, which she was now touching, were hard and callused. Her own hands were slim and soft and pale by contrast.

She pursed her lips. "That probably keeps them from festering, but it must dry them out awfully. What you need is a good dose of wool grease. Lanolin," she explained, catching his frown. "I'll get you some and give it to you next time you stop by."

"No need," he said quickly, wanting no more close examination of his unsightly hands. "They heal up in winter, anyway."

She said no more, but led the way back outside, holding the door open for him.

Back on the porch, they settled down to their tea and cake. Mrs. Devon asked him a few questions about people he knew. Mostly he was content to eat the cake and listen to the two women talking. As soon as they'd finished their tea, the ladies took up their sewing.

He watched Mrs. Devon stitch a piece of white linen. He noticed her taking frequent pauses, stopping as if to rest her wrists and hands. Rianna's progress seemed much quicker by contrast.

At one point, she shook out the cloth, and Noah noticed its pretty, lavender color against her black skirt.

"What are you sewing?" he couldn't help asking.

"Nothing. Just a garment." Rianna bunched it back onto her lap.

Noah was intrigued at her change in manner. She'd never seemed so…he'd almost venture to say embarrassed. "It's a pretty color."

Rianna looked at him, her eyes widened in surprise. Did she think he was color-blind? he wondered in amusement.

Luckily, Mrs. Devon made up for her daughter's sudden reticence. "Yes, isn't it a lovely shade? I finally convinced Rianna to make herself a new gown. It'll be ready just in time for the clambake tomorrow, won't it, dear?"

Rianna assented with her head.

Mrs. Devon continued with a chuckle. "I told her I refused to have her in black any longer. I'm tired of seeing only black and brown in the sickroom. She might be a nurse, but she doesn't have to look it!"

Noah watched Rianna during the conversation and noticed that the more her mother explained, the more studiously Rianna bent her head over her sewing. He found it very interesting to find her so silent.

"I knew this color was right the moment I saw it. It favors her complexion, don't you agree, Noah?"

He imagined how nice it would look against Rianna's auburn locks. He looked from her hair to her down-turned face, and it was then he noticed her heightened color. It dawned on him, she was blushing! He stretched out his legs in front of him, resting his hands on them. "You could be right," he told Mrs. Devon. "Why don't you hold it up, Rianna, so I can see for myself." He kept his tone devoid of anything but innocent curiosity, but he began to savor the moment.

Rianna took a while to comply with his request, continuing to stitch at the garment. Finally, she knotted her thread and broke it off with her teeth. She stuck the needle into the pincushion and removed her thimble. With a final shake of the garment, she stood.

As she held the dress to her front, she finally met Noah's gaze.

Their glances locked, and all thoughts of teasing left

Noah's mind. He forgot his surroundings and ceased to hear Mrs. Devon's voice in the background. His senses were filled with the image of the woman standing before him, transformed by the lavender cloth draped in front of her to the young girl who'd laughed and danced with him so long ago.

Chapter Five

"Look at Mr. Samuels!" Seven-year-old Tad's voice shouted down the entry hall. Everyone turned to look up the stairs as Noah made his way down, wishing he could just turn right around and go back to his room.

"You look like you was going courtin'!" his twelve-year-old brother, Robert, piped up.

Noah could feel his face getting hotter as Mrs. Avery and Mrs. Johnson both inspected him from head to foot.

"He's turnin' beet-red," Tad chimed in.

Before Noah could take the two young ones by the scruffs of their necks and muzzle them, Melanie stepped up to him. "Oh, Papa, you decided to come with us! I'm so glad."

Noah swallowed, not sure when he'd made the decision. "Yes, I thought you might like the company."

"You look handsome, Papa," she said softly, taking in his suit.

He smiled down at her. "I figured I'd better be presentable if I was going to take the prettiest girl in town to the picnic."

She giggled then took a step back and held out her sprigged gown with both hands. "Do you like my dress?"

"I sure do, Mellie."

Mrs. Avery interrupted them. "You look right handsome, Noah."

"Thank you, ma'am," he answered, wishing he could just go unnoticed out to the barn. "You look quite fine yourself."

She smiled prettily, patting her new bonnet. "Thank you." Before she could speak any further, Mrs. Johnson sniffed, pointedly ignoring Noah and turning to the glass in the hallway.

He cleared his throat and faced her back, knowing he'd get no peace until he'd said *his* piece. "Mrs. Johnson."

Mrs. Avery's daughter turned to him slowly, her nose tilted up. "Yes, Mr. Samuels? Did you have something to say to me?"

"I wanted to apologize for any rudeness to you the other day at supper."

She stared down her nose at him a moment before sniffing a second time. "Well, I should say, I was quite offended by your remarks."

Noah bit down. She wasn't going to make it easy, but he'd plod on, if only for his landlady's sake. Mrs. Avery's wrinkled face looked at him so hopefully. "Yes, well, it was inexcusable of me."

"There now, no harm was meant," Mrs. Avery put in. "I'm so glad you changed your mind about accompanying us to the clambake."

He turned to the older lady. "I thought I could take all of you, if it isn't too late." He turned deliberately to the younger woman. "That is, if you don't mind."

She began to soften. "Not at all. It would be most gentlemanly of you to escort us."

Noah felt as if he'd just run through a mortar field. "Well, that's settled then. I'll go hitch up the wagon."

By the time they reached the wide cove where the clambake was being held, Mrs. Johnson had recovered her goodwill toward him. "I told you an outing would do you good," she said as they spread out their blanket on the sand.

As soon as he'd unloaded everything and seen them settled, he took off, joining the men congregated about a large driftwood fire.

"Hey, there, Noah, good to see." He was slapped on the back by some of his acquaintances. "You're looking grand."

Joe ran up to him with a big smile of welcome, and they all talked fishing for some time.

Noah pulled at his stiff collar, unused to being constricted around the neck. He'd removed his jacket and rolled up his sleeves as soon as he'd arrived. The noon sun was directly overhead. The tide was out, and children scampered about the sand. It didn't take him long to spot Rianna among them, her lavender dress like a spring flower against the drab brown of the clam flats. She seemed like a child herself, running among the others.

He shaded his eyes and looked around for Melanie. She was helping Mrs. Avery spread out their things. He sighed, wishing he could get her to join the other children more. But he didn't want to push her and make her feel uncomfortable.

"Hey, Noah, I see you was away fishing. How far out did you go?"

He turned to the fisherman. "Oh, not too far, just beyond Grand Manan." He didn't say he could have stayed out another day, but had felt pulled back to shore.

They continued chatting awhile longer. When Noah turned to look toward the shore again, his gaze searched immediately for the splash of lavender. This time his attention was arrested by the yellow, sprigged figure beside it. His daughter was standing alongside Rianna out on the clam flats, looking intently downward. He remembered Rianna's penchant for searching for treasure. He could hear the faint sound of their laughter across the flats.

He fought with himself to keep from joining them, ignoring the fact that Rianna was the sole reason for his being out today in the first place in his uncomfortable Sunday best. He stubbornly continued standing with the men even though he'd run out of things to say. When some of them suggested a game of horseshoes, Noah jumped to help organize it.

He became aware the moment Rianna joined a group of onlookers. Out of the corner of his eye, he caught sight of the lavender skirt. Even more surprising was seeing her with a child by each hand, one of them his daughter.

He didn't know why the sight of Rianna surrounded by children should be so startling. Was it only because the last time he'd known her, she'd been barely out of childhood herself? The notion of her as a grown woman was something he was still getting used to. The idea of her being good with children shouldn't be so astounding. After all, her vivacious, fun-loving personality would be a magnet to children, like a female Pied Piper.

He focused on the horseshoe in his hand, taking aim. When he made the shot, it annoyed him how pleased he was when she cheered him on.

When the clambake pit was uncovered and everyone began drifting back to their groups to eat, he couldn't help noticing the numerous family members surrounding Rianna. Once again he held back from going over to greet her. He recognized two of her sisters and their husbands who'd come from the nearby villages. Noah, by contrast, headed to sit at the edge of Mrs. Avery's family group.

Melanie skipped up to him. "Papa, may I go sit with Mrs. Bruce and her sisters? Please, Papa?"

She hadn't been this excited about someone since… well, he was the only one she got excited about. "I don't know. She's got a lot of company there."

Melanie looked down, her bottom lip jutting out. "But Papa, she invited me."

He felt caught between not wanting to disappoint her and not wanting her to come to depend on Rianna too much.

"Please, Papa? There are a lot of children there."

He swallowed, feeling the bite of food he'd just taken stick in his throat. "Sure, sweetie. Go on and have a good time."

Her bright smile lit her face. "Thank you, Papa!" Before he could say anything more, she had spun around and was running to the Devon gathering.

More like a clan, he thought sourly, eyeing their laughing group spread out over various blankets and folding chairs.

"Noah, you've hardly touched your food," Mrs. Avery scolded. "What's wrong? Don't you like my potato salad? Isn't the corn sweet? I thought you liked lobster!"

He reassured her everything was fine and took a heaping forkful to show her. The potato salad tasted like mush in his mouth, but he chewed determinedly, trying to stifle the sense of abandonment he felt.

Just then, Mrs. Johnson's youngest son ran up to him. Noah lifted his plate into the air to avoid the shower of sand he kicked up.

"Mr. Samuels," he panted, "can you get together a ball game after we eat—"

His mother glared at him. "Thaddeus M. Johnson, what do you think you're doing? Look at the sand you've thrown all over Mr. Samuels!"

Tad hung his head. "I'm sorry, Mr. Samuels, I didn't mean to."

"That's all right. I know you didn't," he assured the boy. "Why don't you sit down and eat your food and then we'll see about a ball game."

Mrs. Johnson handed her son a plate and turned her attention back to her mother. The two women commented on everyone they'd seen as they ate their food.

When Noah had made a sufficient effort to clean at least half his plate, he laid it aside and stretched out on the blanket, looking upward.

What was he doing here? Who was he fooling? He closed his eyes against the vivid blue sky. She was the same Rianna. It was her way to have a good time, not caring for the feelings of those she left in her wake. The way she was charming Melanie was the same way she'd charmed him. What would happen when she up and left again? He didn't want his little girl hurt.

He knew Melanie felt the lack of a mother, when all her schoolmates had their mothers. All she had was Mrs. Avery, and kind as she was, the woman was only their landlady. Her work kept her too busy to give Melanie all her attention, the way Rianna did. Melanie was blossoming thanks to her time with Rianna, but how long would it last?

Suddenly, he heard Rianna's musical voice and snapped to attention, every fiber of his muscles on the alert.

"Good afternoon, Mrs. Avery. Amelia, how nice to see you again."

"Hello there, Rianna!" Mrs. Avery's voice sounded welcoming. "And Amy and Marianne. How wonderful that you could come to the clambake. It's lovely to see the three of you together. If only your oldest sister were here."

Slowly, Noah opened his eyes and stood, dusting the sand from his trousers and smoothing down his hair, annoyed that she had found him looking like an old codger taking a nap after his meal. That brought up the thought of her elderly male patient and his mood soured further as he remembered Mrs. Johnson's words.

When Rianna and her sisters turned to greet him, he held out his hand and nodded his head. "Good to see you, Amy, Marianne, Rianna."

He tried not to stare at Rianna in her light-colored dress. He'd been right. The shade made a perfect complement to her hair, which glowed with fiery highlights in the bright sun. Her bonnet had fallen back onto her shoulders. Her cheeks were pink and her amber-colored eyes twinkled with suppressed merriment.

He hardly had eyes for the other Devon sisters, although together all three of them presented a lovely sight. "Hello, Noah. It's been a while…how are you doing?" Amy and Marianne returned his greeting with warm smiles.

"Congratulations on your win," Rianna said, when he took her hand in his. "I'd forgotten you were so good at horseshoes."

He shrugged, conscious only of her soft hand in his. Then he pulled his away, remembering how rough it must feel to her.

The Devon sisters remained conversing with Mrs. Avery and her daughter as Noah tried not to stare at Rianna.

Before he could think of anything to say to prolong

their stay, Tad and Robbie both grabbed him by the arms. "Are you ready, Mr. Samuels, for our ball game? You promised when we finished eating you'd play."

"Yes, I'll be right there."

Rianna smiled at the two boys. "And who might you two gentlemen be?"

The two fell silent, their cheeks reddening as they stared up at Rianna.

Noah cleared his throat. "These are Mrs. Avery's two grandsons, Thaddeus and Robert Johnson." He indicated their mother with his chin. "Mrs.—uh—Johnson's boys, up from Massachusetts for the summer."

"How do you do—" she held out a hand to each as if they were grown men "—Thaddeus, Robert. So, you're going to play ball?"

They bobbed their heads. "Yes'm."

Rianna turned to Melanie. "Then why don't you come along with me while the men play ball, and we can go look for some more treasures along the shore." She glanced at Noah. "If it's all right with your papa."

Melanie quickly nodded, putting her hand in Rianna's. "May I, Papa?"

"Yes, sure," he said, torn between wishing for some time alone with Rianna and knowing it was best this way.

The sisters said their goodbyes and continued on their way, greeting other families along the beach.

By midafternoon, the tide was halfway up, and the younger children were out swimming in it. Warmed by the mudflats, the normally cold surf felt like bathwater by the time it reached the sand.

Finally able to extricate himself from the ball game, Noah walked toward the shore. Seeing Rianna out in the shallows with a group of children, he took off his boots and rolled up his pant legs and waded out.

Rianna was swinging a little boy up and down in the water. His head was thrown back as he shouted in glee each time his body hit the surface.

"Auntie Rianna, me next! Me next!" A chubby little girl in pigtails tugged on her dress.

"No! She promised me!" Another little girl pushed her away from Rianna.

"Now, none of that, Lucy," Rianna said firmly.

Melanie stood quietly with the others.

"Haven't you had a turn?" he asked her.

"A while ago. There are too many children for Mrs. Bruce by herself."

With a smile toward Noah, Rianna set down the boy with a final splash. "All right now, who's next?"

Noah watched a whole chorus chime in, then saw how she calmly chose one, and ignored the cries of the others. He looked at the bottom half of her new dress, dragging in the water, and remembered the better care she'd shown her other dress the other day on the beach. Still, he supposed she couldn't very well display her legs today.

He stepped up to his daughter. "Come on, hang on tight." Before she could react, he scooped her up and swung her high then low into the water. She screamed with laughter.

After that, Noah gave a little boy a turn. Soon, between him and Rianna, they satisfied every child.

"All right, who wants to learn to float?" he asked the group, and received an immediate chorus of "Me! Me!"

By the time he and Rianna finished giving each child a

turn, he didn't know who was the more soaked, the children or the adults. He realized he hadn't felt so lighthearted in a very long time.

"Oh, is my back sore!" Rianna groaned with a laugh as they waded back to shore, herding all the children toward the sand.

"Your new dress," he commented when she attempted to wring out the hem.

She shrugged. "It'll dry."

"They're your nieces and nephews?" he asked, gesturing toward the scampering children.

"Most of them! Neighbors' children, as well."

"Yes, I recognized one or two of them."

"Thank you for your help back there."

He shrugged. "You looked a bit outnumbered."

She laughed.

"You don't miss having your own?" he asked. The next second he could have kicked himself for the thoughtlessness of the question as he saw the way she averted her eyes.

She laughed again, but this time it sounded forced. "I'd have made a terrible mother."

He frowned, remembering how drawn children seemed to her. "Why do you say that?"

She picked up a shell at her feet, still not meeting his eyes. "Oh, I'd doubtless be bossy or not practical enough or too demanding. I'm the good 'auntie' type. And I have plenty of opportunity to use my skills in that capacity right now with so many nieces and nephews of my own. Anyway, I believe the Lord has another road for me, and I'm perfectly content following it."

The more she talked, the less Noah believed her. Who was she trying to convince, him or herself? It was the first time he'd glimpsed a vulnerability in her, and it brought out his protective instincts.

Rianna pointed to one end of the beach. "Look, children, they're serving ice cream! Last one there's a rotten egg." With that, she hiked up her skirts and began running toward the crowd, the children dashing alongside her.

Noah followed slowly, indifferent to their taunts when he arrived last, his mind too full of the expression in Rianna's eyes and the tone of her voice when she'd spoken of motherhood. What was she hiding?

Chapter Six

Rianna turned to offer Noah a bowl of blueberry ice cream. Then she knelt beside one of her three-year-old nieces to help the child with her dish. Noah sat on the beach beside her, a toddler on his lap.

Melanie helped another younger child with her bowl of ice cream.

As Rianna struggled to recapture her lighthearted mood, Noah asked her quietly, "Why haven't you ever remarried?"

She glanced at him over her niece's head. He seemed determined to upset her equilibrium at every turn this afternoon, first with his question about motherhood and now this.

Did she miss having her own children? A bayonet piercing her heart couldn't have hurt more. Every day of her life she missed the little one she'd lost, until she'd learned to shut out the thoughts, determinedly, methodically, and busy herself with caring for others.

Now, she assumed a flippant tone. "In case you hadn't noticed, the War of Secession didn't leave many good prospects around for us widows."

"How about your patients? No wealthy widowers among them?"

She stared at him. Did he think, like so many did, that a private nurse was out to get rich from a dying patient? Not Noah!

She decided to test him. "Well, yes, I have had a few come my way. Take old Mr. Whitestone, my present charge." She sighed, assuming a long-suffering look. "Such a fine old gentleman." With a conspiratorial little laugh, she added, "I think he fancies me. Says I remind him of his first wife, Sadie." Removing the empty bowl from her niece and wiping her sticky face with a handkerchief, she observed Noah's reaction. "If Mr. Whitestone has proposed to me once, he's done so a half a dozen times. I tell you, he's wearing me down. He's even said he'll change his will if only I'll agree to be his wife."

"How old is he?"

The curtness of his tone didn't escape her. So, he believed it, too? She looked at her fingernails. "Well, let's see, he's…ninety-one."

As Noah's dark eyebrows drew together in a stern line, Rianna finally could stand it no longer. She fell backward on the sand, bursting out with laughter. "You believed me! How could you?" she gasped between laughs, looking up at him.

The children looked at her wide-eyed and began to laugh and copy her, flinging themselves onto the sand. "What are you laughing at, Mrs. Bruce?" Melanie asked.

Rianna turned to her, thinking how covered with sand her hat and the back of her new gown must be. "*Whom,* darling. I'm laughing at your papa, that's who!"

Melanie turned to her father, as the younger children

turned their attention to playing in the sand. "What did you say that was so funny, Papa?"

His unreadable glance shifted from Rianna to his daughter. "Nothing, sweetie, you go on and enjoy your ice cream before it melts."

The girl continued looking at him with a puzzled expression for a few more seconds. But when neither adult was forthcoming, she took up her spoon once more.

Rianna sat up on one elbow and gazed at Noah.

He was watching the incoming tide. The only sign of any remorse for his contemptible assumptions was the heightened color along the nape of his neck. She was beginning to be able to read the telltale signs of his emotions. Had Charlotte been so adept? Why did the thought unsettle her?

"Actually it's all quite true," she said quietly. "I do have a ninety-one-year-old patient at present who has proposed to me numerous times. But I have turned him down firmly each time, much to the relief of his family and heirs. And I know his proposals have only been in jest, because he's such a dear man."

Deciding she wasn't going to get any kind of apology from Noah, she sat back up, removing her hat and dusting the sand off it. "Anyway, I've grown much too independent since widowhood to make anyone a suitable wife, even if there were a suitable candidate. I make a good living, accept the jobs I want, get to travel a fair amount."

Noah glanced sidelong at her. "Still the same Rianna, aren't you?"

She swallowed, not wavering under his scrutiny. He didn't realize how much his remark hurt. Jesus said that a prophet was respected everywhere but in his own country. How could she expect any better? She bowed her head, giving her pain over to her dear Savior. Hadn't He promised to give her great peace, so that nothing would offend her?

What a long road she'd traveled since she was that fifteen-year-old girl, who'd confided her hopes and dreams to a very grown-up, nineteen-year-old Noah. The girl who couldn't wait to get away from Wood's Harbor didn't have much in common with the war widow who yearned to come back home and have a family of her own.

When Rianna looked up again, she was smiling, and it was in that moment that it occurred to her how much perhaps she'd hurt Noah when as a girl she'd rebuffed his advances. She hadn't thought much about it then. As she recalled, shortly afterward, he'd started walking out with Charlotte, a girl from another village, and the two had soon married. At the time, she'd thought only that his feelings must not have been any deeper than hers.

She spread out her drying skirt. "There's a camp meeting this week. Have you ever been to one?" she asked him, wishing above anything to see some joy restored to his countenance.

He blinked at the change in subject. "No, can't say I have, at least not since I was a child."

Her smile grew wider. "They're fun. Everyone leaves his daily routine for a week to camp out in a field, and just spends that time seeking God. Wonderful things happen. Would you like to come?"

He tugged at his collar, looking away from her again. "I don't know. I don't go in much for religion."

"Oh, it has nothing to do with religion!" When he turned his attention back to her, she explained. "It has to do with hearing from God." Her voice grew eager as she sought to make him understand the wonder of it. "It's a time when you put aside every care you have and just spend some time praising God and waiting on Him—to see His glory revealed. And when it happens, people's lives are changed! Sins we've clung to so long, or that had us bound for ages, are broken by God's Holy Spirit. Only God's power can do that. Do come!"

He shook his head, clearly uncomfortable. "I don't know. I couldn't take a week off from fishing, for one thing."

She spoke gently, "'There is no man that hath left house, or brethren, or sister, or father, or mother or wife, or children, or lands, for my sake, and the gospel's, but he shall receive an hundredfold now in this time.'"

He rubbed his beard and didn't say anything.

Rianna turned at the sound of a child's cry. "Jenny, let your brother go." She rose to separate the pair of toddlers. "I think someone needs a nap."

Noah helped her herd the tired children back to their parents.

After that, she went to spend some time with her sisters and their husbands, with Melanie tagging along. As the afternoon waned, some families gathered their things and started homeward. Others, like Rianna, loath to put an end to the perfect day, stayed on. She sat beside her mother and father, contemplating the sea after her sisters and their families had left.

She watched Noah help Mrs. Avery and her family pack up, and she felt a little bereft knowing he, too, would be leaving. Instead of coming to say goodbye to her, he sent one of Amelia's boys to fetch Melanie.

"Maybe I'll see you tomorrow?"

Rianna heard the hopeful note in the girl's voice. On impulse she bent down and gave her a hug. Melanie's slim arms came around immediately and hugged her back tightly. "Of course you will. Why don't I stop by and ask Mrs. Avery if you can come over and visit a little while. We can finish your doll's gown and perhaps start a new one."

The girl nodded. "Oh, yes, please, may we?"

"Of course."

With a big smile and a final wave, Melanie ran after Robert to rejoin her father. Rianna looked after her, a catch in her throat, remembering the soft, warm feel of her body against hers. A swift longing washed through her for the motherhood she'd been denied.

With a shake of her head, Rianna chided herself for the sudden wave of self-pity. Her life's calling had been another. She turned to place a shawl around her mother's shoulders. "Are you tired, Mother?"

"Just a little, dear. It's been a wonderful day. What a joy to have almost all my family reunited."

As dusk fell, those remaining built up the bonfire. They sat around it, singing songs and hymns while watching the fiery orange sun set across the bay. Rianna was just gearing herself up to leave with her parents when she felt someone looming over her. She looked up in surprise to see Noah bending over her.

A spurt of joy filled her at the sight of him. "I thought you'd left!"

He squatted down beside her. "I did, but I'm back. I helped Mrs. Avery's family home and put Melanie to bed." He shrugged, seeming suddenly ill at ease. "I saw how much you were enjoying yourself, and I thought you might wish to stay on with the younger folks if your parents want to leave. I could see you home."

Rianna smiled in delight, not realizing how much his leaving had affected her until he came back. "Oh, that's sweet of you!"

But he had already turned to her parents. "'Evening, Mr. Devon, Mrs. Devon. If you'd like to call it a night, I could see Rianna home."

Her father yawned. "Yep, well, I was just thinking about having to go home and milk the cow." He turned to her mother with a chuckle. "What do you think, dear? Think we can trust Mr. Samuels to bring home our daughter?"

Mrs. Devon smiled at Noah. Before she could answer, Noah assured Rianna's father, "I'll see she gets home at a decent hour."

Rianna felt like a girl again, cherished and protected. She hadn't appreciated it back then, too eager to be off on her own. She helped her father get her mother into the wagon, while Noah gathered their belongings. After her parents had gone, she and Noah sat together around the bonfire with those remaining and continued singing.

During a lull, Noah turned to her. "I'm sorry if I implied anything unkind about your marrying one of your patients."

Her breath caught, reading the sincere regret in his dark eyes. Then she smiled. "That's all right. It's forgotten. Besides, I should be used to it. That's why I was teasing you a little." At his surprised look, she explained, "You'd be amazed how suspicious people are—especially family members—when a private nurse comes to a house."

"How did you get involved in nursing?"

She gazed at him, enjoying the way the firelight turned his skin golden and reflected off his eyes in the deepening twilight. "It's a long story."

"During the war, wasn't it?"

She nodded, resting her cheek on her clasped knees. "But it all started with Ralph and the reasons I married him." She took a deep breath, seeing into the past as she watched the flames shoot up from the dry wood. Was she ready to tell Noah?

"Reasons you married him?" He sounded puzzled.

She looked over at him. Something about the intense way he had of listening—as if he was not just hearing the words, but understanding their real meaning—made her decide to risk the pain of telling him. "Poor Ralph. I wasn't exactly honest when I married him. I wasn't exactly dishonest either. We were both just fun-loving youngsters. Well, you knew that about me back then."

He nodded.

"I married him to escape the drudgery of factory life."

"I thought you didn't believe in trading one type of drudgery for another."

She smiled. "But you see, Ralph was different. Or at least I thought he was. Neither of us was interested in buckling down and building a home together as married people do. We made grandiose plans—to go abroad in a year, live the life of artists on the continent." She shook her head in tender reminiscence. "Or as the hangers-on to the real artists. I suppose I saw Ralph as my way to fulfill those childhood dreams I had." Then she sobered. "But Ralph and I never had the chance. Before we'd even had our first quarrel, the war broke out and Ralph joined the Union troops."

"He must have been one of the first."

She nodded against her knees. "He was so full of enthusiasm. Finally, a real cause! To defend the nation. He looked quite handsome in his uniform. I continued working at the factory."

She paused, the next part the most difficult to speak about. Thankfully, Noah proved patient, giving her time to tell her story in her own time and way.

"The only thing Ralph didn't know was that I…was—" the words were still hard to say "—expecting at the time."

She heard Noah's intake of breath and met his gaze. His two dark eyebrows were drawn together, his gaze penetrating. "You were with child?"

She nodded, unable to speak for a moment.

"You didn't tell him?"

She looked down at her knuckles. "I didn't know it then myself." Taking a deep breath, she braced herself to go on. "I didn't realize until I started feeling sick. Yet I had to continue working. And then, not three months later, I heard from his commanding officer that Ralph was in a hospital in Washington."

She was silent, remembering those terrifying days and nights. "Ralph lay there, gravely wounded. Infection had set in. He wasn't expected to last the week.

"I handed in my resignation, took all our savings—" she made a humorless sound "—savings for Europe—packed a few garments and took the first train south.

"After living in Lowell I'd imagined myself as somewhat a woman of the world." She shook her head. "I didn't know what a big city was. A city in wartime, with soldiers everywhere, wounded choking the hospitals, fear of invasion any day, prices beyond reach, scarcity…" She could see it all in the flames. "Well, I finally found the hospital. What a horror."

Rianna felt Noah's hand on her shoulder. He was looking at her with understanding in his eyes. "You know," she whispered, "you saw much worse than I did." She shuddered. "I don't know which was worse—the agonizing cries or the stench."

"They stay with you always."

She nodded. With a sigh she resumed her narrative. "In time I found a place to board. A kindly nurse let me share her rooms. She soon realized my condition. I…I was just beginning to show. She was truly a godsend, making sure I ate properly and got my rest.

"But there were so many casualties that soon we both hardly had a moment to ourselves. We spent most of our time at the hospital, I at Ralph's side until he…until he passed away."

Noah cleared his throat. "How long did your husband last?"

"Not long. Three, four weeks. He regained consciousness after the first week, though he was so awfully weak. Then the fever set in again, and he lost consciousness and never woke up."

"I'm sorry." Noah's words were simple, but she knew they came from the heart.

"He was so happy about the baby coming, and I promised him I would come back home as the time drew near. He worried about what would become of the baby and me, but I assured him that my family would take care of us. I was more concerned with making Ralph comfortable.

"If I hadn't had those few weeks with Ralph, I never would have truly had a husband, nor been a wife to him."

"I don't understand."

She took a deep breath, suddenly wishing she could white-wash things more. "Because I was selfish when I married him, just thinking of how he could help me achieve my dreams."

Noah's expression was unreadable, only the reflection

of the fire visible in his eyes. She continued, hoping in some way to redeem herself through her next words.

"But the Lord gave me the chance to get to know Ralph and be his helpmate before he departed this earth."

She smiled—a genuine smile this time. "We were able to talk about the things that really matter. I was able—I like to believe—to make his last days on this earth a little more bearable than if he'd been alone. Most of all, the dear nurse who befriended me was able to lead Ralph, as she had me, to his Lord and Savior, Jesus Christ. Ralph received the assurance of where he was going after he left us." She felt that familiar joy rise up in her. "I witnessed the Lord's grace in those final hours of Ralph's consciousness, when he truly knew God's touch and was no longer afraid of what awaited him."

"What happened to…to your baby?"

The low question forced her back to the pain of the past. She looked away then and again fell silent. Finally, she spoke. "It was after Ralph was gone, perhaps a week, that I got terrible cramps. I stayed in bed that morning and as soon as my friend found me, she called for a midwife. There was little they could do. I don't know what went wrong. Perhaps the strain of working so hard…" She shook her head. "I don't know. I only know it wasn't meant to be."

She drew aside a strand of her hair and forced herself to continue. "Once I was able to, I went back to working at the hospital and stayed for the remainder of the war."

They didn't say anything for a while.

"Did your family know?"

"Yes. They wanted me to come home immediately. I…I couldn't leave then."

"Is that why you never came back?"

She started at the question and slowly met his glance. There was no hiding behind his dark, piercing stare. Hardly aware, she nodded.

Noah pulled on the nets with Joe, bringing up their catch of cod. The slick, shiny fish fell onto the boat's deck. Now the grueling work of gutting and cleaning them before bringing them back into port began.

As his fingers worked over the fish, Noah's mind worked just as feverishly. He couldn't get the evening of the clambake out of his thoughts.

The stark pain in Rianna's eyes when she'd told about losing her child tore at him. It was as if he'd opened up a mortal wound…he who well knew what old wounds were like. How could he have been so clumsy and unfeeling?

As she'd spoken to him of the past, she'd looked just like the girl he'd fallen in love with so many years ago, her skin luminescent against the flames of the bonfire, her hair a thick coil at her nape, its loosened strands framing her face, a promise of its rich fullness.

But what had drawn him even more than her beauty were the things she had revealed to him about her life since she'd left Wood's Harbor.

He knew how hard it was to speak of anything pertaining to the war years. No one who hadn't lived through it could imagine the fear and horror and absolute waste of human lives.

Rianna had seen plenty if she'd nursed the wounded and dying in a D.C. hospital, a city on the front lines, for all intents and purposes. Why had she had to endure even more? The loss of her unborn child. He wouldn't have known it to hear her joyous laughter earlier among all the children.

What had given her the strength to go on?

Noah swallowed back a yelp as a fishhook pierced his finger through the knitted gloves he wore.

Not stopping his pace, he reached for the next fish.

He couldn't help going over Rianna's words about her husband, unsure what to think. It hadn't sounded as if her Ralph was the great love of her life, the way he'd first thought. He paused in his actions with the knife, struck for a second at the similarities between her marriage to Ralph and his to Charlotte.

He had loved and respected his wife. A worthier woman he couldn't have found. But he'd met and married her on the rebound, his only thought to find someone the opposite of Rianna. Charlotte had embodied all that was quiet, steady, thoughtful—the kind of person you wouldn't notice in a room. She'd be sitting in a corner with her stitching, smiling at the others.

He'd come to admire her more the deeper he got to know her, but he'd never felt the flame of passion. The recognition of kindred souls despite their outward differences was something that he'd felt the moment he'd seen Rianna as a young woman—and the moment he'd laid eyes on her again at the old house.

This time it was all the more dangerous. If Rianna fled again, more than Noah stood to be hurt. Melanie had gotten attached, as well. Yet Rianna was no longer a lighthearted girl with a hunger to live life to its fullest. She was a woman who had seen more pain and suffering than most people would see in a lifetime, and who'd shown the compassion and fortitude to help alleviate that pain…and who, through it all, hadn't lost the essence of who she was, a beautiful, vivacious, joyous person. Had she lost the restlessness that had driven her away all those years before? Would her joy remain if her mother's health demanded that she stay in Wood's Harbor?

He frowned, throwing the fish into the crate. The word *joy* wasn't one he thought about often. But it was one he'd heard her use more than once.

Did Rianna's joy have something to do with her new-found religious convictions?

She'd invited him to a camp meeting. He hadn't been to one since he'd been a kid—taken by his grandparents. He didn't remember much of it except running around with other boys his age while the grown-ups sat under a tent, listening to all kinds of preaching.

Perhaps he'd go and see what all the commotion was about. See what it was that put that indefinable light in Rianna's eyes and lilt to her voice when she spoke of her faith.

Chapter Seven

A week later, Rianna looked down at Noah where he sat under the tent on a folding chair in the gathering dusk. He'd shown up at the camp meeting one evening about midweek into it and had sat down beside her during the service. He stood when the others stood, sat when the others sat, looked onto Rianna's Bible when she turned to a Scripture. But that was all. If he felt anything at all, he kept it greatly hidden. Amid the shouts of "Amen!", "Hallelujah!", "Praise the Lord!" he sat unmoved. As soon as the crowds settled down to hear the preaching—good, rousing, don't-shout-me-down preaching—Noah promptly fell asleep.

That's how he was now, as everyone else stood for an impromptu hymn. Impulsively she reached over to smooth his hair, a wave of tenderness washing over her. How exhausted he must be after waking before dawn and spending a day at sea. His hair felt as silky smooth as it looked. Noah started forward, and she quickly removed her hand.

He yawned and sat up, then stood as soon as he noticed everyone else standing. "Sorry, I must have nodded off."

"You must be tired."

He looked sheepish. "It's been a long day."

"You're off at first light, I imagine."

"Yes."

"Why don't you go on home and get some sleep," she suggested again, just as she had several times over the past few days.

He shook his head. "It's all right. I'm fine."

She turned away to resume singing. He was as stubborn as her worst patients. Why did he come, anyway? Night after night, receiving nothing, sleeping through the most moving songs, the fieriest preaching. Rianna had pleaded and pleaded with the Lord to touch Noah, to let him receive an inkling—just an inkling—of what it was all about.

If only the Lord would reveal to him what the gift of salvation, of eternal life, meant. But her prayers seemed to fall on deaf—or rather, sleeping—ears.

She told herself once again to be patient. The Lord would do His perfect work in His perfect time. He'd promised if she asked anything in His name, He *would do it,* and she firmly believed this. Hadn't He restored the joy in her own life after she'd thought she'd lost it forever?

She went back to worshipping the Lord and was soon caught up in the beauty of God's holiness and sense of His presence. She lifted her hands and sang with all her soul.

He'd seen her pain and loneliness after the loss of her baby, and He'd healed her. He'd given her the strength to go on and help others. He'd give her the courage to face coming back home. And now she believed in His mercy to allow her to befriend young Melanie and not allow regrets to taint her relationship with the girl who so much needed a mother, and with the father whom she'd like to see smile again the way he used to at age nineteen.

Noah shifted on the hard chair, always uncomfortable with unbridled shows of emotion in people he knew as quiet and generally undemonstrative. Suddenly, with a few hymns and a preacher spouting Scripture at them, they were transformed into an exuberant, hollering, weeping mass.

After the first night, he was no longer concerned by Rianna's tears, knowing nothing was physically hurting her.

Even though he'd been bone tired from a grueling day at sea, he'd come that night for Rianna's sake. Her joy at seeing him had made it all worthwhile. He was far more moved by her happiness than by any of the singing and sermonizing he'd heard.

People from several neighboring villages sat around him, as preachers from near and far exhorted them. On the preaching circuit, he called it. Despite all their pleas for repentance, their graphic descriptions of hell, their eloquence over heaven, Noah's heart remained as stone cold as it had been since—

Since the war. Since Charlotte's death. Since he'd felt as dried up and lifeless as a weathered shingle.

Rianna hadn't been the only one to leave home. Noah had been away, too, for a few years. But his departure hadn't been by choice. The last thing he'd planned on was to fight a war that had nothing to do with him or his. Just when he'd had a chance at true happiness—a young wife and child, a house of his own to make into a home—he'd been called up to serve his country.

And after the war, what had he come home to?

Widowhood and broken dreams. His grandparents' dilapidated house said it all. Any dreams he and Charlotte had had of fixing it up for their future family were useless by the time he returned.

Noah looked at the people under the tent around him in the glow of the campfires. He didn't begrudge these folks their spiritual experiences. Clearly they were feeling something good. Unfortunately, displays of emotion only made Noah feel his isolation all the more. The loneliness he'd grown accustomed to until Rianna's return now mocked him in its profundity. It didn't matter how many camp meetings he attended. He'd be no closer to filling the void in his life than when he'd returned from the war to find nothing left of his former life.

Rianna had risen and moved away from him, but just then she turned and looked at him, her face suffused with emotion. She stretched out her arm and drew him forward by the hand. He complied, startled momentarily by the feel of her strong grasp. Her smile was radiant.

"Noah, you need to have your joy restored. Let me pray with you." And closing her eyes, she began to pray.

Noah just watched her. She prayed in a way new to him, as if she had a personal acquaintance with her Creator and was free to drop in on Him whenever she wanted. She reminded Noah of a little girl whose father was the bank president. Into his office she marched boldly anytime she wanted, unmindful of his other demands, to perch on his knee, knowing he would make time for her amidst his more important affairs. Noah would almost envy Rianna this bold familiarity, if he didn't find it so strange.

For Noah, God was a distant deity, as far removed from the realities of his life as the constellations he viewed above him in the inky-black sky—there to acknowledge but too far to affect his everyday life in any way.

* * *

A few days after the camp meeting, Noah entered the house for supper to find Mrs. Avery hurrying toward him. "Oh, I'm so glad you're home."

He scrutinized her unsmiling face. "What is it, ma'am?"

"It's Melanie. She has a fever."

He started walking past her immediately, heading for the stairs. "Have you fetched Dr. Peters?"

"I sent Tad and Robert. He should be here any moment."

Noah heard no more, but took the stairs two at a time. He found Melanie lying in bed, Mrs. Johnson sponging her forehead. She turned to him as soon as he entered. "I was hoping you were the doctor. She's burning up."

He leaned over and felt his daughter's forehead.

"It hurts all over, Papa."

He was alarmed at how hot her skin felt, but tried to project calm as he took her hand in his. "I know, sweetie. But Doc Peters will soon be here and give you something to make you feel better." Even as he said the words, he hoped they were true.

Children and adults died every day of fevers. Fear gripped him, leaving him paralyzed.

"I'll sit with her, ma'am," he told Mrs. Johnson.

She rose and set aside the cloth in the basin. "Very well. I hope it's not contagious," she added quietly. "I have my boys to think of, you know."

"Yes, I understand," he said tersely, taking her place beside his daughter.

The next hour passed in a blur. The doctor, whom Noah trusted and had known for years, straightened from his examination and said the dreaded words. "Scarlet fever, most likely. We won't know for sure until tomorrow or the next day if the rash develops." His lips puckered and he drew his thick gray eyebrows together. "We'll have to quarantine her and keep the boys away from her. Let's hope they don't develop it, as well. She'll need constant nursing for a week," he added.

Noah could hardly think straight. At the word *nursing,* his first thought turned to Rianna. But she was busy with her mother.

Mrs. Johnson immediately began getting herself and her sons ready to move to an aunt's in the next village. Mrs. Avery bustled about helping her.

In the midst of this confusion, Rianna knocked on the doorjamb leading to Melanie's room. Noah looked up and felt a wave of relief wash over him.

"I stopped by to see if Melanie would like to come over tomorrow and Mrs. Avery told me." She entered the room softly. "I'm so sorry. But she should be fine as long as she keeps to her bed."

He made room for her as she approached Melanie. She put a hand to the girl's forehead. "Hello, there. I'm sorry you're feeling so poorly. Don't try to talk, darling. I know your throat hurts. I was sick just like you when I was your age."

As Melanie closed her eyes again, seemingly reassured by Rianna's gentle words, Rianna turned to him and beckoned to the other side of the room.

He stood and accompanied her over.

"I spoke with Mrs. Avery. I think she'll need some help. Would you like me to nurse Melanie?"

He stared at her, hardly believing her generous offer. "But your mother—"

Rianna smiled. "I've been meaning to tell you. Mother

is doing much better." Her smile grew. "Ever since the camp meeting, she has shown remarkable improvement."

Before Noah could say anything, she touched his arm. "If you give me permission, I'll go home and pack a few things and come over. The first few days will be the hardest."

He nodded slowly, relieved beyond measure to have Rianna's presence.

Rianna placed the cool compress on Melanie's hot forehead and leaned back. The room was perfectly still, the house quiet. She removed her pocket watch. Three o'clock in the morning. Thankfully, Noah had finally agreed to go to bed. The poor man had been exhausted, his face gray with worry.

Rianna touched Melanie's hand on the quilt. *Dear Lord, I pray for Your mercy and grace for this little girl...show Noah how much You care for his daughter. More than he could ever imagine.* She continued praying for Melanie. She knew well how fragile human life was, but she had also witnessed God's healing grace time and again.

When Rianna took up her shift once more after sleeping a few hours, Noah sat as she had left him that morning, one hand engulfing his daughter's.

She leaned over and touched Melanie's forehead. It was still hot.

"She's all I have."

Rianna started at the sound of Noah's voice, low yet harsh. Her heart went out to him, his features so stern and strong and yet the words speaking of an anguish she could only imagine. She ached to comfort him. Instead, she touched his shoulder gently. "The Lord is merciful."

"Was He merciful to Charlotte?" his voice lashed out immediately. "To your husband—to your baby?"

She could only stare at him. "God's grace is so terribly wide and grand, we frequently don't realize it until later. I don't know why He took Charlotte or Ralph...or my little baby. I only trust that He sees your love for your daughter. I'm praying and believing for her to make it through this illness. We're doing all we can with nursing her. The rest is in the Lord's hands."

He said nothing.

The crisis came four nights later. Both Rianna and Noah sat by Melanie's bed, one on either side. Melanie thrashed about, crying out at times.

Noah looked haggard. He had not taken out his boat, despite Rianna and Mrs. Avery's reassurances that they would take good care of Melanie.

The house was quiet and time seemed to stand still. Finally in the wee hours of the night, Rianna noticed Melanie bathed in sweat. She felt her forehead. It felt normal. She turned to Noah with a smile. "The fever has broken."

Without a word, his own hand reached out and he touched his daughter's forehead. "You think it's broken for good?" He sounded skeptical. She well understood his fear of getting his hopes up. How often she had seen it at a patient's bedside.

"Yes, I believe Melanie is over the worst. Why don't you get some sleep and I'll sponge her off and change her nightgown."

"No, I'll help you. You need sleep, as well. You've been here 'round the clock."

"I've managed to catch some sleep on the cot you set

up for me." She indicated the narrow bed at one end of the room. "I've grown used to sleeping anywhere over the years," she added with a smile.

He nodded, his eyes looking beyond her words and probably seeing the war years.

Together, they soon had Melanie in a clean night-gown. They watched her for a moment sleeping a more peaceful sleep.

"Now, you get some rest. I know you'll soon need to go back out in your boat, and it would do you no good to fall ill from neglect." As she spoke, she shooed him out of the room. With a few more protests, he finally left, after making her promise that she would let Mrs. Avery take over at first light.

When he'd gone, Rianna knelt by Melanie's bed.

In the few weeks she'd spent time with the child, Rianna had realized how easily she could imagine Melanie as her own. Their friendship had felt as natural as if they'd always known each other.

Rianna bowed her head.

"Dear Lord," she prayed in a soft voice, "thank You for sparing this girl's life. You know how much Noah needs her…and how dear she has become to me…" she ended on a bare whisper.

Chapter Eight

"Tell me what Mrs. Bruce used to be like when you first knew her."

Noah looked from his daughter, who'd asked the question, to Rianna, whose raised eyebrows told him the question had taken her as much by surprise as it had him.

Before he could answer, Melanie gazed up at him from her bed, where she sat propped up by lots of pillows. "Don't you remember, Papa?"

Noah couldn't help smiling at his daughter, who seemed to get better each day. He glanced over at Rianna, his smile lingering. If not for her, who knows what the outcome would have been. No one could have given more selflessly than Rianna. Melanie's own mother couldn't have shown more love and care for Melanie during her illness. Rianna had truly become a woman of depth and maturity, someone he could trust with his heart and his daughter.

He rested against the small rocker by his daughter's bed, easing his long legs out in front of him and beginning to rock slowly before answering. "Well, let's see, Rianna was in grammar school with me. She was about four years younger, so she was a little girl in pigtails when I was just becoming a teenager. Her oldest sister was more my age and in my year in school." He paused, enjoying watching the heightened color in Rianna's cheeks as he spoke of her and her family. "She was sharp. All the Devon girls were, weren't you?"

Rianna smoothed the front of her skirt over her knees, making a small sound, half laugh. "I don't know about that."

"Sure you were, always at the head of your class, all of you. Of course, I hardly noticed Rianna back then," he said with a chuckle.

"Of course not," she agreed. "You were too busy horsing around with the older boys and girls."

"I like it when you call her Rianna. It's such a pretty name. Is that what you used to call her?"

He nodded, watching the way Rianna cast her eyes downward, her long, auburn lashes brushing her cheeks. "Yes, 'cept I didn't call her much of anything till she started growing up."

"Were you sweet on her, Papa?"

His rocker came to a stop. "Not back then. That came later." For the first time, it was no longer painful to admit. He chuckled as Rianna stretched forward to adjust Melanie's quilt around her. Was she made uncomfortable by his words? "I mean, she was just a pesky girl as far as I was concerned. Sort o' like the way Robbie and Tad feel about you. All I was interested in at that time was going out to sea with my pop."

"Oh." She sounded disappointed.

Rianna settled back in her chair. "Your father was single-minded in his desire to follow his grandfather and father out to sea. He was the handsomest boy in Wood's

Harbor and yet, he didn't give any of the prettiest girls a second look, too focused on growing up and becoming a fisherman to notice their little ploys to get his attention."

His gaze sharpened on Rianna, surprised at her assessment. Had she even noticed that much back then? "How would you know so much?"

Her lips curled up coyly. "Oh, I had eyes in my head…and three sisters who would talk." She burst into laughter at his surprised look.

"When did you ask Mrs. Bruce to dance?" persisted Melanie.

Noah fell silent, the only sound in the room the slow creak of the rocker. His thoughts went back to that first dance, remembering it more serenely than he had since seeing Rianna again.

Now it seemed so far away. He couldn't help smiling, rubbing a hand over his beard. "It wasn't till Rianna turned about fifteen that I began noticing her—as a young lady, I mean."

"Was she pretty then?"

He chuckled. "Oh, yes."

Rianna's cheeks turned a deep pink.

It wouldn't hurt to tell Melanie. It would be like a fairy tale. "I remember a particular dance at Grammie and Grampie's. I think they didn't want me to be lonely, growing up without my parents and having no brothers or sisters, so they were always having socials, as they called them.

"That one dance—I was about nineteen. Rianna stepped into the parlor. She must have been the prettiest girl there with her thick, auburn hair just falling around her shoulders like sea foam and tied back with a big bow. She had a new dress on, down to her ankles. It was the first time I'd seen her wear a lady's gown. She looked all grown-up." He shook his head, unable to take his gaze from Rianna, who had picked up her mending and seemed intent on it, the way she had when he'd watched her sew her lavender dress.

"She was standing in the doorway," he said softly, picturing it all in his mind. "Her face was flushed a pretty pink, just like she looks now, her lips half-parted as she watched the dancers on the parlor floor, as if she wanted to join in but didn't quite dare."

Rianna's gaze had flown up when he'd begun describing the scene, and now she seemed as riveted as Melanie. "Then Rianna looked across the room and smiled at me. It was the most dazzling smile I'd ever seen."

Her eyes had held a mischievous glint as if she knew something he didn't. He'd known in that moment that she would be his wife.

"I walked across the room with one thought only in mind, to ask her to dance. It seemed like I was meeting her for the first time."

The room was quiet as the two listened to him. When he paused, his daughter asked, "What did you do then?"

A deep sigh escaped him, as if he'd forgotten to breathe during his travel back in time. "Well…we danced quite a bit with each other that evening. In between, we talked. Seemed I'd never talked so much with another soul."

Rianna smiled at Melanie. "Your papa was always a bit of a loner. I guess he had to be to be content all those hours on the boat or in the woods in winter."

"After that evening, I'd look for Rianna at each social. We'd dance and then we'd talk."

"Your papa told me all about his dreams to be a fisherman, and I told him about mine to see the world."

Once again, the silence stretched out between them. "What happened then, Papa?"

His daughter's voice brought him back to the part of the memory he preferred to forget. "I'll let Mrs. Bruce finish the tale." How would she tell it?

Rianna looked back down to her sewing. "Oh, the dance would end. Everyone would say good-night and thank their host and hostess. Your great-grandparents were the most hospitable folks around to the young people. As I recall, I used to walk home with my sisters, humming the last tune we'd heard."

Noah slowly rocked, his expression impassive as he listened to her words. Did she really remember it that way? Had she forgotten everything else so completely?

It was clear that season of their lives hadn't meant as much to her as it had to him. He glanced at Melanie and was relieved to catch her yawning wide enough to crack her jaw. Hopefully, she'd soon be asleep and this conversation would be only a vague memory when she woke up. The way it needed to remain.

With an effort he stood up from the rocker, the soreness in his back a reminder of the hours he'd spent bent over his nets at sea. He'd put in extra hours the last day or so, once he was assured of Melanie's recovery.

"I think it's time you got some sleep, sweetie. There's been enough talk of the past for now." He bent over Melanie and kissed her cheek.

"Good night, Papa," she said drowsily.

"Good night, Mellie."

Rianna adjusted the bandanna around her head and picked up her stick. She was tired, but she mustn't quit now.

Her father had taken her mother to see the doctor and Rianna had promised herself she'd be finished by the time they returned. Only a few more rugs to go and she'd be done with housecleaning for the day. She whacked at the rug hanging on the line and kept at it.

"Good afternoon."

Rianna whirled around, stick in her hand.

"Noah! I didn't hear you walk up."

"I could see that."

She became conscious of how she must look, stick held up like a weapon, head wrapped in a red bandanna, her dress enveloped by a smudged apron. Her free hand came up to her head, and then she saw the humor of the situation.

She brought her hand to her mouth and began to laugh. Once started, she couldn't stop. She clutched her waist, laughing all the harder at the bewildered look on Noah's face.

He was carrying something wrapped in newspaper.

"Is—is th-at for me?" she gasped through laughter, gesturing with her hand.

He nodded, a smile beginning to form on his lips.

"Than-k you!" Regaining her breath, she dropped her stick and stepped forward. "You must sometimes think I'm no nurse at all, but a patient escaped from a lunatic ward."

He was looking at her so warmly, she suddenly glanced away, focusing on the newspaper bundle in his hands. Ever since they'd spent so much time together taking care of Melanie, there had been an easiness in their manner and Noah had seemed more relaxed.

"Not at all. It's good to see someone laugh like that." He cleared his throat. "You always seem to find something funny about the most commonplace things. As if you're full of that joy you talk about."

"You could be, too."

"Yeah, well…" He looked down at his parcel. "I brought you some haddock. Just off the boat."

She took it from him. "Oh, thank you! Let me set it in a cool place. We'll have it baked for supper." She began to turn away before pivoting back. "Would you like to stay for tea?" She hadn't seen him in a few days. While she knew he'd had a lot of catching up to do now that Melanie was well on the mend, she'd missed his company. It had been nice looking across Melanie's bed and seeing him there, both of them doing all they could for the little girl.

He didn't quite meet her eyes. "I've had a lot of thinking to do."

She nodded. They'd been through a lot in the past couple of weeks, and they'd never had a chance to talk about the camp meeting. She thought of all he'd witnessed there. Between naps.

"What's so funny?" he asked.

"Nothing. I was just remembering the camp meeting the week before last."

He smiled sheepishly. "I wasn't very good company, I'm afraid. I guess religion just doesn't take with some people."

She shook her head at him. "I told you, it has nothing to do with religion. Anyway, if you'd like to tell me what you've been so busy thinking about the past few days, why don't you go on in while I set this in the icehouse."

He gestured to the clothesline. "Want me to bring in your rugs?"

She smiled. "Sure."

When she came back, she found him beating one of the remaining carpets. "You don't have to do that!"

"I don't mind." He looked down at her. "Besides, I'm stronger than you are."

She met his gaze, wondering how she could have ever found his eyes without humor. "I'll go fix tea."

She hummed as she replaced the clean carpet then checked the water in the kettle. Good, it was still hot. Since she'd been back from her time at Mrs. Avery's, she'd watched for Noah every afternoon at teatime, expecting to see him walking by from the harbor. Funny how she'd grown accustomed to his presence.

"There, that does it. Where would you like me to put these?" Noah stood in the back door, holding the neatly folded rugs.

She smiled gratefully. "Oh, just set them there on the bench. I'll lay them out later."

As she reached for the teapot, she felt him approach behind her. He put his hands on her shoulders and turned her toward the room.

"What—"

"I have a better idea." He steered her toward the table.

She did as he commanded, mystified as to what he was about.

"I didn't mean to make more work for you. Why don't you let me make *you* a cup of tea."

Unused to being waited on, she watched, bemused, as he prepared the tea.

"Sugar pot?" he asked her.

She pointed.

"Cream?"

She indicated the doorway to the cellar.

He brought everything to the table and poured out her tea.

"Would you like a piece of pie?" she asked him.

"No, thanks. Just the tea will do."

All of a sudden she felt nervous. Was it because it was the first time she was all alone with Noah? Was it because they'd spent so much time by Melanie's bedside, seeing each other day and night?

She remembered the bandanna she still had on and reached up to pull it off. She saw him looking at her hair and put a hand up to it self-consciously, wondering how mussed it must appear.

She lowered her hand and laid the bandanna on the table. "As a professional nurse, there's usually plenty of other help in a house to take care of the housekeeping. I'd forgotten how much there is to running a house oneself."

"Here you're doing both, nursing and housekeeping," he remarked.

"Mother's getting stronger," she said, brightening. "That's where she is right now—at the doctor's office to discuss her improvement. I think the camp meetings did her good."

He didn't say anything, so she took a sip of her tea.

"Melanie's growing stronger every day," she added to fill the silence. "I don't think there will be any lasting effects of the fever. She's very anxious to get out of bed now and come over."

"I'm very grateful for all you did for her. If not for you—" Noah looked away as if unable to say more.

"I didn't do any more than anyone else would have. Besides…" She looked down this time. "I've grown very fond of her."

She could feel his gaze on her. Finally, he sighed. "I don't have as much time as I'd like in summer to spend with her."

"I understand," she said softly. "I think she does, too. She loves you very much. You are so blessed to have her."

He nodded and didn't quite meet her eyes. Was he embarrassed by the fact that his child had lived and hers hadn't? Since meeting Melanie, there were moments when the pain of her loss hit her afresh, but she'd given it over to the Lord during the camp meeting, and she trusted His grace to aid her. Before she could think how to reassure Noah, he lifted his gaze to hers. "Why didn't you ever come back before now—I mean, after the war…when enough time had passed?" His stumbling question made it clear he meant after she'd mourned the loss of her unborn baby.

She found it impossible to pull away from the directness of his look. His questions always demanded honesty from her. "I…don't know. Mother never needed me before," she said with a shrug.

As he continued regarding her with those eyes that seemed to see through her, she felt compelled to probe herself more deeply. "Pride, I suppose. Who wants to return home a war widow, without even a child?" Although she kept her tone light, she knew he saw beyond the humor.

"Besides, what would I come home for? To sit around and think about my loss? At least away—" she gestured with a hand "—I could make myself useful." She paused, tracing the bandanna's design with her fingertip. "It's different now."

"How?"

"I like being home." She couldn't help the note of longing creeping in.

"Do you really think you'd be happy living here?"

Why did he sound so skeptical? Instead of answering him, she clasped her hands on the tabletop and looked across at him, deciding to pose a few questions of her own. "I might ask you how you like living at Mrs. Avery's, when you could live in your own house, such a pretty house by the sea?"

He looked down into his teacup. "I tried living there for a while. After the war…after—" He cleared his throat. "After Charlotte. A lady in town who'd been looking after Melanie since I'd been gone agreed to keep her a little longer. With the way Charlotte had…passed away…well, I just wasn't ready to…to set up housekeeping yet for the two of us."

He took a deep breath as if bracing himself to get over a large hump. "I soon realized Melanie needed me. So, I moved in with Mrs. Avery. She'd recently lost her husband and had to take in boarders. She's been good with Melanie." With a sheepish smile, he said, "Mrs. Avery keeps me civilized. When I was alone, I'd forget to shave, change clothes, get my hair cut."

Rianna sat riveted, listening to his stark words. So much needed to be filled in…so much was clear from what he didn't say. "Why haven't you remarried?" she asked softly then gave a short laugh. "There are certainly no lack of nice widows about since the war."

He looked at her a long moment then answered more bluntly than she'd expected. "I didn't want to go through that again."

She knew he was talking about Charlotte's death. "Was it so very bad?"

"I don't know. I wasn't here. While we were sitting out the winter outside Richmond, my wife was dying of consumption up here. I didn't get a scratch on me, and Charlotte wasted away."

Rianna shut her eyes. "Oh, Noah. I'm so sorry." She had seen all the guilt he still carried around for his wife's death in those brief words he'd spoken.

He said nothing, just sat staring down at his cooling cup of tea. Rianna reached across the table and took one of his hands, wanting only to comfort him. The moment she did so, she felt their roughness, and remembered her promise to treat them.

She stood immediately and went over to a cupboard. She came back with a jar of lanolin. "Give me your hands," she said, standing at the end of the table next to him. He was too startled to argue. She grasped one hand and began dabbing the ointment on it. "I don't know how you can let these go. They look awfully painful to me." She rubbed the palm and back first then proceeded with each finger.

"You'll probably soften them too much then I'll have to toughen them up all over again," he said in a gruff voice.

She tsk-tsked as she set down one hand and took up his other. She repeated the same procedure, back, palm, fingers, working the ointment around every finger, reaching down well into the base of each one.

She looked up at him, on the point of saying something, when she stopped. He was staring at her, with an unmistakable look in his eyes. She'd seen that same look in the faces of dozens of wounded soldiers when confronted by a pretty, caring nurse. Their eyes held raw longing. It had never touched her before except to stir her to compassion. Now she dropped his hand like a hot iron and turned away.

She heard him scrape his chair back as she replaced the top of the jar with shaking fingers.

"I'd better be off." He walked to the door, taking his hat from a hook. "So long."

"Yes, goodbye," she answered, intent on the jar. "Thank you for the haddock," she called out as an afterthought, but he'd already slammed the door behind him.

Oh, Lord, oh, Lord was all she could think, her hand to her mouth. She walked to the window overlooking the backyard, unmindful of the vegetable gardens and fruit trees in her view, seeing only the look in Noah's eyes.

Did he really feel that way for her? Did she want him to? Although she'd been drawn to Noah since the first day she'd seen him again—and enjoyed renewing their friendship—she hadn't let herself think beyond that.

Why? What was she so afraid of?

Ever since Ralph's death and her miscarriage, she hadn't allowed herself to think of remarriage. First, there had been the war years, then she'd thrown herself into her work, convincing herself that was her life's calling.

Why did the feelings Noah stirred in her scare her so?

The thought came slowly, like the unfurling of a flower. Was it that she felt unworthy of being given a second chance at love and marriage…and possibly motherhood?

Had Ralph's death so soon after their marriage—followed so quickly by the loss of her unborn baby—left her feeling that God was punishing her for some failing of hers?

No! She clutched her mouth. She'd never blamed God. But the thought wouldn't leave her. She'd told Noah of God's goodness and grace. Had part of her felt penalized for something she hadn't done? "Dear Lord, forgive me…." Was that why she had condemned herself to a life alone and away from home?

Her thoughts turned to Melanie, a little girl who clearly needed a mother's love. Rianna's heart swelled, wishing she could fill that role. The feeling startled her with its vehemence.

And what of Noah? He was the first man since widowhood to make her long for things she thought long dead.

He drew her the same way he had so many years ago. Back then she'd spurned him, afraid of the feelings he awakened in her. Nothing would keep her tied to Wood's Harbor, she'd vowed, not when there was a whole world out there beckoning.

And now?

She knew she could never string Noah along—never again as she had when she'd been a thoughtless school-girl—not if she wasn't ready to reciprocate his feelings.

She'd never meant to hurt him, but she hadn't been ready to settle down back then.

Was she now? Her heart responded with a sudden longing that was her answer.

Chapter Nine

Rianna lingered by the gate, ostensibly to pick some flowers for the table, but every time she heard a step down the road, she couldn't help glancing up to see who it was this time.

Would Noah stop by when he got off his boat? Or had she rebuffed him with her fear? Did she want him to come? Would he act as if yesterday hadn't happened at all? Did she want that?

For so many years, she'd believed she must be on her own that the thought that Noah might love her both thrilled and terrified her at once. All she knew was she wanted—needed—to see him again. Then everything would sort itself out.

Hearing a pair of footsteps, she jerked at the flower she was clipping. She looked up and saw Noah and Joe approaching. Carefully, she finished clipping the stem and placing it into her basket. Feeling more skittish than a young woman with her first beau, she stood, laying down the basket and smoothing her apron.

As she stepped toward the gate, she saw that she needn't

have worried about rushing to catch them. Noah and Joe both stopped.

"Afternoon, Mrs. Bruce," came Joe's chipper tone followed by Noah's quieter, "Afternoon, Rianna."

She put on her best smile and stepped forward. "Hello." Before she could invite them both for tea, Noah turned to Joe.

"You run along. I'll see you tomorrow."

Rianna and Noah both watched the departing boy's back. After he'd disappeared up the hill and there was no more reason to direct their attention that way, the two turned back to each other.

"Ria—"

"Noa—"

They both smiled self-consciously before Rianna, willing herself to be calm, said, "Go ahead."

He cleared his throat. "I wanted to ask you whether—" He stopped then started again. "Whether you might like to accompany me to the dance over at the Farmer's Club? Tomorrow evening."

Rianna looked into his eyes, and she was back more than ten years ago—the last time Noah had asked her that question. It had been a few weeks that they had been dancing together at each one of his grandparents' socials. Noah made her feel like a grown woman, and she had been proud to be singled out by such a tall, handsome young man. And even though she'd known him most of her life, that night he was looking at her differently and she was seeing him differently. They'd danced and laughed and talked, as usual. And she'd never enjoyed herself so much. And then he'd gone and ruined it all by asking her to a Farmer's Club dance. She knew what that meant. It meant she would be "walking out" with him exclusively. Eventually he'd ask her parents for her hand, and her future would be sealed.

No, she'd thought at the time, she wouldn't go the route of so many young women. She was going to be different. No fisherman or farmer's wife she. She was going to seek her fortune at the mills down south. And she'd told him so in no uncertain terms, and watched his confidence deflate and his enjoyment dissipate in a few brief moments.

Rianna was back in the present, wondering if Noah remembered any of it. Why was he willing to take a similar risk again?

She looked into those unsmiling eyes and knew he remembered. They both knew the implications of such an invitation now. They might be ten years older and widowed, but a man and a woman didn't go out together without an understanding.

Rianna's fears of the day before returned and she opened her mouth to say "no" but found herself saying instead, "I would be honored to accompany you, Noah."

He nodded, and the two smiled hesitantly, a little fearfully, at each other, as if sealing an accord.

Then Noah cleared his throat, breaking the tension of the moment. "Good then. I'll come by and pick you up around six tomorrow evening. Is that all right? Should I ask your mother or father?"

Rianna's smile grew a little wider as she shook her head. "Noah, I'm a twenty-seven-year-old widow. You do not need to ask my parents' permission."

He answered with a smile, a freer, more relaxed smile than she'd seen on his face in years. With a touch of his hat, he bid her goodbye and set off down the road.

She watched him until he was out of sight, and heard him whistling the way Joe had. She hadn't heard him whistle before, either.

The next morning as she sat in the sun, drying her hair in anticipation of the evening's festivities, her father approached her.

"You look awfully grave on such a beautiful morning," she said to him. "What's the matter?"

"You tell me." With that, he held out an envelope to her. "You got a telegram."

"Me?" Taking out the sheet of paper from inside, she unfolded it carefully and began to read. "Oh, no!"

"What is it, dear?"

She met her father's concerned eyes. "It's my patient, Mr. Whitestone. They say his end is near. They want me to come back immediately. He's been asking for me." Shoving the paper into her pocket, she began to turn away, already thinking of all the things she'd have to do before leaving. "I must go—but, Papa, how can I?"

"We'll be all right here, dear. You know your mother is nearly better. You go do what you have to."

She knew she had to go, but for the first time, she felt reluctant to do her duty as a nurse. There was so much calling her to stay here in Wood's Harbor…

She sighed deeply. "I wouldn't go if the situation weren't so grave. I need to know he's accepted the Savior. I've prayed so much, but he's been so hard."

Her father put his arm around her. "I understand. Let's go tell your mother."

They moved toward the door, and then Rianna remembered. "Noah! Oh, Papa, what about the dance? What'll I tell him?"

"He'll understand."

"I know. It's just that—" How could she voice her fears to her father? Would Noah understand, or would he think she was pushing him away again? Or worse, outright deserting him? And what of Melanie? Would the little girl understand that she wouldn't forget her? That she'd be back—hopefully soon?

She had no time to think of it anymore just then. There were a million things to do before the steamer left at dusk.

All day she thought of Noah and Melanie, knowing she must see Noah as soon as he got back from fishing to explain the situation to him. As she ran around putting things in order, her mind was ticking off the hours until his return.

"Mama, how can I leave you right now? I'm going to talk to Mrs. Myers down the road to see if she can come in every day to do the heavy work."

Mrs. Devon nodded. "Don't worry about me. The women at the church will look after me, as well. Besides, there's something I haven't told you."

"What's that?" Rianna came to sit beside her mother. "Is something wrong?"

"Oh, no. Quite the contrary. I know you've realized I've improved, but I haven't wanted to tell you just how much better I'm doing until I was really sure."

Rianna widened her eyes. "What is it?"

She held out her arm. "Yesterday, I woke up and realized all the numbness was gone from this arm."

Rianna stared at her mother, her mouth opened in wonder. "Oh, Mother!"

Her mother nodded. "Jesus healed me. I knew He had that night when everyone prayed for me. Each morning since then, I've felt a new strength, a vitality in me that wasn't there before."

"Oh, Mother, praise be to God!" The two women hugged hard as they laughed and cried together.

"Oh, Mama, I don't want to leave now!" she wailed when they sat apart once again.

Mrs. Devon smoothed Rianna's hair. "I know you don't. But haven't you said you've been praying for Mr. Whitestone's soul for a long time now?"

She nodded.

"I don't think there's many folk who harden their hearts against their Maker in those final moments. Don't you want to make sure there's someone there with him who can testify one last time?"

"Of course. That's why I'm going."

"Besides," added her mother, "you can always come back here afterward. You needn't be such a stranger this time."

Rianna nodded, thinking of the additional reason she wanted to come back home now.

She went to see Mrs. Myers, but didn't find her at home. Her heart sank when she was told to come back at four. Just when she'd be on the lookout for Noah.

By four, she had her bag packed, supper on the stove. All that remained was to change into her traveling clothes for the steamer at six. She dashed over to Mrs. Myers, but was told the woman hadn't yet returned. She was expected back any moment. Rianna waited for her half an hour, taking a peek out the window every few minutes in case Noah walked by. But she didn't see him.

By the time she ran home, everything arranged with the

good lady, it was five o'clock. Shading her eyes against the late-afternoon sun, she gazed toward the harbor. With a sharp pang of disappointment, she recognized Noah's boat, moored and empty.

How had she missed him?

She had no time to dwell on it. Gathering up her skirts, she hurried up the stairs to change, mindful that it should have been her new lavender dress she would have been wearing instead of her dark serge traveling outfit.

Noah whistled all the way home. The Devon house seemed deserted when he passed by, but then he hadn't really expected to see Rianna. He glanced up at the second-story windows, wondering if she was getting ready.

When he came through his own door, he was glad to see the kitchen empty except for Mrs. Avery.

"Hello there."

"Where's Melanie?" he asked.

"Well, now that she's all better, Amelia stopped by and invited her for a ride over to my sister's. Poor child has been getting quite restless. They'll probably stay the night. I hope you don't mind?"

"No, of course not."

Mrs. Avery peered at him. "You're looking pleased with yourself. Good catch?"

"Yes." He laid some cod in the sink. "They're all cleaned."

"Oh, thank you, dear."

He stood a moment, hesitating. "Mrs. Avery, mind if I use the kitchen after supper? I thought I'd take a bath."

"Why, no. Go right ahead."

He cleared his throat. "I thought I'd go on down to the Farmer's Club this evening. They're having a little to-do."

"Yes, of course." Mrs. Avery patted his arm. "You go on and have a good time. I'm glad to see you gettin' out. Since Ria—Mrs. Bruce has come back…I mean—" She turned and busied herself at the counter as if she'd said too much. "She's such a nice young woman. Still in her prime."

Noah didn't say anything, afraid that if he did, he'd wake up and find it all a dream.

As he went about heating some water and pouring it into the tin tub, he couldn't help smiling at his fear the day before when he'd asked Rianna to the Farmer's Club. He hadn't felt this scared since he'd been nineteen and had asked her the first time. His smile disappeared, thinking of the look in her eyes. She, too, must have been back at the time. But the woman who'd said "yes" this time spoke with the quiet certainty of someone who knew her own mind.

Noah began whistling, thinking that perhaps this time, things would be different. After scrubbing and soaping till he shone, he rubbed himself dry. Thankfully he'd just gotten his hair cut before the camp meeting, but now he trimmed his beard and nails. He paused a moment to look at his hands. He hadn't continued Rianna's treatment, so they looked about the same. But they had sure felt good that day after her ministrations. He thought that was due as much to the feel of her fingers massaging his as any ointment.

He dressed in his best broadcloth suit, which he hadn't worn since the beach picnic. He combed his damp hair, tidied up the kitchen then went out into the garden to pick a few flowers for a posy, laughing at himself as he did so. He hadn't done anything even remotely resembling courting since he was nineteen.

After Rianna's decisive rejection, he'd made up his mind he was through with courting. Then he'd met Charlotte, a girl as different from Rianna as night from day. He'd proposed after a couple of months, and put the whole procedure of courting firmly behind him, relieved he'd never have to face it again.

Now he was thirty-one, and he felt more awkward than that nineteen-year-old boy. A lot more was at risk. But he couldn't contain the hope that swelled in him when he thought of the woman who'd accepted his invitation the day before. The woman who'd been by his side through Melanie's fever. The way she'd looked at him yesterday promised much, much more than he'd ever dared hope.

He bid Mrs. Avery good evening, and stood patiently while she exclaimed over him. Nothing could mar this evening for him.

He took the wagon over to the Devon house. As soon as he neared the house, he received his first inkling that things weren't quite right. Rianna was standing with her father by the gate, as if on the lookout for him. As he descended the wagon, he noticed she was dressed in black. He'd expected to see her in her lavender dress at the least, not looking as if she were going to attend a funeral.

"Evenin', Mr. Devon, Rianna."

Mr. Devon nodded his head before turning to his daughter. "I'll wait for you down there." With those words, he began walking down the street toward the harbor. It was then Noah noticed the portmanteau he carried in one hand.

"Noah." Rianna turned to him as soon as her father was out of earshot. "Something's happened. I wanted to see you as soon as you got in from fishing, but there's been so much going on—"

He could feel his heart begin to thud against his chest,

but he kept his face and voice emotionless. "Slow down. What's happened?"

She took a deep breath. "I have to go back to Mr. Whitestone this evening." At his frown, she added, "Mr. Whitestone, my patient. You remember my telling you?"

At his nod, she continued. "I received a telegram today that he's very ill. They say…" She paused, swallowing. "That the end is near." Her amber eyes seemed to implore him. "I have to go back right away and be with him. You understand, don't you?"

He nodded, the gesture automatic, as he was still unable to comprehend fully what she was saying. All that seemed to register was that she was going away and not attending the dance with him.

"Oh, I knew you would!" She grabbed one of his hands and gave it a squeeze. It was then she saw the posy, which he'd forgotten he still clutched. Before he could hide it from view, she grasped it. "Is this for me?" She brought them up to her nostrils. "Oh, Noah, how sweet of you. Thank you." With another squeeze to his hand, she affixed the posy to her buttonhole. "I'm so sorry about the dance tonight. I really wanted to go."

"It doesn't matter."

"Will you tell Melanie goodbye for me?" She looked genuinely distressed. "I haven't had a moment all day to run over to Mrs. Avery's and say goodbye."

He shook his head. "She's not there anyway."

"Oh, where—"

"Off with Mrs. Johnson for a visit to her aunt's." His answers were abrupt, his mind on one thing only. Rianna was leaving. And now a new worry formed in his mind.

What would Melanie think when she discovered her new friend had up and left without warning?

"Oh, thank you. Will you…will you tell her I'll miss her…and that…" She hesitated then plunged on, "That I'll write to her? If that's all right with you?"

His eyebrows drew together. She'd write to his daughter? He'd believe that when he saw it. Before he had a chance to express his doubts, her father called her. "Come on, dear, or you'll miss your boat."

Rianna gave Noah one more look, as if pleading with him. "I have to go. Would you…would you walk with me down to the landing?"

Again, a mechanical nod. He followed her out the yard, feeling like a tin soldier, obeying commands. The three of them made their way down past the wharf to the steamboat landing. A few other people already stood congregated. Moments later, someone spotted the ship entering the harbor, churning its way toward them.

Rianna felt awful, torn at having to leave Wood's Harbor just when she'd begun to hope for a future there. She stole a peek at Noah's stern profile.

Most of all, she ached at the thought of leaving the man who'd begun to mean so much to her again. There remained so many things to say to him. And she felt awful about not having a chance to bid young Melanie goodbye. Would the girl understand? How would Noah explain it to her? He hadn't answered her when she'd asked if it was all right to correspond with Melanie, but he looked so forbidding she didn't broach the subject again.

As she studied his face, his eyes fixed on the approaching steamer, she wished she could leave him something—but what?

She could read nothing from his countenance. It was as unyielding as the slate rocks edging the harbor. She didn't dare offer him empty reassurances. The truth was, she couldn't promise him anything. Her life was not her own. She'd guided her life for so many years on which needy patient the Lord would lead her to next that she hadn't dared think that perhaps now He would guide her to a home and family of her own.

Oh, but why did Noah look so devoid of emotion? He didn't even look at her, just stared out to sea. If she couldn't make him any promises, what *could* she give him? The answer popped into her head: her Bible.

No!

She normally carried an extra New Testament in her reticule, for the purpose of giving away. But she hadn't carried one since her return to Wood's Harbor. All she had was her own dog-eared, marked-up Bible, which the nurse had given her when Rianna had sat at Ralph's bedside, and which she'd carried ever since.

It was like a part of herself. But the thought persisted, even as they lowered the gangplank and the few passengers disembarked.

Her father touched her elbow. "Come on, sweetheart, if you want to get a good place. It's quite a ride to Bangor."

She'd have to change steamers there for the overnight one to Boston. She nodded, but still didn't move. It was as if something held her to the ground until she complied with the urgings in her heart. It was always so when the Lord was telling her to do something.

No, Lord, not my Bible. I'll write Mother as soon as I arrive and tell her to buy Noah a brand-new one.

Only stillness greeted her silent plea. A stillness that held no peace.

Already the few people waiting with her began to board.

"Well, Rianna, I guess this is it." Her father turned to her, and she embraced him. "You'll let us know as soon as you arrive? We'll be praying for you and Mr. Whitestone."

She nodded, but couldn't speak. Then he released her and she knew it was now or never. Still, she couldn't bring herself to go up that gangplank. "Mrs. Myers says she'll come in every day," she told her father. "I've told her I'd send her her wages."

"Don't you worry about that. We'll settle up here."

"No, Papa. I want to. Please."

He nodded.

"You'd best get aboard."

She turned to Noah, wanting to touch him, but suddenly afraid, feeling bereft at the moment of both his support and the Lord's.

She reached into her reticule and extracted the worn black book. Quickly she thumbed through it, taking out her own markers and placing them where she wanted Noah to read.

"Rianna," said her father.

"I'm coming." She still had no inkling of what was going through Noah's mind, but she now felt she had the Lord's support. *For by Thee I have run through a troop; and by my God have I leaped over a wall.*

"Here, Noah, I want you to have this." She was obliged to place it in his hands, almost forcing him to take it. "I want you to take care of it for me. It's very precious to me. Please." She smiled but received no answering smile. "Please read it sometime." His hands were as cold as a granite slab. She tightened her grip. "Thank you for being such a good friend." She looked at him warmly, but felt she wasn't reaching him at all. On the spur of the moment, she reached up on tiptoe and gave him a peck on the cheek. "Goodbye, Noah. I'll be praying for you. Give Melanie a kiss for me."

Her father hurried her aboard then came back to stand beside Noah. The gangplank was raised, and the steamboat made its way back out the harbor.

Noah stood through it all, feeling nothing. He sensed Mr. Devon's gaze on him, but he didn't return the look. He didn't want anyone's pity. But all the man said was, "She's a good woman, son."

Noah made no reply, simply turned on his heel and walked off the landing.

Chapter Ten

Noah marched down the clamshell-crushed road, along the main street and up the hill, not slowing until he reached his rooms. The faster his pace, the stronger his rage grew. The only words going through his mind were, *The Lord giveth, and the Lord taketh away. The Lord giveth, and the Lord taketh away.* Over and over in his mind.

He'd taken away Charlotte, and now He'd taken away Rianna before anything had even had a chance to start.

When Noah finally reached his room, he noticed he was clutching the Bible Rianna had given him. He glared at it a second before flinging it across the room. It slid down the wall and landed facedown, its binding split open.

"Well, He's not going to take from me anymore! There's not going to be any more to take from me!" Noah surveyed the room in front of him, the rage in him swelling so greatly it would explode if he didn't find an outlet for it soon. If he didn't respect Mrs. Avery so much, he'd begin destroying the things before him right then and there. Before the temptation overcame him, he flung off his clothes, pulling at the tie and tearing away the stiff collar, finally leaving his one good suit in a heap on the floor. When he was back in his work clothes, he slammed out of the house, keeping up the rapid pace until he came to his own property—the house by the sea.

He fumbled with the rusted padlock, swearing at it and kicking at the door. Finally he was inside the abandoned house. What came to him in a vivid flash was the night so long ago when he'd asked Rianna to dance. The house had been redolent of the scent of *Rosa rugosa,* large bouquets in every corner. It had taken him a long time not to notice that scent anymore.

The parlor had been full of young people, but Rianna had stood out like a princess among them. But it had been more than her appearance. Her personality—vivacious, lively, enthusiastic—had enchanted him. And later, when they had sat together on the back porch, hearing the sound of endless waves in the dark, drinking lemonade, they had talked and talked and talked.

He who'd never been much of a talker, especially around females, had opened up as never before, confessing his hopes and dreams for the future—to save up for a boat of his own and to help his grandfather when he grew too old to sail.

And Rianna had confided her dreams to him of going away and seeing the world. She'd devoured books that had opened up a world to her and made her hungry to explore it. He should have known then how things would end.

When he'd asked her to that farmer's dance a few weeks later and she'd turned him down, her words and expression had left no doubt in his mind that she was not interested in any kind of future with him. And it appeared that was still the case.

Shaking his head to clear it of those unwanted memories, Noah looked at the house in loathing. Suddenly, he started grabbing anything at hand and throwing it. He overturned tables, flung chairs against any furniture too heavy to budge, threw shelves of books to the floor. Spotting a crack in the plaster on a wall, he whacked a chair against it until a whole section came off, leaving the naked laths exposed. When there was nothing left to destroy, he slid to his knees on the floor, trying to hold back the choking feeling in his throat.

But it wouldn't be restrained. Like a flood tide, the years of loneliness and bitterness surged within him, refusing to be suppressed any longer. Finally, a sob erupted, and he couldn't stop the tears. His shoulders shook and his chest ached with the wrenching sobs.

By the time he returned to Mrs. Avery's, the house was dark and quiet. He'd survived the war, he'd survived Charlotte's death and his own feelings of responsibility for it. He'd survive this.

Glad he didn't yet have to face his daughter with her inevitable questions over Rianna's departure, he headed to his room.

Despite physical exhaustion, he couldn't fall asleep as he normally did as soon as his head touched the pillow. Rianna's smiling face teased him every way he turned, through closed lids and opened. Finally, exhaustion won out, and he fell asleep.

It seemed as if he'd just shut his eyes when he was awakened suddenly. His body was so accustomed to rising at four that he expected it to be that hour, but after a few seconds of lying in the darkness he sensed it was earlier. He finally turned up the lamp and read the clock face. A full hour too early to get up. Already his eyes felt gritty from lack of sleep. As he reached to lower the lamp, his gaze fell on the Bible resting awkwardly against floor and wall. He ignored it, plunging the room once more into darkness. Though he tried to fall asleep again, it was a vain hope. He finally rose, dressed and went to the kitchen to eat his bowl of porridge.

He followed the same routine every morning except Sunday, when he got up a little later than usual and Mrs. Avery fixed him a big breakfast. He knew the routine by heart, he could do it in his sleep. He wondered if he would be doing it until the day he died.

That afternoon when he returned from fishing, Melanie was waiting for him. She ran up to him as he lifted the latch at Mrs. Avery's gate. "I'm back, Papa! I missed you yesterday, but we picked so many blueberries." She giggled and stuck her tongue out at him. "My tongue was all blue from eating so many. I'm going to help Mrs. Avery and Mrs. Johnson can them."

He touched her head, glad she'd been too busy to notice Rianna's departure. "Hello, Mellie."

When she paused for breath, looking up at him with such love and trust, he was at a loss how to proceed. Did she know? "I missed you, too." Would she take Rianna's departure hard? They'd grown close in the short time Rianna had been back home.

Home. Was Wood's Harbor still home to Rianna? Could it ever be again?

Melanie took his hand in hers and swung it as they turned to walk to the house. At the porch steps, he stopped and sat down, tugging her down to sit beside him.

"Let's sit a minute before we go inside."

"All right, Papa." She sighed in contentment. "I hope Tad and Robbie don't see you yet. I like sitting with just you."

"I do, too, sweetie." They sat quietly for a few minutes as Noah collected his thoughts. Fishing had been hard today, and not only because of his lack of sleep the night before. He'd had trouble keeping his mind on track. But he was mindful the boys might run out any minute, so finally he took a deep breath. "I have something to tell you. Actually, a message to give you."

She sat with her chin in her hands and turned a look full of curiosity at him. "A message for *me?*"

He cleared his throat, looking away from her innocent wonder. "It's from Mrs. Bruce. She…she had to go back."

Melanie scrunched up her eyebrows. "Back? You mean to nurse the old man?"

He looked down at the paving stones between his boots and picked up a loose pebble. "Yep. Back to her nursing job. The old man's real sick, I guess."

"That's too bad." Melanie looked ahead of her again. "I'm going to miss her. She was lots of fun."

He glanced sidelong at his daughter, wondering what she was thinking. "She told me specially to tell you goodbye and to say how sorry she was not to be able to tell you in person." He remembered what else she'd said, about writing to Melanie, though he didn't put much stock in it and decided not to mention it. "I'm sure she'll miss you, too." The words sounded weak. He wished he could give her something more, but he wasn't willing to give Melanie false hope. That only deepened his anger toward Rianna the more, for putting him in this position and for playing with his daughter's feelings.

Melanie said nothing for a few moments. "Do you think she'll come back soon?"

The question he'd dreaded. "I don't know. I guess it depends on her patient. He…he really needs her right now."

Melanie firmed up her mouth, and he recognized the gesture in himself, before nodding.

"Well, I'd best go to the pump and wash up." The worst was over. Melanie seemed all right with the news. A child's memory was a lot shorter than an adult's. She'd probably have forgotten Rianna by the end of the week.

As for himself… He got up, feeling like an old man. He didn't want to think that far ahead.

Noah glared at his clock face. Three o'clock. Again his gaze fell on the Bible. He turned on his other side, burying his head under the bedclothes.

Sheer exhaustion had made it easier to fall asleep at night after a few grueling days on the water, but each morning it was the same, as if someone were waking him up an hour earlier for the sheer pleasure of torturing him with too little sleep. He became grumpier and grumpier, not addressing anyone unless absolutely necessary. He could see the fear in Joe's eyes every time he had to ask Noah something.

The only one he strained to treat normally—even delicately as if she were a fragile seashell that might crush with the least pressure—was Melanie. She seemed her usual self. He looked for any signs that Rianna's absence had affected her, but he was away all day, so it was hard to tell.

He didn't bring up Rianna's name deliberately, but Melanie seemed to have no problem mentioning her. Whenever she thought of something the two had done together or of something Rianna had said, Melanie talked about it.

"See, Papa, it's almost finished," she said one evening, holding up a doll's dress. "Mrs. Bruce helped me cut it out and showed me how to sew it."

He stared more closely at the familiar shade of lavender. "Let me see it, sweetie." He fingered the soft material, remembering Rianna at the seashore, playing with the children, unmindful of the salt water drenching her hem. "It's very pretty. You've done a fine job sewing it."

"Mrs. Bruce sewed the hardest parts."

"I see." He handed the garment back to his daughter, feeling almost as if he was letting go of Rianna—or a little part of her—once again.

After a week of interrupted sleep, Noah, spying the Bible in his line of vision for the seventh morning in a row, flung back the bedcovers. He stalked over to it, fully intending to remove it to some location where it would be impossible to see.

He picked it up. It had fallen open at one of the markers Rianna had placed in it. His gaze fell on the psalm that was underscored with ink. *Oh Lord, Thou hast searched me, and known me. Thou knowest my downsitting and mine uprising, Thou understandest my thought afar off.*

Riveted by the words, he couldn't stop reading. When he finished the psalm, his fingers riffled through the thin pages, seeking more. Rianna's other marker was lodged securely at the beginning of the Gospel of St. John.

Noah kept reading, only coming to with a start when he looked at the clock and saw it was four o'clock. He dressed and was on the point of going downstairs when he saw the

Bible on his night table. As an afterthought, he grabbed it up, deciding he could read while waiting for the coffee to boil.

He read as he ate his porridge, propping the book against the kerosene lamp.

And thus began a new routine. Each morning his body awakened a full hour early, and he spent that time in bed reading Rianna's Bible. And no longer did he feel fatigued, but rather invigorated, as he set off toward the harbor.

When he returned from the boat one afternoon more than a week after Rianna's departure, Melanie came running down the front walk to him, waving something white in her hand.

"Slow down there before you fall."

"Papa! Papa! She wrote to me. I received a real letter from Mrs. Bruce!"

Noah could hardly believe what he was hearing. He felt unable to move and waited for his daughter to reach him.

Melanie skidded to a stop and showed him the envelope. "See, Papa?" She held it out to him.

As if it might crumble and disappear as soon as he touched it, he put his hand out slowly. But the thick paper held. He studied the handwriting on the front, noting that he didn't know her handwriting. It was addressed in a neat script to Miss Melanie Samuels. In the upper corner was a return address in Massachusetts. Somehow, that made it more real, dispelling the notion he sometimes had that Rianna had disappeared off the face of the earth, the way he'd felt the first time she'd left.

"Do you want to read it, Papa? She sent you a special hello."

"Did she?" His voice sounded odd, unsure.

"Yes, Papa. May we sit on the steps and read it together?"

"That'd be fine." He let her lead him along the path, feeling like a sleepwalker.

Once again, the two sat side by side on the front porch steps. "Mrs. Avery helped me read it the first time 'cause there were some words I didn't know." Melanie spread the letter flat on her knees and began to read in a clear voice.

"'Dear Melanie, Greetings from Massachusetts. First of all, I want to say how sorry I am that I was not able to see you to say goodbye before I left Wood's Harbor. Everything happened so quickly I hardly had time to pack and catch the evening steamer. I'm sure your father, though, gave you my message.'"

The letter went on to recount her voyage in simple enough language for an eight-year-old to read, but the descriptions were vivid enough that Noah could picture it all. He couldn't help smiling at some of the funny incidents along the way. He could almost hear Rianna's voice and laughter underlying her account. Then her tone became more serious and she told about Mr. Whitestone and how ill he was. Lastly, she asked about Melanie and her activities. Then she ended with, "'I hope you will answer my letter. I want to hear all about your life in Wood's Harbor. Please give Mrs. Avery, Mrs. Johnson, Tad and Robert my best. I hope they are all well.

"'And please give your father a special hello. I hope he is well and happy. I know you are the best daughter anyone could have and are his little helper.'"

Well and happy. Rianna's wishes for him fell dully against his ears.

"Here, Papa, would you like to read it yourself?"

He took it without replying and read it through again, each word tasting as sweet as fresh water did from the rain barrel on his boat when he was surrounded by the salty sea.

* * *

Every few days Melanie received a new letter from Rianna and promptly replied with Noah's help. Noah didn't know why he didn't pick up a pen himself and reply to her greetings for him, but something held him back. She had left, and he didn't want her to know how hard he'd taken her departure. He was also afraid that somehow he'd express a desire to know if she'd ever return and was terrified of hearing words to the negative.

Instead, he felt as if he was writing to her secondhand through his daughter's pen, and that in some sense she was replying to him in the same way.

One afternoon as summer was waning, Noah walked back to his grandparents' old house. He regretted his angry outburst and wanted to see how much damage his loss of temper had caused. In silence, he walked through the downstairs rooms, surveying the evidence of his hurt and disappointment over Rianna's desertion.

He was glad to see the damage was mostly superficial, not beyond picking up and cleaning up and effecting a few repairs. The longer he lingered in the old house, the more he examined. He knocked on some beams, looked at the ceilings for evidence of dampness, went down into the cellar to check the floorboards from below. He found no major structural weakness from the years of neglect.

He stood again in the main sitting room, watching the afternoon sun stream through the picture windows overlooking the bay. The golden light shone onto the wide floorboards, re-creating a pattern of squares from the windowpanes. Despite the bits of plaster strewn about, the upturned furniture and motes of dust, the room exuded a warm welcome.

The unformed thoughts that had brought him to the house and caused him to look it over, began to gel in his mind. Maybe it was finally time for him and Melanie to have a home of their own. But his doubts came immediately to the fore. Why should he fix the place now? To what purpose? To make a home for Melanie without a mother to look after her... He was gone too much for that to be possible. And there was only one woman with whom he'd care to share a home and a life.

"Arise and build, son."

The words were so distinct, Noah turned to see if someone was in back of him, but there was no one else in the room. He rubbed his ear, doubting what he'd heard. Had the verse from Scripture just been in his head because he'd recently read it?

But he couldn't forget the words.

In the following days, he returned to the house to measure and make notes. On impulse, one afternoon he took Melanie with him. "What do you think if we fixed this place up and lived here ourselves?"

Melanie's eyes began to shine as she looked around her. Then she clapped her hands together. "Oh, Papa, a house of our own?"

He nodded, not realizing how much his daughter had missed having her own home.

Melanie frowned, gazing up at him. "But who will take care of me when you're fishing?"

He rubbed his beard, not having an answer to that. "I don't know, Mellie. We'll have to see about that."

She gazed out the window overlooking the bay. "I wish..."

He walked slowly up to her and laid his hand on her shoulder. "What do you wish, sweetheart?"

She didn't look at him. Finally, when he thought she wouldn't answer, she said, "I wish Mrs. Bruce would come back."

He didn't know what to say. Her voice sounded so forlorn. All he could do was squeeze her shoulder and say silently, *I wish she would, too.* For the rest of the afternoon he tried to distract her with talk of the practical side of repairing the house.

Despite trying to temper his optimism, his excitement grew as he began repairs. He cleaned out the woodstoves and chimneys and built up the fires one morning to get the dampness out. He pried out the nails that had kept the windows shut, and flung them all open on a warm October morning. As he carted more and more building materials to the place, he knew people were talking. It didn't take much imagination to know what they were saying.

Poor Noah, who's he fixing up that house for? Rianna's gone and turned him down again, and the poor man still hasn't learned.

As he lifted rotted boards and hammered new nails into fresh lumber, he often felt like the patriarch he was named after. They'd thought he was a fool, too, building that giant ark in the middle of dry land.

He divided his days between fishing and rebuilding, his thoughts often of Rianna. He was no longer angry at her. He thought of the sunshine she'd brought into his life, without his even realizing it. He remembered her easy laughter, her capacity to enjoy the simplest things. He remembered the nostalgia in her voice every time she spoke of being home, an unvoiced desire to return to her native town for good. He'd distrusted it before, as part of her enthusiasm of the moment. If she wanted a way to come home, he would offer her one.

Chapter Eleven

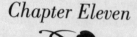

Boston, Massachusetts

Noah got down from the cab, and faced the mansion before him in the lamplight. He turned to the cabdriver again. "Are you sure this is the right address?"

"Sure is."

Noah stood under the massive portico fronted with elegant columns and hesitated at the heavy black door. Two lamps burned at each side of it. Although several windows along the wide front of the house were lit, he could make out no signs of life through the gauzy curtains framed by heavy drapes.

He'd see it through only because he'd come so far, but any lingering hope he'd had evaporated the moment he saw the size of the place where Rianna lived and worked.

He couldn't help comparing the modest house he'd been working on with so much enthusiasm and love to the imposing mansion dwarfing him, where Rianna had servants at her beck and call.

A butler opened the door to his knock. "Yes?" came the frosty greeting.

"I'm looking for a Mrs. Rianna Bruce."

"She's no longer in our employ."

Had he missed her? Not sure whether to feel relief or fear, he asked, "Could you please give me her current whereabouts?"

The man showed him to a side parlor. After a few minutes he came back with a piece of paper. "She just left us the day before yesterday. I believe she is now at this address."

Noah felt a surge of relief that she was still to be found in the city. He climbed back aboard the cab and gave the driver the new address. This time, he stood outside a brick town house of more modest proportions. No lights through the windows softened its square dimensions. When he rang the bell, it was answered by a stern-looking woman.

When he asked for Rianna, the woman eyed him suspiciously. "It's a bit late in the evening to be entertaining gentlemen callers."

Noah hid a smile, remembering Rianna's description of dragon-lady landladies. "That's all right." Unable to think of a better excuse, he said, "I've been sent by her family."

The woman looked him up and down and finally stepped aside. With a jut of her chin, she directed him up a dark flight of stairs. "Third story, second door on your right."

"Thank you, ma'am."

At the top, he stood outside, his heart hammering, his hand poised above the dark wood door.

Rianna went to the door, wondering what Mrs. Thompson could want of her. When she opened it, her hand flew to her mouth. "Noah!" she breathed. His tall frame filled the dark hallway. So many nights she'd dreamed of just such a scenario, for a moment she thought she must be asleep.

A sudden fear filled her. "It's not Mother, is it? She's not—"

Noah shifted on his feet. He was dressed in a heavy overcoat and hat. That's when she realized he was clean shaven. He looked about ten years younger—almost as young as the man who'd first asked her to dance.

He cleared his throat. "No, she's fine. She sends her love."

"And Melanie, is she all right? I just had a letter—"

"She's fine. Also—ahem—sends you her love."

He sounded nervous. Did he think she wouldn't welcome his visit? She almost burst into laughter at the mere thought. "Oh, my goodness, come in!" she urged a second later, opening the door wider.

Once inside, Noah removed his hat and ran a hand through his hair.

"Then who—what—" She stood against the door, her hands closed about the handle. He looked so tall and handsome standing there, overwhelming her little sitting room.

"I brought you your Bible." As he spoke, he fumbled in the pocket of his greatcoat then extended it toward her.

"My Bible?" She looked at it in wonder, reaching for it. "You came all the way here to bring me my Bible?" She looked at him in disbelief and suddenly could hold the laughter in no longer. She felt such overwhelming joy, she couldn't contain it.

But instead of joining in her laughter, he seemed more ill at ease than ever.

On impulse, she stepped forward and reached up a hand and cupped his cold cheek. "You shaved."

He colored, his eyes never leaving hers, and cleared his throat. "Always do in the winter."

"That's right," she answered softly, still not removing her hand. It felt so good to be touching him. It made him seem *real* and not some dream she'd conjured up in her loneliness. "You told me that. It makes you look the way you used to." With regret, she let her hand fall back to her side.

She couldn't think why he had come all this way— unless…unless he cared something for her. But he'd never written, not so much as a line in all the months she'd been away. "Are you sure everything's all right? Melanie didn't say a word—"

"It was…a sort of surprise."

Her eyes widened. She felt herself coloring as he continued to look at her in that intent way he had. Would he see her lonely existence, her yearning to come home…to make a home for him and his daughter…?

He cleared his throat again. "I've been going to church."

She looked searchingly at him. "Just 'going,' Noah? Have you been meeting God at all?"

His dark gaze shifted away, and she could see it was not easy for him to talk about it. But as he began to tell her what had happened to the Bible she had left with him, her heart swelled with wonder and joy.

When he finally came to the end, again he fell silent and just looked at her.

"What is it, Noah?"

"Melanie wondered when you might be coming back to Wood's Harbor."

She wished she could hold on to the doorknob again, but she'd stepped away from it. "I—I...I'm not sure. My job has only just ended...."

He nodded, then looked down at the brim of his hat. "Would it help if you had a...an invitation?"

"An invitation?"

He raised his head to her again. "Yes."

Was he giving her an opening? "Ye-es, perhaps it would."

She watched him swallow and knew suddenly it was as hard for him as it was for her. "The reason I've come..."

When he paused, she encouraged him with a smile. "Yes, Noah?"

He cleared his throat and started again. "Rianna, the reason I've come—Rianna, will you marry me?" The last words were said in a rush, as if in desperation.

Rianna met his gaze one eternal instant before shutting her eyes. *May I, Lord?* Reassured, she opened them, only to find Noah's tortured gaze still on her. She couldn't resist teasing him then. She moved her hand up to his forehead. In her best nurse's voice, she said, "Noah, are you all right? Do you have a fever?"

He looked taken aback an instant, before he narrowed his eyes at her. She couldn't help the laughter bubbling out of her. He reached for her, and with a laugh, she spun out of his grasp. But a second later, he caught her and swung her up high in his arms.

"Noah! Put me down! Put me down this instant!" But even as she scolded, she wrapped her arms about his neck.

He only tightened his hold around her. "Not until you answer my question."

Her laughter subsided, and the two stood still. "Noah, I would love to marry you."

She waited in anticipation, not daring to breathe as he looked deeply into her eyes, his own the color of rich, black coffee. Then his head slowly came down to hers and his lips met hers. Her own parted, as she felt the soft warmth of his mouth touch hers.

Home. She was home at last.

"Oh, Rianna," he whispered against her lips, his mouth skimming hers, "how I've missed you."

"I've missed you, too, and Melanie." And then she could speak no more.

A long time later the two sat close together, Noah's arm around her, in front of the coal stove. "So, Noah," she began, her fingers playing with the hair about his ear, "why didn't you ever write to me?"

He rubbed his clean-shaven jaw. "Too scared, I guess."

She stroked his face lovingly. "Scared? You fought in a war. You risk your life at sea each day. You, Noah, scared!"

He stopped her hand an instant, covering it with his own. "When it comes to you, I'm terrified." His smile disappeared. "Rianna, I just came from where you used to work." His eyes searched hers. "The place was grander than I imagined. Are you sure you can be happy with the kind of place I can give you?"

"Oh, Noah, you silly," she replied softly. "Don't you know me any better by now? Don't you know how happy it would make me to make a home for you and Melanie, wherever it is, however small or grand?"

"Well, Melanie will sure be pleased. She was real happy when your first letter arrived." His look sobered. "Thank you for taking the time to write her. It meant a lot to her... and to me."

She touched his cheek. "Her letters gave me as much

pleasure, I'm sure." Her lips firmed once more. "And, they were my *only* source for news of you."

He flushed under her gaze. "I kept wanting to write you. But I was so afraid I'd only want to know when—and *if*—you were coming home and you'd tell me you weren't coming home again—"

"Oh, Noah, didn't you realize how much I cared?"

"I just couldn't bring myself to believe you could."

She shook her head at him, but before she could say anything more, he captured her lips in another long, deep kiss.

Afterward, he spoke up, "I'm fixing up the house."

Noah would never tire of reading those expressive, cider-colored eyes of hers, now so alive in the lamplight. One minute they were mischievous, the next so tender as to break his heart. Her eyes lit up now with the excitement of a child. "Your grandparents' place? That's wonderful!"

"It's coming along pretty well. You were right. It's in better shape than I thought. Melanie's been pretty excited with the thought of having a home of our own." He swallowed. "And she's told me more than once she hoped you'd come back soon…and take care of her."

Rianna's eyes softened. "Did she? Do you think she'll mind having me for a…stepmother?"

"I think she's been praying for you to be her mama."

"Oh, Noah—"

He hugged her to himself. "You'll make her a wonderful mother." Seeming to know she needed reassuring, he continued, "I've never seen anyone so good with children. Melanie will be blessed with you as her mother. You never left her side when she was so sick. You know how to have fun with her, too."

Rianna looked down, but he could tell by her heightened color that she was pleased with his words.

"The house is almost finished," he added after a moment, "though it needs a woman's touch with furnishings and such. We probably can't move in till next summer. Can you wait that long?"

"Of course." She became serious. "But I can't wait that long to marry you."

He read the look in her eye and tightened his hold. "Good. I feel exactly the same."

"Would you mind very much if we stayed with my parents a while until our house is ready?" she asked him when he loosened his hold on her.

Our house. He liked the sound of that. "Whatever you want is fine with me as long as we're married."

She smiled. "How did you decide to start work on the house? The last time I spoke with you about it, you didn't express any interest in it."

He swallowed, feeling her intent gaze upon him, he who was so unused to talking about the things closest to his heart. "Well, you made me change my feelings about that. I began to hope that maybe, someday—" He colored as he began talking of his deepest emotions. Before he could go any further, he felt her soft hand stroking his cheek again, which made talking all the more difficult. He cleared his throat. "I began to hope, that is, to hope that maybe someday you might…might…"

"Love you?" she finished for him.

He glanced at her, nodding. "I was going to say, 'return my affections.'"

Rianna nodded. "I just thought I'd help you get over those difficult words."

He swallowed. "They're not difficult. It's just that I'm a little rusty with them."

"You'll have to start practicing then."

She kept looking at him until he nodded. "You want me to start right now?"

"I wouldn't mind."

He took her face in his two rough palms. "I love you, Rianna, with all my heart."

"I love you, too, Noah."

"Oh, Rianna," he whispered raggedly as he bent his head to kiss her again, this time more leisurely than before. This time it was as if each was taking the time to explore the feel of the other. When they finally broke apart, he sighed heavily. "I hope you don't expect a long, drawn-out engagement."

She laughed her throaty laugh. "As soon as you can get the license, I'll be waiting at the altar."

He squeezed her shoulder as he rested his head against the chair back, overwhelmed by the joy he felt filling him.

After a while he was able to continue his story. "As I was saying, I didn't dare hope you might return my feelings, and then when you left all of a sudden—"

She took his hand in hers and pressed it in encouragement. "Then I walked back to the house, feeling so angry."

"Angry? At me for leaving?"

"Partly. But mostly at myself for being such a fool again where you were concerned."

"Oh, no!"

"But then, later, much later, when I went back out to the old house, I began seeing it through your eyes—seeing it how a lady might. It made me realize that when you left, I hadn't exactly given you any reason to stay—or to come back."

"I'll say!" she answered. "What was I supposed to think? You didn't react at all that day I left. That hurt," she said softly. "Anger, anything, would have been preferable to the indifference you displayed on the wharf."

"If you could have seen inside me that day, you wouldn't say I was indifferent. My heart was anything but. I just wanted to rip it out, if only to make it stop feeling." He rubbed his face again, as if dispelling a bad dream.

She smoothed back a lock of his hair. "Oh, Noah, I'm so sorry."

"Anyway, as I walked around the old place, I began to see it as you had, with possibilities. Then—" He laughed. "You'll think I'm crazy, but as I was standing back from it a ways, looking at the sitting room one last time, I heard someone behind me say, 'Arise and build, son.' It was almost—" He gave another self-conscious laugh. "It was almost like a papa encouraging his son. I even turned around, but of course, no one was there.

"So, I began to fix it up. Melanie was all for it. She had more faith than I did that you'd come back. I often felt like the old Noah, building that big old ark and not a cloud in the sky. Here I was rebuilding a house, and no bride to fill it. My girl had up and left me."

Rianna put her hands around his nape and lay her head against his chest. "I hadn't left you. I would have come back, you know, if you hadn't beaten me to it."

He looked at her through half-closed lids. "So, when were you planning to come back?"

"Soon." Again that impish expression as she smiled up at him. "I'm a woman of means, you know."

"You don't say," he answered, playing along.

"As of a week ago." She sobered. "Remember how I

told you about dear old Mr. Whitestone wanting to marry me?"

"You didn't finally break down and accept, did you?"

She giggled, shaking her head. "He was such a dear. He died in peace at last. At peace with his Maker against whom he'd railed so long." After a few moments, she continued, her fingers playing with a button of his jacket. "The dear old man left me a little something in his will. Nothing so much that his family would object to, but a nice little nest egg for me." She looked at Noah significantly. "Enough for me to give up nursing and come back home."

"So you really wanted to come back?"

"Yes." She laughed. "And if you hadn't taken me back, I'd have conspired with Melanie to make life absolutely miserable for you until you came to your senses."

He chuckled, stroking her hair, gaining confidence as he began truly to believe she returned his love.

"You will make a wonderful mother—and I don't mean with just Melanie."

He enjoyed watching the color suffuse her face from cheeks to forehead. "Are you going to give me children, Noah?"

His fingertips traced her cheek. "I'll do my part. I think the Lord will do the rest."

Her momentary shyness turned to joy as she smiled at him, that radiant smile that he'd missed so much.

A loud knocking at the door startled them both. "Mrs. Bruce! Are you in there?"

Rianna lifted her head with a look of exasperation. "Yes, Mrs. Thompson?"

"Mrs. Bruce, let me in. I must insist!"

With a sigh, Rianna arose and smoothed her skirts and

hair. "Just a moment." When she opened the door, the land-lady came bursting in as if she'd been leaning on the door.

"Oh," she said when at last she spotted Noah. He arose and inclined his head. "Are you still here?" Before he could answer, she turned to Rianna. "I must tell you I don't ap-prove of gentlemen callers after eight o'clock. It's only because he said your family had sent him that I let him come up at all."

"It's all right, Mrs. Thompson," she replied, looking to Noah with an unmistakable twinkle in her eye. "May I in-troduce you to Mr. Samuels, my fiancé?"

Mrs. Thompson's mouth fell open then snapped shut. "Well, that's different. Still, you understand—"

Before she could go any further, Noah spoke up, "Mrs. Thompson, could you tell me where I could get a room for the night?"

"How long will you be staying?"

Noah looked at Rianna. "How long do you need before you can leave for Wood's Harbor?"

She didn't hesitate. "I can leave tomorrow."

Noah breathed a sigh of relief. "Good." He turned to Mrs. Thompson. "I only need it for tonight."

Mrs. Thompson offered him a room in her own build-ing and he followed her out. As he turned to bid Rianna good-night, watched all the while by her landlady, he bent down to give her a quick peck on the cheek, knowing he'd have a lifetime of more satisfying good-nights.

"I'll see you tomorrow bright and early," whispered Rianna, her hand squeezing his.

"You'll be making one little girl very, very happy," he said. "As well as one lonely widower," he added with a small smile.

She returned his smile. "I can't wait."

Noah followed Mrs. Thompson down a couple of landings to another room.

When he was finally alone in the darkened room, he lifted his hands heavenward, and said, "Thank You, Lord."

Epilogue

"Mama, may I hold little Josh, please?"

Rianna smiled at Melanie before looking down at the precious bundle in her arms. Joshua Noah Samuels had been born two weeks ago, and it was hard for her to trust anyone with her baby. "All right, dear, if you're very, very careful."

"I'll be right beside her."

Reassured by Noah's words, Rianna relinquished the sleeping infant to his father then watched as father and daughter, their two dark heads together, murmured over little Josh.

Finally, Noah stepped back a fraction, allowing Melanie to hold her new brother. Josh continued sleeping, only a soft sigh signaling the movement.

"I'm so glad I have a little brother. Maybe someday I'll have a little sister, too."

Noah and Rianna looked at each other and chuckled. "Maybe," replied Rianna as Noah echoed, "I hope so, sweetie."

Rianna rocked on the wooden rocker Noah had made

for her over the winter when they knew they were expecting a new baby. She looked around at the comfortable parlor room with a warm fire burning in the woodstove. Everything was neat and tidy again, as in the days when Noah's grandparents had lived in this house.

Outside, a cold northeastern wind blew across the long, dry grass and whipped up whitecaps on the gray ocean, but inside she was safe and warm with the man and the children she adored.

"What are you thinking?" Noah touched her softly on the shoulder.

She looked up at him with love in her eyes. "How blessed I am to have come home."

* * * * *

Dear Reader,

I used to spend childhood summers on the coast of Maine. Down the road, overlooking a bay, stood a dark green, shingled farmhouse with a barn alongside.

An elderly couple lived there. He made a living clamming, lobster fishing, raking blueberries, logging—all seasonal occupations, and she had been a nurse when she was younger. When I knew her, she made the best clam chowder and rhubarb cobbler.

The house has stood empty for many years now, its windows shuttered. There are still some remnants of her flower garden each spring and summer, but mostly it's wildflowers that blossom in the surrounding hills.

The house inspired Noah's old homestead in my story. Maybe someday someone will restore and inhabit the real life farmhouse here on the downeast coast of Maine.

I love to hear from readers. Stop by my blog, http://ruthaxtellmorren.blogspot.com, or Web site, www.ruthaxtellmorren.com, and drop me a line with any comments you might have on *A Family of Her Own*. You can also mail me at: Cutler General Delivery, Cutler, ME 04626.

Blessings,

QUESTIONS FOR DISCUSSION

1. How is Noah's heart like his grandparents' old house?

2. What is Noah's memory or perception of his old sweetheart, Rianna?

3. What is Rianna's perception of him?

4. Like many veterans, Noah doesn't like to talk about the war. How does Rianna's nursing experience in the war help draw them closer?

5. How does Noah see that Rianna is not the same girl he met so many years before?

6. How is she similar to that girl?

7. Why does Rianna think she was not meant to have children of her own?

8. How has that rationalization helped her overcome her feelings of unworthiness caused by her widowhood and miscarriage?

Here's a sneak peek at
THE WEDDING GARDEN
by Linda Goodnight,
the second book in her new miniseries
REDEMPTION RIVER,
available in May 2010 from Love Inspired.

One step into the living room and she froze again, pan aloft.

A hulking shape stood in shadow just inside the French doors leading out to the garden veranda. This was not Pop-bottle Jones. This was a big, bulky, dangerous-looking man. She raised the pan higher.

"What do you want?"

"Annie?" He stepped into the light.

All the blood drained from Annie's face. Her mouth went dry as saltines. "Sloan Hawkins?"

The man removed a pair of silver aviator sunglasses and hung them on the neck of his black rock-and-roll T-shirt. He'd rolled the sleeves up, baring muscular biceps. A pair of eyes too blue to define narrowed, looking her over as though he were a wolf and she a bunny rabbit.

Annie suppressed an annoying shiver.

It was Sloan, all right, though older and with more muscle. His nearly black hair was shorter now—no more bad-boy curl over the forehead—but bad boy screamed off him in waves just the same. He was devastatingly hand-some, in a tough, rugged, manly kind of way. The years had been kind to Sloan Hawkins.

She really wanted to hate him, but she'd already wasted too much emotion on this outlaw. With God's help she'd learned to forgive. But she wasn't about to forget.

*Will Sloan and Annie's faith be strong
enough to see them through
the pain of the past and allow them to open
their hearts to a possible future?
Find out in THE WEDDING GARDEN
by Linda Goodnight,
available May 2010 from Love Inspired.*

Love Inspired®

Former bad boy Sloan Hawkins is back in
Redemption, Oklahoma, to help keep his aunt's
cherished garden thriving and to reconnect with the
girl he left behind, Annie Markham. But when he
discovers his secret child—and that single mother
Annie never stopped loving him—he's determined
that a wedding will take place in the garden
nurtured by faith and love.

REDEMPTION RIVER

Where healing flows...

Look for

The Wedding Garden
by Linda Goodnight

*Available May 2010
wherever you buy books.*

www.SteepleHill.com

REQUEST YOUR FREE BOOKS!

2 FREE INSPIRATIONAL NOVELS
PLUS 2
FREE
MYSTERY GIFTS

Love Inspired.

HISTORICAL
INSPIRATIONAL HISTORICAL ROMANCE

Love Inspired.
HISTORICAL

INSPIRATIONAL HISTORICAL ROMANCE

Widower Tyrone Justice has a simple plan—to convince schoolmistress Caroline Hudson to take in his children as wards. Instead, she requests a marriage of convenience! It makes sense, both for the children and for the love-wary couple. Yet, happiness lies within reach—if they'll take a chance on the unplanned gift of love.

Look for

A CONVENIENT *Wife*

by

ANNA SCHMIDT

Available May
wherever books are sold.

www.SteepleHill.com

Steeple
Hill ®

LIH82835

Love Inspired.
HISTORICAL

TITLES AVAILABLE NEXT MONTH

Available May 11, 2010

A CONVENIENT WIFE
Anna Schmidt

LOVING BELLA
Charity House
Renee Ryan

Love Inspired

Thanks to his uncle's posting in the church bulletin, all of Dry Creek, Montana, thinks Conrad Nelson wants a wife! But he's just fine on his own—until Katrina Britton drives into town. It's not long before even Dry Creek's confirmed bachelor realizes they're meant for each other!

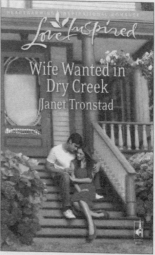

Look for

Wife Wanted in Dry Creek
by
Janet Tronstad

Available May wherever books are sold.

Steeple
Hill®
LI87596

www.SteepleHill.com